RUNE AND FLASH

INSIDE THE DREAM PRISON

RUNE AND FLASH: INSIDE THE DREAM PRISON
Copyright © 2022 by Joe Canzano. All rights reserved. Printed in the United States of America. No part of this book may be used or reproduced in any manner whatsoever without written permission except in the case of brief quotations embodied in critical articles and reviews. For contact information visit Happy Joe Control at www.happyjoe.net.

Happy Joe Control books may be purchased for educational, business, or promotional use. For contact information visit www.happyjoe.net.

Library of Congress Control Number: 2022905022
ISBN: 979-8-9859132-0-0

Cover painting by Jill Caporlingua at gallerychaos.net

Photo of painting by Jaime Shombert

"Just gimme some truth."

- John Lennon

RUNE AND FLASH

INSIDE THE DREAM PRISON

JOE CANZANO

😊 Happy Joe Control

www.happyjoe.net

Chapter 1

Markla didn't care for the dark. Why did they need to be creeping around in the woods at night? The trees all looked like gnarled monsters, and the moon stared down like an evil eye, and couldn't they attack this place in the daytime?

The Serenity Six Dream Station would still be around when the sun came up. It would still be around on a weekend, too—in case someone didn't want to save the world on a school night. But she was the only one still in school, and being just sixteen years old no one seemed to care what she thought, anyway.

Dru was two years older and he was up ahead. He was stomping through the forest, snapping twigs and swishing his feet through every pile of dry leaves. If the darkness gave them a certain element of surprise, it was totally lost by all the noise they were making. They were supposed to be warriors in a primitive and ancient tradition, schooled in the art of silent attack—but now the idea made Markla roll her eyes. We're as clueless as the enemy, she thought. Any second now someone was bound to walk into a tree and knock himself unconscious.

The thought almost made her laugh, but she bit her lip instead and stepped lightly over a thick root. She was tiny, and slender like a branch, and she wouldn't be walking into anything. Then Dru held up his hand and whispered in a fierce tone.

"Stop!" he said.

Markla didn't stop right away. Instead, she tossed back her hair and crept to his side. Markla's hair was a shade or two darker than midnight, and it was always tangled and messy, and most of the time she liked it to hang down because it covered a small scar near her left ear and another star-shaped one on the right side of her forehead. But tonight it seemed appropriate to let her scars show.

They were standing at the edge of the dense forest. Somewhere nearby, an owl hooted and her heart leaped. She brushed a mosquito from her bare arm and peered across a grassy clearing. Did she really want to do this? Well, she did have a steel club slung across her back, and so did Dru, and so did the other three people who'd come trudging through the woods on this humid autumn evening. They were staring across the field at a knob-like building that resembled an observatory. There was no kind of visible fence around the place, but it was supposedly equipped with sensors that would detect anyone who crossed a certain perimeter—unless the system was disabled by someone inside.

Dru wiped some sweat from his forehead. He motioned for everyone to crouch down, and in the darkness three silent figures followed his instructions. But Markla remained standing, and so did he, and he turned to face her like she knew he would. Even in the moonlight, she could see his blue eyes, thick dark hair, and chiseled facial features—and yeah, he looked good. But just because Dru was sexy didn't mean he couldn't be infuriating, especially when he said, "Maybe you should wait here."

"What?" She felt her stomach tighten. "What are you talking about? You want to leave me behind?"

Dru smiled. "Markla, no—that's not how it is. I know you're tough, but you're also small, and we could use a lookout."

"That's stupid," she sputtered. "That was never the plan. I'm part of the group, and now you want to leave me here all alone?"

"No one wants to do that. It's not like that at all."

"If you leave me here by myself, I'll be alone, right? I can count to one."

Dru sighed in dramatic fashion. Behind Markla, the three others remained silent, like they were waiting for the argument to end. And it did end, the way it always ended. Dru reached out with his big hands and squeezed Markla's shoulders as he looked into her eyes and said, "I would never leave you behind, Markla. You know that."

She was quiet. "Okay," she finally said. Then she shrugged. "So what are we talking about? Let's go."

He laughed. "We can't go yet, honey. We have to wait for the signal."

Right. She knew that, and she hadn't meant it literally. Then there was a chirping sound, and Dru was staring at a wafer-sized device in his hand.

"Okay, this is it!" he said. "Are we ready to do some damage?"

Everyone murmured that they were—and then they put on their masks. The masks were all different colors, none of them natural skin tones. They were blue, red, orange, and green, and other than the vibrant hues, they were plain and featureless and strapped securely to the front of the face. Markla's mask was dark purple. When all the masks were in place, the whole group started running across the field. Dru was in the lead, moving fast. Markla knew she could pass him, but she also knew he wouldn't like that so she let him stay in front. She stayed close behind, with her long hair flying, and it felt wonderful; running was one of the most primitive things a person could do. The building had no windows on the ground level and just a single door built into its smooth exterior. The door slid open, and there was a pudgy guy standing there. He had nervous eyes and wore a dark blue jumpsuit. "Everyone's upstairs!" he hissed. "Three people and that's it."

"Great," Dru said. "Let's go."

Everyone followed him. They bolted past a glass desk and the gleaming station logo on the wall and then ran up a winding flight of stairs. They raced down a short hallway and burst through another door into a cramped room filled with black consoles and blinking lights—and two men and a woman sitting at a table in the corner, eating oranges and crackers. They were all wearing blue jumpsuits.

"It's our world now!" Dru screamed. He pulled out his club and charged.

Markla froze. The people at the table just stared with open mouths—but then one guy leaped to his feet and Dru swung at his head. The guy stepped aside, avoiding the blow, and then grabbed a chair and blocked the next strike. Then he cursed and lunged toward Dru, slamming the chair into Dru's chest and knocking him to the floor. The man was big like a bear, and he held the chair high and swung it hard—but Dru rolled away just in time. The chair hit the floor and smashed into pieces.

Now the three guys behind Markla dove into the fray, swinging wildly. Meanwhile, the woman in the corner hurled an orange at Dru as he staggered to his feet. The "chair guy" was being pummeled, and the other guy was trying to run, and the woman was cursing and throwing some dishes that smashed against the wall. Everyone was shouting.

Markla started shouting, too, and swinging. But she was in a daze, and her heart was pounding, and she didn't swing at any people—she swung at the consoles. Wasn't that what they'd really come to do? To send a message about this technological disease that was infecting the world? Her metal club hit the glass console in front of her and it shattered. She hit it a few more times and moved to the next one. And then there was the sound of an alarm ringing. It shrieked through her head like a spike.

What? Supposedly, the security system had been disabled. Something was wrong.

The woman and one of the men ran from the room. The guy who'd used the chair was on the floor in a pool of blood. Markla looked at him, and a wave of nausea washed over her. Meanwhile, Dru was cursing and waving his arms.

"Smash everything!" he said. "Destroy it all!"

"No!" came a voice. It was the jittery guy who'd let them in. He was their spy, and Markla knew his name was Tiber, and now he said, "You need to get out now. We all do!"

Dru hesitated while the alarm kept screaming. Markla said, "He's right, Dru. Let's go!"

Dru snarled and seized Tiber with both hands. "Why is the alarm still on?"

"I don't know," Tiber said. "But we need to go."

"But the alarm was supposed to be off!"

Everyone was shouting now. "Let's go, Dru! Let's go!"

"But we've hardly done any damage! And we didn't do the motto!"

"I'll do it!" Markla blurted. "You guys keep smashing stuff."

Dru hesitated again and then gave her a little smile. "All right," he said, and he reached into his knapsack and tossed her a can of spray paint. "Go!"

Markla bolted back into the hallway and down the stairs. Painting the motto was purely symbolic, but then again so was the entire attack; after all, smashing up one dream station wasn't going to bring down the government. She ran into the main entry area, right near the reception desk. She grabbed a chair and slid it into position so she could reach up higher. Her pulse was racing. This was a crazy thing to do but she was glad to get out of that room—and besides, everyone would love it. But she had to be quick.

She leaped onto the chair and in a few seconds the motto was splattered across the wall in fuzzy red letters: *"FIGHT BACK!"* She paused for a moment to examine her work, and for an instant she was filled with pride. And then someone tackled her from behind.

"Oof!" she said and hit the floor hard. The can of paint rolled across the floor.

It was a guy dressed in black, some kind of security person. Why hadn't he been accounted for by Tiber?

Markla twisted onto her back, and now the guy was on top of her, and he was swinging his fists, and she tried to block his hands, but he was big and heavy—and now he was hitting her, and then he had a forearm across her neck. His dark eyes were raging as he looked down at her.

"I've got you now, little girl," he said with a snarl. "You're finished."

She tried to slither away but she was pinned under his bulk. She couldn't breathe, and she was gagging, and his arm was crushing her throat. She felt trapped, smothered, helpless—and then she wriggled her right hand free, down to where she had a dagger strapped to her hip.

She was struggling for air and things were getting hazy. She couldn't do it, no way, no chance—but then her fear and panic turned into rage, a rage that blossomed inside her like a mushroom cloud. *Not today! And never again!* With one desperate motion, she grabbed the weapon and drove the blade into the man's neck.

His eyes bulged. She yanked out the blade and did it once more. He gasped and went limp.

Markla pushed and twisted and slid out from underneath him. She got to her knees, coughing and gulping air and then coughing again. The room was spinning, and she was once again filled with nausea—and her hands were slick with blood. She stared with wide eyes at the blood on her clothes, and on the floor, and all over the dead man. *What did I do?* But now someone else was in the room. It was one of the guys she'd seen upstairs, along with the woman—and he had a weapon in his hand, a black stick. Markla started to move, but he leaped forward and shoved it into her ribs.

She felt an agonizing jolt and everything went black.

Chapter 2

Everyone was talking at Seaview Secondary School. In the halls, in the courtyard, in the restrooms, the dissonant whispers grew to a roar.

"She was in 20 Eyes," Dimitri said. "She murdered six people." Rune looked up at Dimitri and stared. Everyone looked up at Dimitri because he was tall like a tree. He was also gawky and skinny and pasty-looking and tended to laugh at things no one else found funny. Right now Rune was standing with Dimitri in a crowded hallway, the one with wide windows overlooking a windy ocean, near a place where a great city had supposedly stood 10,000 years ago. But Rune wasn't thinking about ancient history.

He shook his head. "I don't believe it," he finally managed to say. "Markla wouldn't kill anyone."

Dimitri laughed. "What do you mean?" he said, sounding smug. "You hardly know her. You just think you do because you've been in love with her forever."

"That's not true!" Rune shot back. He didn't blush easily, but now he felt his olive skin turning red, and he spun away so fast that his long hair moved like a whip. It was the color of charcoal and hung to his shoulders.

I've just been thinking about her a lot lately.

Dimitri laughed again. "Maybe you can visit her in prison. You can sneak her a bomb inside a bunch of roses." Then he gave a snort and said, "I'm sure you'll find someone else. Plenty of girls like you."

Do they? Rune thought. But he didn't have time for Dimitri's envy. He had other things on his mind.

It wasn't true that he hardly knew Markla. In fact, he never remembered not knowing her. They'd been classmates since first grade, and friendly in a "school friend" kind of way—and of course he'd noticed her because she was noticeable. But this year he'd paid extra attention to her because…he just had. He sat right behind her in math class—and yeah, she was interesting, and he always tried to say something clever to her when the class ended. But he was just being nice, and he usually said, "Hey, see you tomorrow." He'd used that witty line lots of times.

Meanwhile, the swirl of chatter and hearsay was drowning Rune like an ocean. Markla Flash was involved in a plot that had killed five people, or maybe four. No, wait—it was three, or maybe two. The victims had been stabbed to death, or slaughtered in some primitive way that was the trademark of 20 Eyes, the subversive organization that threatened the country. And now it was obvious she was in that group. After all, she didn't dress like other Sparklan girls; she was mainly known for oversized flannel shirts covered with cat hair. She didn't wear makeup, and she liked jewelry made from pebbles and seashells, and her long hair was always tangled and messy. She'd quit the Run Team, even though she'd been a tough competitor, and she'd stopped socializing with other kids at school—not that she'd ever done much, anyway.

Rune doubted Markla ever gave him much thought. *Why would she?* But maybe now it was for the best.

Dimitri nudged him with a bony elbow. "They'll probably bring her to the Dream Prison after she's sentenced. They'll get someone nasty to write for her. One of the top people, for sure."

Probably, Rune thought—and it was sad. Markla was smart, but if all this talk turned out to be true she'd be sent to the Dream Prison and sentenced to nightmares, probably a high number. Rune was familiar with the creation of nightmares, since he was a student at the Cold Brook Dream Academy. But so was Markla, and Dimitri, too. They spent some days here in normal classes for "advanced" sixteen-year-olds—but three days per week, they went to the academy where they were training to be dream writers. Dreams were so much more interesting than reality.

As he walked down the hall, Rune glanced through the windows at the rocky beach and watched the rolling waves, and he wondered where Markla was right now. He wondered what she was seeing. He was still thinking about her as he slid into a desk in his morning history class, with Dimitri in front of him and Janna to his right. In this class, Markla used to sit in the far corner of the room, where she'd been barely visible to Rune—unless he craned his neck. Meanwhile, Dimitri kept talking to Janna, who was striking with her deep blue eyes, coppery skin, and honey brown hair hanging down. They were both talkers, much more than Rune.

Dimitri grinned. "Well, it's one less person to worry about in the Dream Project."

"Nice," Janna said. "Were you worried about her?"

"Hey, Markla's weird, but she's not dumb. One of us should break into her dreambank and see what she was working on, now that she doesn't need it."

"How would you do that?"

"There's a GoBug script that can do it. It's illegal—but Rune has it."

"Rune, is that true?" she said. "Are you hanging out with the smashers again?"

Rune gave her a blank look. At the mention of the Dream Project, his ears had perked up. The project was a major competition at the school, and everyone wanted to win—especially Rune. And it was true, he sometimes connected with "smashers," people who collected and traded special scripts that could do all kinds of wild things, some of them illegal. But Rune wasn't a bona fide smasher—it was just a hobby. And yes, he had a script that could supposedly break into anyone's dreambank. But he'd never tested it on anything difficult. Not yet.

He gave Janna a smile and a little shrug. "I don't know," he said. "But maybe I should let Dimitri try it. His best chance of winning would be to steal something."

Janna laughed. "Hear that, Dimitri? Rune's going to let you steal Markla's LiveDream. Who knows what you might end up with. Probably something scary."

"She's a good dream writer," Rune said. "She's got good stuff."

"Yeah, right," Dimitri said with a grin. "And how much of her 'stuff' did she show you?"

Rune gave Dimitri a cool stare, but Dimitri didn't seem to care. "She was always crazy," Dimitri said.

"That's true," Janna replied. "But she's still innocent until proven guilty."

Dimitri scoffed. "Didn't you get into a fight with her once?"

"We were ten, Dimitri, and it was my fault."

"She punched you in the nose—you were bleeding. She hit you hard."

"Yeah, but that's because I called her a 'piglet' and put orange paint in her hair. I felt bad, and we made up a week later—sort of. But I think she's hated me ever since. Anyway, regardless of what she did, she still has rights."

Dimitri gave a snort. "You're not the only one she fought with. It's a pattern. First a punch in the nose, then a dagger through the heart. Isn't that right, Rune?" Then he gave Janna a sly look as he added, "She's a Basic. Rune likes Basic girls."

Rune didn't respond. It was a common joke that Markla was a "Basic"—one of those strange people known to live in the woods away from the world.

Janna answered in a sharp tone. "Leave Rune alone!" she

snapped. "You don't know what he likes, and you don't know the whole story about any of this." Dimitri laughed yet again, but Rune knew it was a hollow laugh. Dimitri didn't like to argue with Janna; he was usually too busy trying to impress her. At this point Mr. Kyla asked for everyone's attention. He was their teacher, and he was strong like a box of barbells, and he loved to talk about how their nation of Sparkla was superior to previous societies. Sparkla wasn't just a democracy—it was a direct democracy. Through the use of technology, people could easily vote on any issue that was deemed important, without lawmakers and bureaucrats in between looking to aid their friends and cronies. According to Mr. Kyla, this was why Sparkla was such a paradise. It was a lush green country that stretched down the continental coast and westward to a great river, and it contained far more trees than people. It was a land that knew how to manage its resources—and a place where the will of the people was always done, blah, blah. All in all, Rune hated this class. It was a lot of tedious talk about the world.

Mr. Kyla's voice boomed throughout the room. "Everybody quiet down," he said. "I know there are crazy things going on today, and we've all heard about them—but we have a lot to cover. Important stuff."

"Right," Rune thought. And now he recalled how Markla hated this class, too, but for different reasons. She'd claimed it was "propaganda for the toads." And how had he responded? He'd laughed and said, "Hey, I'll see you tomorrow."

He closed the notebook. Mr. Kyla was still talking but he didn't hear a word.

Chapter 3

Markla wiped her teary eyes. She was in a room the size of a bathroom shower stall with drab stone walls and a hard metal chair—and she'd never felt so alone. Meanwhile, on the other side of a thick glass window, her mother Sharli was shaking her head.

Markla gave her mother a quick look. Markla had been adopted, and she did not physically resemble Sharli. Yes, they both had black hair and the olive skin so common in the country of Sparkla—but Markla's eyes were dark green, like a pond in a forest, while Sharli's were a more traditional shade of brown. Also, Sharli was tall and bulky. She's so much bigger than me, Markla thought, and it was something she'd always remember—being six years old, and her mother staring down.

Markla wiped her eyes again and took a deep breath. All right, let's get through this, she thought. Her mom was talking and crying at the same time, and the words seemed far away.

"Markla, how could you?" she said. "How could you join a subversive group? How could you murder someone? When did you turn into a monster?"

Markla blinked a few times. There were so many things she wanted to say, and she wanted to throw the words and watch them cling to her mother's face like the stickiest mud in the world. She wanted to scream and explode—but she didn't. If her mom hadn't figured it out by now it was pointless.

I'll just sit here and be quiet, she thought. *Can I do that? I will. I will.*

Markla stopped crying. She took another deep breath and spoke in a soft voice.

"It's good to see you, too, Mom."

Sharli hesitated. Then her eyes flashed like fireworks. "Always with the snotty remarks," she said. "Always with the attitude—why? Was your life so bad? This wasn't my fault, do you hear me?"

"No one's blaming you!" Markla spat. "It was my choice, and why do you care? You're not even my real mother. You're no one's mother."

Sharli froze for a second, and then her mouth dropped open. "I can't believe you said that. After all I did for you."

"Is that so?" Markla said. "Like what? I know what you did for me—and I'm not the only monster in the room! You never cared about me or Tommi at all."

That went well, Markla thought. *Quiet as a bomb.*

Sharli shook her head. "I don't know what you're talking about," she said. "And by the way, it's not like you were the best daughter in the world. But you never think about that, do you?"

Markla banged her fists on the window. "Why am I even talking about this? I hate you, and I will *always* hate you! Get out of here and leave me alone! Again!"

Sharli leaned toward the glass and spoke with a low snarl. "Your life was never that bad, Markla. You exaggerate so much. You want to talk about Tommi? How do you think he feels today? He has to go to school and hear how his sister is a murderer! But you were always causing trouble. Now you want me to leave you alone—fine. I'll leave you here to rot."

She leaped from her chair so fast it fell over, but she barely seemed to notice. Then she said, "You don't know what I went through, Markla. You're too young to understand, and a lot of it was your fault! My life would've been so much better without you." She whirled and motioned to a chunky female guard wearing dark glasses. "I'm done here. I want to leave." The guard's face remained blank as she nodded and escorted her to a door. Sharli didn't look back as she hurried away.

Markla listened to the echo of her mother's footsteps and then put her head in her hands. Had her mom really deserved that? Yeah, for sure—in fact, she deserved worse, much worse. She's the one I should've killed, Markla thought—along with a few of her loser boyfriends. But at the same time, guilt was gnawing at her. It felt like a small rodent was chewing on her insides.

She never loved me, Markla thought. *And I made everything worse—I did.*

The guard came over and said, "Back to your cell. Let's go."

The guard shoved Markla down a bleak hallway that led deeper into the prison. Markla stared at the heavy metal shackles on her wrists and thought about Dru and the others in 20 Eyes. Was Dru worried she would give up secret information? She clamped her jaw shut; she wouldn't say a word. Dru will be proud of me, she thought.

Then she thought about her twelve-year-old brother, Tommi, and the things her mother had just said. Would he really think she was a monster? Probably. *I just hope he feeds the cats. I think he will.*

The guard led her to another dreary cell and undid the shackles. "Get in." Then the guard closed the hefty door and it clanged shut.

Markla sat on a metal bench. Her chest was heaving. She tried to calm down but it was useless. Was all this real? *Please, can this be a dream?* She knew it wasn't.

She should be in math class now. Rune would be trying to talk to her, and she'd be wondering what he was thinking. He seemed to like me, Markla thought, but he never really said anything—and that was too bad because he was smart and good-looking. He wrote the best dreams, and he wrote the scariest nightmares. In fact, he seemed too nice to write some of the things he did. But of course she didn't know everything that happened in his house, just like no one knew what happened in hers.

She suppressed a sob. All this was pointless now. Rune, Dru, Tommi, her mother—she'd probably never see any of them again.

Chapter 4

The school day was over and Rune slipped fast through the crowded halls. He burst out of the building and jumped onto his flyboard. It was a standard size board; it was longer than his arm, thinner than his hand, and it rose off the ground to the height of an ankle. In an instant, the reverse gravity generator caused it to cling to his feet and he was off, zooming down the tree-lined streets and fumbling to get the GoBug in place behind his ear.

The GoBug was gold, and about the size of an almond, and it worked by proximity. There was no wire that connected it to his brain, but when he heard the chime inside his head, he thought "Rune Roko, dreamer"—his name and *stream code*—and he was connected.

Now he could see whatever mindstreams he'd joined. With help from the GoBug, his mind made it seem like the three-dimensional images were hanging in the air a short distance from his eyes. But they were not actually there, and to any casual observers Rune would appear to be staring at nothing. Meanwhile, the same observers might be viewing mindstreams of their own. If they were all tuned to the same stream, they would all see the same images—but they would only see them in front of their own faces. No one could tell what anyone else was seeing.

Whoah! He swerved to avoid hitting a cat. The animal paused to give him a dirty look. It wasn't a great idea to watch a stream while riding a flyboard, but today he couldn't wait until he got home.

Go to news Rune thought, and then *go to Markla Flash*, and *add 20 Eyes*. Now he saw a group of newspeople sitting there like well-dressed manakins, discussing the incident—and there was an image of Markla! She had a faraway look in her eyes. She also had a bloody lip and swelling on the side of her face, like someone had hit her.

Rune felt a flash of anger. Then he frowned as a commercial

cut into the stream. Commercials were a new addition to mind-streams—the population had voted in favor of this change, and it meant people could now choose to watch commercials in exchange for free LiveDreams. This commercial was for Sky Oat cereal, and he ate it all the time.

GoBug off.

He could scan for news about the attack later. He kicked the flyboard up a notch and flew through the quiet streets of his town, a place called Cooly Strip. The Strip was part of a peninsula just west of the mainland, and it was covered with piney forests ringed by sandy beaches and a sky-blue sea. He knew from Kyla's dull class that this area had been called many things during the last 10,000 years, from Liberte to Nova Scotia, but now it was just another part of Sparkla. There were few houses on his street but this was common. In the entire nation of Sparkla that stretched down the coast to the topical zone, there were less than one million people.

By the time he got home his head felt light, like he was floating. He leaned the board up against the small and tidy-looking house. It was the color of sand, and like most Sparklan homes it was constructed from wood and blocks made from plant fibers. There were ample windows, and the roof gleamed with thin green tiles that converted sunlight into electricity. His mother Maya was in the living room when he arrived, sunk down into the cushy sofa with her GoBug. She was wearing a fuzzy purple bathrobe and drinking herbal tea from her favorite mug, the delicate one that featured a picture of a rose. She was pretty in a disheveled way, like a piece of birthday cake tossed onto the floor. She was also submerged in a LiveDream. Maya spent a lot of time in LiveDreams—a lot. She didn't see Rune at first, but then the LiveDream ended and her eyes seemed more aware. She looked at him and smiled.

"Hi, Rune. I didn't realize it was so late. I was supposed to wash my hair." Her dyed blond hair was tied in a ponytail; her natural color was walnut brown. "How was everything today?"

"It was okay," Rune said. "What LiveDream were you in?"

She gave a little laugh. "It was dumb, but it was romantic. It was just a dream." She smiled. "Do you ever write romantic dreams, Rune?"

The question caught him off guard. "No," he said. "I never tried that."

"You should. That's what the girls like, and it's good to do what the girls like."

For an instant, Rune thought about Markla, and how she'd never written a romantic dream—at least none that he'd seen.

"Not all girls write romantic dreams," he said. "I know one who doesn't."

"She will," Maya said. "She'll write that dream one day, Rune." Then she smiled again and said, "Who knows, maybe you'll write it with her."

For the second time in one day, Rune's face turned red. And now his mom was laughing.

"Is this the girl you're always talking about?" she said.

"What? Who?"

"You always mention 'a girl you know,' and I'm wondering if this 'girl you know' and that 'girl you know' are all the same girl—and hey, are you talking about Markla Flash?" Maya watched Rune's reaction and laughed again. "Oh, she's a wild one, Rune. I saw her last week on a flyboard, zigzagging all over the place, doing crazy tricks. You've always liked her, haven't you? She's a cute little thing."

"Yeah, she is," Rune blurted. "I mean—no, that's not her. There is no girl." Then he mumbled, "Markla's just a friend." Obviously, his mom hadn't been watching any news streams today and that was good. Meanwhile, she was still laughing. Then she glanced out the window as a blue car glided to a stop in front of the house. Like most vehicles in Sparkla, it used an anti-grav generator to float a short distance about the ground. Maya watched it park and her smile faded.

"Your father's home," she said. Then she sighed. "Let's get the party started."

Rune had a sinking feeling. Blog Roko was tall, and he held his head high as he walked through the front door. He'd been a Warrior Captain in the Sparklan army before taking his job with the police force, and Rune often thought he should've stayed in the army. He did not look like Rune. His dark hair was short and combed into a neat block, and his body was wide, and he wore shiny black boots that stomped on the ground when he walked and sent creatures running for cover. He also wore the perfectly pressed indigo uniform of the nation's police force, along with a gold sash that indicated his position as a Centurion.

"Hello, Rune," he said with a grunt. Then he looked at Maya. "So, how was the sofa today? Anything big happen over there?"

Maya eyed Blog for a second and then got up. "I was about to wash my hair," she said.

Blog grunted. "It's good to have a plan. Maybe tomorrow you can comb it."

Maya shook her head and put down her teacup. "It's great that you're home early, Blog. You can start your nasty comments sooner than usual."

He smirked but said nothing. She sighed and left the room, and Rune heard the bedroom door click shut.

It's true, she doesn't do much, he thought. *But she doesn't do any harm, either.*

Blog walked into the kitchen, opened the refrigerator, and wrapped his shovel-like hand around a bottle of ale. Rune started walking fast to his room, but then Blog said, "Wait a second. I want to talk to you."

Rune swore to himself. "About what?" he said, trying to sound calm. It was always the best way. But he guessed another sermon was coming, another blast of hot air from his father's face about his future and his duty and how he needed to "be tough"—unless it was about something worse.

Blog splashed some ale into his mouth. "We arrested a girl from your dream class. She was a member of 20 Eyes."

"Yeah, I know."

"And she's already been found guilty. That's why the new system is so good. Criminals don't get time to stall."

"They also don't get time to defend themselves."

Blog laughed. "What criminal told you that? People voted for the new laws, and for good reason. They realized we had to get tougher, and that's what makes Sparkla a great country—the people are the lawmakers. Of course, we have Interpreters to explain the consequences of the more complex stuff, and we have the Territory Keepers to evaluate all the daily petitions—but once the National Keeper puts it up for a vote, it's a simple 'yes' or 'no' answer from everyone, and the GoBugs make it easy. And that's why it's your duty to be informed about what's going on around you, Rune. So, do you know her?"

"No," Rune said quickly—maybe too quickly. "I know who she is…but I don't really know her."

Blog studied him. "That's good," he finally said. "It's not good to know scum like that. And it's not good to be involved with all this dream stuff. You need to start thinking about your future."

"I *am* thinking about my future. I'm going to be a professional dream writer. I keep telling you that."

"I know, and I keep telling you it's stupid. Only a handful of people make any money doing that—and besides, people in that industry have no honor, no code." Blog paused and then said, "Did you enter the Dream Project at your school?"

"Of course I entered."

"Did you win?"

"They haven't announced anything yet."

Blog shook his head. "You've still got time to open your eyes. Let someone else write all that sappy garbage that makes your mom cry tears of joy, boo hoo."

"She doesn't always cry. She didn't always spend so much time in LiveDreams. Not until you made her miserable."

Rune braced himself. Had he gone too far? He was sweating—and he clenched his fist. Because if Blog came at him, he was going to fight back. Maybe.

But Blog just took another swig of ale. "Is that what I do?" he said. "I didn't put her where she is now. She spends her whole day looking at those dreams. When I met her, she had dreams of her own. But now she's an addict, and you want to be one of the people who keeps her that way. Reality is a tough thing for most people, Rune—you need to be strong, and dreaming makes people weak. It makes people forget what's real. I'm just trying to help her, and I'm trying to help you."

"Your idea of 'help' is mostly telling me what I can't do."

"The truth always helps people who can face it. Don't lie to yourself—nobody likes a weak man. In fact, one of the reasons your mother married me was because I was *not* weak. It's about making tough choices, real choices. But nothing in a LiveDream is real. You did real things before, like the Run Team, but what happened? It got hard and you quit."

"That's not why I quit. I had other stuff to do."

"Like what? Spend your time with dream writers—like that no good girl."

"She's not 'no good'!" Rune shot back.

Blog cocked his big head and stared. "I thought you didn't know her."

Rune stared back. He hesitated, and then he said, "I know her. I know her well. And I like her."

Rune whirled and stormed out the front door. He waited to hear the heavy sound of his father's feet coming after him. But it didn't happen.

Rune breathed a sigh of relief. He'd escaped. For now.

Chapter 5

Markla kept her face blank as two bulky female guards escorted her through the prison. Inside, she was shaking like a leaf, but she wasn't going to show it. The guards shoved her into a small room with blank gray walls, an examination table, a few pieces of shiny equipment, and no windows. On the floor was a black mat.

One of the guards pointed at the floor. "Strip and stand on the mat."

Markla hesitated but then did as she was told. She wasn't modest, and she had nothing to hide. But then she felt a flash of fear because she knew people were sexually assaulted in prison—and wasn't this a bit soon? *Can't they give me a couple of hours so I can maybe find a rope and hang myself?*

But they didn't assault her. Instead, they looked her over and then studied a three-dimensional image of her body that appeared near the wall, a ghostly gray shape designed to show inorganic devices concealed in hard to reach places. They grunted with satisfaction before tossing her some undergarments and a pair of blaring yellow jumpsuits. As Markla put on the underwear she noticed the guards had names stitched onto their blue shirts. Crolle was dark-skinned with wavy black hair and lots of eyeliner while Dano was light-skinned with cocoa brown hair and a face that looked incapable of smiling. Before Markla could put the jumpsuit on, Dano unsnapped a banana-sized black stick from her belt.

"Do you know what this is?" Dano said.

Markla knew but didn't answer. She braced herself, and there was a sizzling sound, and then Dano jammed the end of the device into Markla's stomach.

Markla shrieked—the pain was horrific, like every cell in her body was going to explode.

Both guards laughed. "This isn't a normal stun stick," Dana said. "This thing is used for discipline, and it will keep you conscious—and in agony, if that's what we want. So follow the rules." Then Dano gave Crolle a sideways glance and said, "Hey, she killed one of ours, right? Maybe we should give her a few more jolts. Hold her down on the table. I'm going to make her cry like a baby."

Markla's heart started pounding, and she clenched a fist, ready to fight. Go for the eyes, she thought. *If they kill me, they kill me!* She was ready to move—but then another woman came into the room. She was slender, with brown skin and braided black hair, and she wore a white coat over her uniform, like a doctor. As soon as she appeared the guards stopped their torture talk.

The doctor gave Dano a sharp look. "Don't abuse the prisoner," she said. "She's going to get plenty of that in the dream room."

Dano shrugged. "We were just fooling around," she said. "She looks like she can take it."

The doctor noted the guard's comment and glanced at Markla, who was still wearing just a bra and panties. She examined two jagged scars on Markla's shoulder blade as well as a collection of others on her back.

"Did 20 Eyes do this to you, honey? I hear they have quite an initiation process."

Markla said nothing. Yeah, 20 Eyes had done some of it. *But not most of it.*

The doctor pulled out a silver object the size of a pencil. "You're obviously no stranger to pain," she said. "I doubt this will bother you much." She grabbed Markla's hand and jabbed the object into her forearm, and it was true, Markla wasn't bothered by it. "That's a tracking device," the doctor said. "I've imbedded it under your skin. It's not too deep, but don't try to remove it. We'll know, and believe me, the punishment won't be worth it.

So now we know where you are at all times. Remember that."

The doctor left and Markla finished putting on one of the jumpsuits. Since it was still warm outside, Markla chose the lighter version with short sleeves rather than the heavier one where the sleeves were full-length. She fumbled with it a bit but kept her hands from shaking. A minute later she was being escorted deeper into the prison, and as she looked around her heart sank. The place was like a giant cave made of bars and clanging doors. Her wrists were shackled, and she could feel the eyes staring as she passed a row of cells—or was she imagining it? Stop being so paranoid, she thought. *Why would anyone care about me?* She was just one more animal heading into a cage. And the cells did look like cages. The doors were just frames of metal bars that hid nothing. She was going to be on exhibit all the time, like a creature in a zoo.

Markla kept walking and forced her eyes straight ahead. She didn't want to look into the cells and see anyone looking back—she didn't want to see her future, not yet. If she could postpone the thought for another minute that would be fine.

The guards led her across a walkway that overlooked an open area. She looked down and saw other prisoners below, both men and women, sitting at tables and hanging around. She knew the famous Dream Prison was co-ed, and this made her stomach squirm. The men and women's cells were in separate parts of the prison while everyone was allowed to mingle in common areas. Maybe I'll fall in love, she thought, and she imagined a guy coming up to her and saying something corny like, "Hey, do you come here often?" and she would reply, "Only after I kill someone—how about you?"

She shook her head at the grim joke. Then the guards took her through a few checkpoints and into the women's zone. They went past another row of cells along another walkway and then stopped in front of a cell with an open door. "This is your new home," Dano said. "Follow the rules and don't cause any trouble. You can go to the yard this afternoon. Right now I guess you can do a little decorating." Then she laughed and walked away.

Markla scanned the cell and felt her spirits fade even more. It was so small, like something for a dog. The bed was a stiff-looking metal frame covered by a thin mattress close to the floor. Attached to the wall right near the end of the bed was a metal toilet and a tiny sink, and a section of shelves—and that was it. She suddenly felt sick and lightheaded and wanted to sit down, but for some reason she didn't. Twenty years, she thought. *Twenty years.* On the upside, she was the only one in the cell. In fact, all the cells only held one prisoner each. Well, she didn't want to see anyone and she didn't want to talk to anyone. She was going to sit in this cage like a mute for twenty years—or maybe not.

A scrawny woman was coming toward her, a pale woman with stringy dark hair that was streaked with gray. She also had smeared black makeup around her eyes that made her look like a raccoon, and it seemed like she wanted to talk. Stay calm, Markla thought. *She might not be as crazy as she looks.* The woman seemed to sense Markla's anxiety and stopped walking before she was too close. She smiled and spoke in a voice that sounded like the quack of a duck.

"Hi, I'm Nan," she said, staring with gray eyes that did not blink.

"Hi. I'm Markla."

"I know who you are. You're really young—and small. But you'll be okay because of your friends. You just need to meet up with them."

Markla wasn't sure what to say. So she said nothing.

Nan leaned closer and spoke fast, quacking now like she was nervous to get the words out. "They asked me to check on you and tell you a few things—mainly, watch out for the guards because you killed a government guy, right? These guards are all government people, and you killed one of theirs and they'll be coming at you, especially Dano and Crolle because they're the worst so watch out for them." Then her eyes opened wide and she added, "But don't worry, you came at a good time. You need to meet up with Bross and Blu, that's all. They're the ones who told me to find you. You'll see them in the yard—Bross and Blu. They'll explain what's going on."

"Thanks," Markla said. "But I just got here." Then she motioned toward her cell and said, "This is what I have going on."

"Are you in shock?" Nan said, and now Markla studied her face, and she could see this woman was probably younger than she looked, despite the gray hair. Nan continued, "Lots of people are in shock when they first come. Then they get used to it. Then you get the dreams, and it's worse—but you get used to that, too. But it's good to have people who can help, especially at first. Do you want a hairbrush? I have an extra one."

"No, thanks. I'm fine."

"Okay, okay. Do you want me to show you around? I can show you things. I've been here a while. I know a lot."

Markla hesitated. She didn't want any help from this lady, but then again she probably did know a few things—and there was no point in making enemies on her first day.

"Sure, that would be great," Markla said.

Nan showed Markla the dreary communal shower. She told her about the dining hall, and she sat with Markla when a chime sounded and they went there for lunch. Markla felt queasy and ate nothing. Meanwhile, Nan told Markla lots of things—mainly about herself, and how she'd hated her parents growing up, and how she'd hated her sister, and how she'd hated her school, and how she hated pretty much everything, and then she cried about something, but by that point Markla was mostly thinking about how she was going to get away from Nan. Then they went to the yard.

The prisoners moved like a herd through a narrow area between two of the stone buildings that ended with a high fence and a gate that led to an open yard beyond. While they were walking, Nan said, "Be careful when you're in a group, Markla. It's easy to get killed in a group. Someone will stick you and the guards won't care."

This got Markla's attention, and her eyes shifted quickly back and forth, watching everyone. But nothing happened and they were soon in the yard.

The yard was a wide fenced area, roughly square, that was located in the center of the complex of buildings. It was partly paved and partly covered with grass. Markla noted the distance from the iron fence around the yard to the main stone walls of the prison. How long would it take to run across that grassy field? She'd been a fast member of the Run Team, especially considering her size, and she figured she could cover the ground in about fifteen seconds—on her flyboard, maybe five. But that would be a long five seconds with people in the gun towers blasting away. And then there was a lofty stone wall to climb—impossible. Well, it was just a thought. It was important to keep hope alive.

She wanted to be alone now, but Nan was sticking to her like a bad disease. Then Nan motioned with her head and said, "There's Blu. He's the guy you need."

Blu was a dark-skinned guy with short kinky hair and bulging arms. He was handsome in a sinewy way and looked at least a dozen years older than Markla. He had a couple of other guys around him, shorter guys who had long hair—a skinny white guy and a stocky brown-skinned kid with a big smile. Then Blu saw Markla and waved for her to come over.

"Come on," Nan said, "Let's go." Markla didn't want to

go—but she did. When they got near Blu he grinned and then spoke in a deep voice. "Nan, me and this girl need to talk."

Just like that Nan left, and Markla felt relieved. Blu and his friends looked more dangerous than crazy, and Markla preferred it that way. He was studying her a bit, but for some reason Markla wasn't afraid. In fact, she felt defiant. I'm not going to be scared in here for twenty years, she thought. She'd been scared all morning, but now she was tired of it. *Whatever happens, happens.*

Blu was handsome, and he had teeth like pearls, and he grinned once again and said, "So you're Markla Flash. You're even smaller than I expected. You took out a security guy? Good for you."

Markla shrugged. "I didn't want to do it. It just happened."

"Oh, yeah? Well, a lot of things can 'just happen' to you in here if you're not careful. If you don't have friends."

"I'm not always good at making friends."

Blu laughed. "That's okay. I love a person with the right enemies. So, who doesn't like you, besides the government?"

Markla cocked her head and stared up at him. "My mother hates me. What does that mean?"

"It probably means you don't know her too well. Or maybe you're a little hard on yourself. Or maybe she just has no clue." Then he gave a snort and crossed his muscular arms. "But you're in the Eyes. You don't need her."

"Yeah," Markla said, and she stood up a little taller. "I'm in the Eyes."

"And you're a fierce little thing, aren't you?"

"No. I'm not like that. But I guess I shouldn't say that, right? I guess everyone in here needs to act tough all the time."

"Yeah, more or less—but Dru vouched for you. He said you were his 'little wildcat.' "

"Dru?" Markla blurted. At the mention of Dru's name her

heart leaped. "You know Dru? You talked to him, and he mentioned me?"

Blu grinned. "Sure, I know Dru. We communicated. He also told me you were smart, and we should make sure to include you in our plans." Then he turned toward the other two guys and said, "This is Bross and Plano. We're all in." The two guys each gave Markla a friendly nod.

She guessed they were both in their early twenties and seemed affable enough. But it was the thought of Dru that filled her with hope. It made her feel a little closer to the outside world.

"What else did Dru say?" she said.

"He said, 'stay strong, soldier—and get to know your friends.' That would be us." Then Blu paused and said, "We've all been in here about two years. We've got about fifteen members here in the men's section, and three over with the women. But now with you there, that makes four, and that's good because they could use some help. Rose is the one in charge over there, and you'll meet her soon. You're definitely the youngest one we've got... Dru also said our spies found out that someone from the government—probably Aldo Xantha—used the latest LiveDream tech to change the images of your crime, so be prepared for that. And be prepared for what's coming."

Markla narrowed her eyes. "What's coming?"

Blu looked around and lowered his voice. "We're busting out of here."

Chapter 6

After storming out of the house, Rune considered his options. There was the flyboard and there was the shed.

The shed was made from old timber, and it was located just inside the woods at the far end of the Roko's backyard. It was a sturdy structure surrounded by trees and covered with creeping vines, and it hadn't been used by his parents, so Rune had turned it into his "drum space." He'd swept it clean and painted the walls a shade of ice blue and then brought in some lighting orbs as well as a portable heater for cold nights. No one ever bothered him in the shed, and he rarely told anyone it existed. It was a place where he could bang away the world. Tonight he banged harder than usual.

When the moon was high and his hands were aching, he headed back to the house. The yard was flickering with fireflies, and his mind burned with thoughts of his father. He moved carefully to the side door of the house and stayed very still, listening. From some nearby bushes came the hum of crickets and the soft rustle of a scurrying animal—but there was no sound coming from inside. Blog always went to bed early, but would he be sleeping now? Or would he be waiting for Rune like one of the roaring monsters in the nightmares Rune created? *Come to think of it, all my monsters are big, loud, and mean.*

Rune slipped into the shadowy kitchen. Then he tiptoed into the living room and froze. His mother was sitting on the sofa but her back was turned. She had a GoBug behind her ear, and she was submerged in a LiveDream. This was normal enough. As he crept past her, he wondered what dream she was in. I hope it's something romantic, he thought.

Rune didn't have any brothers or sisters. Blog and Maya had decided to have only one child, and Rune often thought this was unfortunate. It would've been nice to have someone else around to absorb a share of Blog's sermons. Rune made it to his room and tried to sleep. He tossed and turned for a while but finally drifted off.

Suddenly, his eyes snapped open. *What time is it?* He sat up fast; it was just before dawn. He blinked a few times and then grabbed the GoBug from under his pillow and quickly slipped the device behind his ear.

Go to news! Go to 20 Eyes! Go to Markla Flash!

Instantly, Rune saw two polished-looking newspeople, a man and a woman. They both wore a look of alarm, like they were sitting on sharp objects. The man had a deep and urgent voice.

"So, what do we really know about this attack?" he said.

The woman opened her blue eyes wide. "These subversive groups usually have a primitive way of thinking, and they're proud to reject technology. But they're hypocrites because they actually use technology all the time, and this is another attempt to try and stop what the public demands—more options for the LiveDreams and the GoBugs."

Then a shoe commercial appeared, and Rune swore. There was nothing new about Markla, and he already had Air One shoes. He sunk back down into his pillows, waiting for Blog to leave the house.

Finally, Rune heard Blog's boots thumping toward the front door. A few seconds later, Rune was racing into the bathroom for a quick shower. Maya wouldn't wake up for a while, so Rune ate his usual breakfast alone in the kitchen—some oatmeal with sliced bananas and raisins, and then some rye toast with peanut butter and raspberry jam. He frowned at the sight of heavy rain pelting the kitchen window. He'd be taking the bus to the Dream Academy instead of his flyboard.

The bus resembled a bulbous glass beetle floating above the

ground. As Rune hurried through the rain and stepped into the vehicle he saw Dimitri motioning to him, and he hesitated. Rune was in no mood for more jokes about Markla—but Janna was sitting in the double-seat in front of Dimitri along with Trilla, who was always friendly and sweet. So Rune sat down next to Dimitri, right near the two girls.

"It's today," Dimitri said with a grin. "They're going to announce the winner of the Dream Project."

The words hit Rune like a punch in the chest. "Really?" he said. "Already?"

"Yeah, it's true," Janna said. "Didn't you see it? Diana posted it this morning. So maybe one of us will go pro."

Rune hadn't seen it; he'd been too busy checking for news about Markla and whoever she'd murdered. Now he told himself to stay calm and act casual—but it would be difficult. He'd been working on his LiveDream entries for months, but were they good enough? He was never happy with them, and they could be so much better, and maybe they were terrible. In his mind, he heard his father blabbering about the low success rate for dream writers—and was he wrong?

Pro dreams were created by high-level professionals and sold to the public. Through the use of a GoBug, a person could purchase any dream they liked and have it streamed directly into their consciousness. A well-written LiveDream allowed the user to experience it as if it were reality, and top LiveDream writers were celebrities who earned big money. But it was difficult to create pro-level dreams. It wasn't just about the story or the images; it was about making people feel submerged. The more skilled the dream writer, the more real the dream would seem. The winner of this contest would have their dream entered into the national dreambank for purchase, and they would also get a royalty as well as free publicity. Winning the contest could lead to serious opportunities, and what would Blog think about that?

Rune laughed to himself. Blog wouldn't be too impressed but it might shut him up for a few seconds—and Rune would be on his way to something better.

Dimitri was smiling. "I'm going to win," he said. "You people are playing for second."

Janna rolled her eyes. "Sure, Dimitri. I'll keep that in mind when you lose—by a lot."

"You think you've got me beat?"

"I think everyone has you beat. I'm sure Rune has you beat."

Dimitri gave a snort. "Rune's got nothing."

"Rune writes great dreams and you know it."

Dimitri bristled while Rune just shrugged. "Thanks, Janna," Rune said. "But your dreams are amazing. I guess we'll see what happens."

Janna grinned at Rune. He smiled at her and tried to relax, even though Janna was his biggest competitor. Her dreams weren't overly original, but they were quite realistic. Then for an instant, Rune thought about Markla. No one will ever see her dreams, he thought, and he felt so sad—even though he guessed she'd been no threat to win the contest. He'd seen several of her dreams, and they were filled with dark smothering spaces, and eerie figures who lurked in the shadows, and then black outdoor skies bursting with vivid colors that were blinding and chaotic. Markla's dreams were disturbing yet they weren't exactly nightmares. They were bizarre abstract visions that made no sense to anyone but her—*and why did she show me those?* He'd complimented her originality, and he'd pondered her dreams quite a bit, and now he wished she could be here to share them.

They filed off the bus and headed through the rain into the Dream Academy, a squat gray building in a lush wooded area on the outskirts of Cooly Strip. Rune was quiet as they entered one of the classrooms near the lab, and he tried not to frown at the sight of Aldo Xantha standing in front of the class. Aldo was the Director of the Dream Academy and the brother of the nation's president. For some reason, Aldo always wore a short white coat like the kind worn by Sparklan laboratory technicians. He was also short and skinny with a pasty face and curly reddish hair tumbling down. It was rumored to be replacement hair—but why would anyone replace real hair with that stuff? It looked like rusty seaweed. Yet the hair was trivial compared to the InfoLenses.

The round lenses resembled goggles, and Aldo wore them constantly. The lenses continuously gathered data and fed it into Aldo's GoBug for analysis, and they made Aldo look like a cross between a robot and an insect. Rune turned away fast as Aldo stared in his direction, and now he saw Diana Drogo enter the room.

She was their principal instructor, a pixie-sized blonde about the age of Rune's mother. She was pretty but often had dark rings under her eyes, like she'd been awake all night. Today she smiled at Rune. Everyone knew she liked Rune, and he wished she'd make it less obvious. He was tired of everyone saying he was her favorite. Then again, Rune really wanted to win the Dream Project, and if being her favorite helped he wouldn't complain.

Diana was smiling at everyone now. "We have an announcement," she said. "As you know, we have a winner for the Dream Project. But first, let me say you shouldn't be upset if you didn't win. Everyone wrote fantastic dreams, and you've all got great potential, so just keep working at it." Then she paused—and Rune realized he wasn't breathing.

Diana said, "The winner of the Dream Project is Janna Krolla."

Janna let out a shriek and clapped her hands to her face.

Rune turned fast to look at her, and he smiled—but inside,

he felt like his heart had dropped into a crater. So that was it, he thought. *But how?* Janna's dreams were so...safe. In fact, they were insipid. They were predictable and stupid! *I knew I should've redone that second one! My father is right. I'll never get anywhere with this stuff.*

Rune slid back in his chair and kept the fake smile on his face. Meanwhile, Dimitri was grinning and congratulating Janna, along with everyone else—and Diana was still talking, saying that they'd all get to experience Janna's dream.

Rune felt like he was far away from the room. He felt like he was in a trance, and the last thing he wanted to do was watch Janna's banal vision. The last thing he wanted was to start comparing it to his own dreams, and then see all the obvious flaws in what he'd done. But everyone was told to activate their GoBugs, and everyone did—and an alert sounded. *What now?* Apparently, an important news bulletin was coming through the government news stream, something of national importance. The same two newspeople Rune had seen earlier were now in front of everyone's eyes.

No one was obligated to watch but since Diana had used her thoughts to switch from Janna's LiveDream to the news stream, everyone did. The news people were still talking about 20 Eyes. "What a vicious murder!" the woman said.

The guy nodded. "Yeah. This is exactly why people voted to speed up convictions. Why wait when you can see the truth? Since this footage has now been released to the public, we're going to show it. This is not eye-capture footage, this is from a security camera—and I have to warn people, it's barbaric. If you have young children connected, you might want to switch them off."

Rune braced himself. But why was he nervous? Suddenly the images from the dream station raid appeared before everyone's eyes—three masked figures in a control room. Rune could tell the images were from a camera rather than a GoBug because they didn't jerk around. The GoBug had a popular 'eye-capture' feature that allowed it to turn anyone's vision into a recording, but since people moved their heads a lot the recordings would often give viewers motion sickness.

Now the intruders were shouting and using thin metal clubs to pummel a man on the ground. The man was screaming as the clubs smashed into his ribs, his chest, and his bloody face—but they showed no mercy. Then another masked person appeared and Rune caught his breath. The lithe little figure appeared to be a girl of Markla's size with her same lawless dark hair, and now she was pulling out a dagger. She dropped down and stabbed the unmoving man in the throat. Blood spurted across the floor, and it was sickening to watch. Then the image cut to another scene, and the girl was being tackled as she tried to run from the room. The mask was torn away—and yes, it was Markla.

Diana turned off the broadcast.

There was silence in the room. People stared at each other like they'd been struck dumb, and Rune realized he still wasn't breathing—or thinking about the Dream Project disaster. I can't believe it, he thought. *I can't believe she did that.* He stared at the chair where Markla used to sit.

Diana cleared her throat and said, "All right, I guess that ruined the mood—but I'm not sorry. It's good to know what we're fighting, even though it's stressful. But life goes on, and luckily, Janna's dream is all about relaxing. So, should we try it again?"

People were still recovering but the murmurs in the room indicated yes. They wanted something to wash away the brutality they'd just seen. Rune glanced at Janna. Janna and Markla had never been friendly, but Janna appeared to be shaken. Then Diana waved her hand over a console, and the room melted away, and everyone was inside Janna's LiveDream.

Rune found himself on a serene stretch of beach, not too different from the one down the road. Think about the beach, he thought. *Forget about Markla!* Rune took a deep breath and tried to submerge himself in the pleasant imagery, and he couldn't deny it did feel like he was there. It was a gorgeous day, with the sun hanging high like a burnt orange, and the clouds drifting by like puffs of cotton, and the water lapping at the warm sand. It was relaxing, but he wasn't interested at all. He was still thinking about Markla, and the grisly murder—and now here she was again!

He caught his breath once more.

She was wearing blue denim pants, and a loose pullover shirt the color of rust, and a single seashell hanging from a silver chain around her neck. Her messy hair was blowing in the breeze, and she was smiling, and Rune couldn't deny he liked what he saw. Markla wasn't conventionally beautiful but she was cute in her own way. There was something about her.

"Hi, Rune," she said. "I was wondering when you'd dream about me. Can you help me? I'm in trouble. I need help."

With a jolt, Rune ended the dream.

His heart was beating fast. He was back in the classroom, and he whipped his head around and saw everyone else was still in Janna's dream, relaxing on a balmy beach, waiting for the next event to appear—and looking contented enough. But then he saw Diana, sitting behind her desk and staring at him. She raised her eyebrows, as if to ask what was wrong. Rune looked away from her gaze, pretending he hadn't noticed it. He did not restart the dream.

With all LiveDreams, Rune knew there were certain blank spaces put it—placeholders that would be filled in by the mind of the dreamer. So no LiveDream was exactly the same for any two people. In fact, it could be vastly different, depending upon the thoughts of the dreamer. The dreamer could set options to exclude any thoughts that were scoring high on a stress scale, but Rune hadn't set any options and obviously Markla was on his mind. And then he had another thought: *I wish I could help her.*

Aldo was back in the room now, and he pointed at Rune and crooked a finger, motioning for Rune to come. Rune felt a flash of anxiety. Was Aldo angry he'd quit the dream? Rune stood up and clenched a fist and followed Aldo into the hall. Aldo was smiling, but Rune felt himself starting to sweat. When Aldo smiled, it often seemed unreal, like the smile was a digital dash shining on his buggy face.

"Rune, let's go to my office," Aldo said. "They can watch the dream. We've got something to talk about."

Rune kept sweating, wondering if Aldo could know what he'd just seen. But there was no way. Besides, thinking about Markla was not a crime, and Rune had nothing to do with 20 Eyes—or with Markla. Nothing at all.

Stop panicking! This is nothing, he thought, and he managed to show no emotion as he followed Aldo into a nearby office. As he walked, Rune stared at the top of Aldo's head and noted he was taller than Aldo. Aldo sat behind a broad desk in a wide wooden chair with a high back and ornately carved arms. Rune lowered himself onto a plain metal chair that was the only other piece of furniture in the room.

Aldo eyed Rune from behind his InfoLenses, and suddenly Rune tried not to laugh. Aldo seemed lost in the chair, like a big-eyed bug with ludicrous red hair sitting on an oversized throne.

"Rune, are you nervous?" Aldo said.

"No."

Aldo chuckled and tapped his InfoLenses. "Your heart rate is elevated. I can see that."

Rune glanced at the weird glasses and didn't respond.

"That's fine," Aldo said, looking smug now. "You can maintain your illusion of calm. People love illusions, Rune. Long before LiveDreams were invented, people loved illusions, and they still love them.They want to tell lies, and they want to be lied to, because lies are more convenient than reality—and they're also more fun. You write LiveDreams, Rune, and so you write lies. And your lies are some of the best I've ever seen."

"Thanks—I guess."

"You're welcome. In a LiveDream, you can be anything you want to be. You can be beautiful, you can be a king, and you can make any girl love you—at least for a while." Aldo sighed and sat back in his chair. "So, you're probably wondering why you didn't win the Dream Project."

Rune shrugged. "Lots of the other dreams were good. Janna's a great dream writer."

Aldo gave a snort. "The other dreams are garbage, and so is Janna's. But she writes wonderful garbage, and the average Sparklan will love the way it stinks." Then he laughed and said, "The average person is pretty average, Rune—and that's why you didn't win. You're a great writer but you don't write the kind of garbage the public loves."

"I don't?"

"No, you don't. But Janna does."

Rune was quiet. He didn't know what was going on, but he wasn't going to insult Janna or her dreams.

"Nothing to say?" Aldo said. He nodded with approval. "You're a careful young man. Anyway, I want to talk about your dreams—and your future." He paused, but when Rune didn't respond he continued. "As you know, your classmate Markla Flash was arrested yesterday. Fifteen minutes ago, she was sentenced to twenty years in the Dream Prison—and one thousand nightmares. How would you like to write nightmares for Markla?"

Rune felt the room spinning. He had to hold onto the chair. But he kept his face blank.

Aldo kept talking. "Rune, very few people have the ability to write LiveDreams that feel real; it takes a special combination of skill and imagination, and a rare ability to manipulate the scripts at a high level. And nightmares are even more difficult. But you write scary dreams that are totally immersive—and disturbing." Aldo stopped and smiled once again. "Diana tells me you want to be a professional. What does your father think about that?"

Rune was still reeling. He just shrugged again.

Aldo chuckled. "I know your father, and he's a fine officer of the law. But I also know what he thinks about LiveDreams."

"He's not a big fan," Rune muttered.

"Yes, I know. And this could be your chance to change his mind, and then maybe get out on your own. You'd be working in the Police Unit—part-time, since you're still in school. But instead of coming here three days a week, you'd go to the Dream Prison where you'd help fight crime."

"I'd be working with the police?"

"Yes, but you'd never see your father," Aldo said, and he paused and looked sly. "You'd be working on a more advanced level than him. Of course, you'd still come here on some days to complete your studies. This is part of a new program to recruit young people into government service. We think you'd be perfect for this job, and she'd be a great place to start."

Rune wanted to speak, but no words came. Certainly, Blog would hate this plan.

"But I know Markla!" Rune blurted.

"I know you do," Aldo said, and his voice was more soothing now. "But it's good to have some knowledge of your subject. Are you concerned about using nightmares as a correction tool? It's what the public wants, Rune. It's what they voted for, and it's the modern thing—and remember, *the future always wins*. Markla made some bad choices, and no one can help her now, but you would be greatly helping yourself by taking this offer. Keep in mind, the Dream Prison isn't just a prison; it's the center of activity for all things involving LiveDreams. The Dream Center is inside the prison, and great research is done there, and that's where you'd be working." He eyed Rune and sat up in his kingly chair. "You don't need to tell me today—but remember, when opportunity knocks, some people complain about the noise. Others grab it and run. Right now, opportunity is knocking hard."

A storm was whirling through Rune's head. This was crazy. But it was also a one-in-a-million shot.

"I'll do it," he said.

"Perfect. You can start tomorrow."

"Thanks. And thanks for giving me the chance."

Chapter 7

Markla sat on her rock hard mattress with her head in her hands. She'd been incarcerated for one day, and she'd already met a crazy woman and gotten involved in an escape plan. She didn't know the details of the plan, but she was having doubts about it. She also realized the main reason the plotters were talking to her was because of her particular crime—they liked what she'd done.

Popularity through murder. Not the best way to meet people.

But if she did get out, she could see Dru again. Dru, who was strong and sexy like an ancient warrior. Dru, who'd contacted some friends in here and told them to look out for her. Dru—who'd run from the Dream Station and left her behind.

Could this get any worse? Of course it could. After all, this was the Dream Prison, and she hadn't seen the worst part yet—the nightmares. Markla had lots of experience with nightmares; she often awoke in a terrified state. But these dreams could be even more extreme, and they were coming. She did some basic arithmetic. One thousand nightmares spread over twenty years meant 50 nightmares per year—or one nightmare every 7.3 days.

She shuddered. She'd heard the anticipation was worse than the punishment, and she'd heard about all the suicides, too. Her eyes were heavy with exhaustion but she gave a weary glance around her bleak cell for the hundredth time. No, they hadn't left her a piece of rope. But *I've got plenty of time to find one,* she thought.

Luckily, there were laws and rules governing the nightmares. There could be no type of sexual torture for her specified crime—in fact, it was strictly forbidden. And as she thought about this, it also occurred to her that maybe she should've given in to Dru's advances. How embarrassing to die a virgin, she thought—but did he really care about her? She wasn't sure. And what if she'd done it, and she'd been terrible at it, and then he'd lost interest in her? She would've been crushed. Well, if she survived her sentence, she would be free at the age of 36. She imagined herself running an ad on LoveSearch: *Thirty-something-year-old woman looking for romance. History includes no lovers and one person knifed to death.*

She almost laughed, but not quite. Then she considered the kind of nightmares that *would* be sent her way. She put three fingers to her throat. How many times would she be stabbed there? Yeah, that guy in the Dream Station might have killed her—but had it been necessary to stab him in the neck? She could've stabbed him somewhere else and maybe escaped, and he might have lived. Why hadn't she done that?

She banged her fist down on the mattress. *He definitely would've killed me!* The guy had been a "toad puppet," and now there was one less puppet in the world, and that was fine. But then she sighed and blinked back a tear. She'd murdered someone, and she'd gotten rid of her freedom, too—and ruined her life.

Her heart leaped as two female guards appeared outside her cell. They wore dark blue jump suits and stared at her with cold eyes, like the eyes of lizards. All the guards here looked brutal and unsympathetic—but they weren't here for a social visit. Instinctively, she knew. It was time.

"Let's go," one of them said. "It's time for your first dream."

Markla felt a little shaky as they shackled her wrists and led her out of the cell and across the walkway. But she tried to look tough, even as she heard people calling out to her; they were yelling from their cells. It all seemed like a blur, and the messages were mixed.

"You're in for it now, little girl!" There was laughter. "Get ready to die!"

But there was also, "Hang in there, honey! Stay strong!"

Does everyone know where I'm going? she thought. Of course they did.

They shoved her into an elevator and it went down, down, down. She gritted her teeth. Don't show them you're scared, she thought. But now she felt queasy, like there was a frog inside her stomach She took a deep breath and told herself to stay calm—stay calm. When the elevator opened, she was pushed into a dim hallway and marched to a wide wooden door encircled by heavy steel bands. The door opened into a circular room made of grey stone blocks. It was dark and dank inside, and the ceiling was high. It was like standing at the bottom of a deep well. Markla looked up and saw two metal hooks on the ceiling about a shoulder width apart. Obviously, nothing good was going to happen here.

"Put out your hands," one of the guards said. "It's time for the real fun."

Markla followed directions. Then the guard touched a button on the wall and there was a clanking sound as a pair of chains lowered the two hooks from above. The guards attached the shackles on Markla's wrists to the hooks, and the hooks were raised again—but not to the point where they lifted her from the floor. They went just high enough so that she had to stand on her toes with her arms stretched out above her head—and she couldn't use her hands to remove the GoBug they attached behind her ear.

"Don't try to shake it off," a guard said. "If that happens, you'll get the whip—and you don't want that, believe me. We'll strip you naked and beat you half to death, and then you'll still have to redo the nightmare. Do you understand?"

Markla just stared at her and nodded.

The big guard turned to go. But then she paused and said,

"They usually start you off with an easy one—probably something unguided. But when the guided ones start, that's a whole other story. Have fun."

The guards left and the door clanged shut.

Markla was alone in the dark with a thousand scary thoughts racing through her mind. She was classified as a 'violent criminal,' and while certain things were not allowed, a lot of other things were perfectly fine. The guard had mentioned "the whip," but that could still happen in a dream. She could be killed in a dream—and probably would be, every time. She could be burned alive, boiled in oil, bludgeoned to death, torn to shreds by wild animals—the possibilities for a horrible death were endless. *It's inhumane!* But was it? When this was done, her body would be unmarked. The general population had voted for this, and it was a popular form of "correction." The law had passed with overwhelming support. She'd killed someone, and many people assumed she was getting what she deserved. Maybe it was true.

Suddenly, she heard a chiming sound in her head, like a gong of doom. Markla felt her heart racing as the nightmare began.

Chapter 8

Blog stopped eating a monstrous pile of noodles and put down his fork. Right away, Rune knew he'd made an impression. It was tough to get Blog to put down an eating utensil.

"So you're going to be working at the prison?" Blog said. "You're part of the Corrections Unit?"

"Yeah," Rune replied, trying to sound casual. "I'm going to be writing nightmares."

Maya's face burst into a smile. "Rune, that's fantastic!" she said.

Blog scowled. "Why is it fantastic? Neither of you have any clue what happens there."

"What do you mean?" Maya said. "Rune wants to be a pro dream writer, and it seems like a good place to start."

"It's not," Blog said, and now his mouth looked like an angry gash carved into his big pumpkin head. "The prison isn't a good place for you, Rune. You don't belong there."

"What are you talking about?" Rune said, and his voice shook with anger. "You're always telling me to be tough. You didn't want me to write sappy dreams—but now I'm going to help with law enforcement, and you're mad?"

"That job's not for you. You're not taking that job."

"Yes, I am."

"No, you're not."

"Why?" Rune snapped. "Are you jealous? Because I'm going to do something creative? Something better than beat people up all day?"

Rune braced himself.

Blog glared. "Is that what you think I do? You've got a lot to learn."

Blog rose to his feet, and Rune started to duck—and then

Blog's hand shot out and swatted a glass of water from the table. Maya shrieked as it flew across the room and shattered against a wall. Then Blog swore and swiped Rune's plate of rice and beans to the floor.

Blog stood there, looming like a monster. "You think I'm the bad guy, don't you, Rune? Well, you're wrong. But since you're so much smarter than me now, maybe it's time you make your own decisions. Maybe you need to find your own path—even if it's a path with no guts or integrity. I'm done coddling you." He turned and stomped out of the room.

Rune watched him go. Then he shook his head, wondering when all the "coddling" had started.

Maya sighed. She was disheveled as usual, with her partially blond hair tied in a chaotic ponytail. "Well, that was sweet," she said. "And he wonders why I don't cook more often." Then she grabbed Rune's hand and squeezed. "Don't listen to him, Rune. It's great that you got this job. You're going to do really well. I can't wait to see the dreams you write for me someday."

Rune looked at her but he didn't respond. Instead, he started cleaning up the mess. Maya helped him, and when they were done she sighed again and said, "Don't let your father bother you, Rune. I know it seems hard to believe, but he usually means well." Then she smiled and added, "Anyway, he'll get over it." She pulled a GoBug from the pocket of her fuzzy purple bathrobe and headed toward the bedroom. "I'm in the middle of a good one," she said. "Try and get some sleep."

Rune followed her with his eyes, and for an instant he realized he was glad she was his mother. Then he went to his room, and later he did try to sleep. But he just ended up staring into the shadows, thinking about Markla.

What was she doing right now? Probably nothing too enjoyable, he thought, and it was his job to make it worse. Rune couldn't deny he felt sorry for her—even though she was part of 20 Eyes and a murderer. Why had she done it? It was a thought filling his brain. And he recalled a day when they'd been eight years old, and she'd found a kitten on the way to school and brought it to class with her, and their teacher had told her it couldn't stay. So Markla had gone home with it, and she hadn't come back to school for a week—not until the School Administrator had gone to her house. Even at the age of eight, Markla had been making waves.

He imagined having a conversation with her about the "kitten incident," and she was telling him about herself, and then he was telling her about a dream he was writing, and somehow her major crime wasn't important. Then he had a vision of them riding their flyboards over the sand near the ocean. She was good with a flyboard, maybe even as good as Rune. One more reason to like her.

He frowned. *Maybe Dimitri is right—I do think about her...a certain way.* And he had to stop doing it and just do his job. After all, she was the reason he might become a professional dream writer. She was his ticket out of here—or at least a start.

He closed his eyes, but he slept little.

Chapter 9

Markla sat on her mattress and shivered. The nightmare had been quick, and now she was back in her dreary cell. But her mind was still reeling. These were not like organic nightmares—or even like real dreams. In fact, they weren't true "nightmares" or "dreams" at all. Everyone called them that, but they were different. They were more powerful and lingered longer—and she remembered every instant.

In her mind, she saw the nightmare again.

She was chained to a stone wall. The shackles were heavy and tight, and they were holding her legs as well as her wrists, and she could barely move. Then there was a tall man in a black mask with a grin on his face and a knife in his hand. There was no doubt he was going to cut and stab her—and he did. First he slashed her cheeks, and she felt the sting, and then he slashed her forehead, and the blood burned as it dripped into her eyes. Then he held the blade up and let her stare at it. He gave a low laugh, and he placed the tip of the blade on her left eyeball, and he slowly pushed. Markla screamed—the pain was instant, and it was agonizing. But he didn't push the blade in too far—only far enough to blind her in one eye. The other eye was left untouched so she could continue to see the knife coming at her again and again, and she was punctured in so many places, and the attack went on and on—yet she did not die. She could only gasp and scream, desperate for death. Finally, the masked man pulled out a dagger just like the one she'd used to commit her crime. He smiled and waved it in front of her—and then plunged it into her neck.

She shuddered, remembering the jolt. Was that what her victim had felt? It had been more shocking than painful. But it had also been plenty painful. Could she really withstand 1,000 more of these dreams? Dru had told people she was 'a wildcat', but she knew he was trying to win her some respect inside the prison. She was nothing like that, and she could never survive twenty years of this. She had to get out of here.

She shook her head and frowned. Then again, she'd passed the test to get into 20 Eyes, and it had involved withstanding a certain amount of physical abuse, and she'd handled it. In fact, it hadn't seemed that terrible to her. So maybe she could survive—maybe. And while the prison nightmare had been unpleasant, she'd seen worse LiveDream nightmares. The key word dream writers used was *immersive*. How real had the dream felt? Certainly, the pain had seemed real enough, but the experience as a whole hadn't surrounded her in an authentic way. She'd experienced much stronger versions of reality through other dreams—and she recalled Rune's nightmares, the ones he'd let her try. Now those had been immersive. His nightmares had felt real.

What was Rune doing right now? *I'm sure he's not thinking about me, unless he's really stupid.* Maybe he was on his flyboard, or playing the drums—she recalled how he played percussion instruments, real ones made of wood. Back in First School he'd played for the class, and she'd always wanted to ask him about it since she played the wooden flute herself. But she hadn't asked because she'd never played with anyone else, and Rune played with the school band—where Janna played the synth and was always flirting with Rune, no doubt. Janna would make a great toad someday. She was a toad already.

A bell chimed, and Markla jumped. But it was only the bell that meant it was time for dinner. It was time for the herd to go to the dining hall, but she wasn't hungry. The guards were shouting and clomping around, and people were lumbering past her cell. Some of them looked inside but none of them said anything. She assumed a guard would come and tell her to go, but no one came. Suddenly, it was very quiet. It was like nothing was alive. Was this normal? She hadn't been here long enough to know—but she had an instinctive feeling something was wrong.

Now what? she thought. All of her senses were on alert, and then two women appeared.

Markla braced herself. They both looked about ten years older than her, and they were also bigger. Of course, everyone in here was bigger than Markla—but these two were much bigger. They were as huge as the guards but they were not guards. They were prisoners, and they were smiling like a couple of crocodiles.

They both had phony died hair; one blonde and the other a putrid shade of pink. One of them was opening the door to Markla's cell.

"Hi, Markla," she said. "My name's Sorla. So, you're new here. We've come to welcome you."

For an instant, Markla had a vision, a flashback from long ago, and it was so real—and for an instant she couldn't breathe. Someone was coming to hurt her—again. Someone was going to beat her—and she hadn't been doing anything wrong, not this time! Or had she? She was only six years old, and she didn't know, and it wasn't clear, and she felt so powerless! And then she was being pummeled with a wooden spoon, and then a belt, and supposedly she'd fallen down the stairs, and who would believe that? But people had believed it, and no one had asked any questions.

Markla hated these visions. She hated the way they exploded in her head and left her gasping for air. She buried these thoughts. But now here they were again—and suddenly, she wasn't scared. Suddenly, her pounding heart was filled with rage, not fear. She knew what it was like to get hurt, and she'd been hurt enough today.

The other woman spoke as Sorla walked into the tiny cell.

"I'm Samantha," she said. "Are you looking for the guards? They won't help you."

Markla wasn't looking for any guards. She was looking for a weapon. But there weren't any sharp objects lying around.

Markla tried to keep her voice even. "What do you want?" she said.

"Oh, nothing," Sorla said in a smug tone. "We're just going to beat you for a while, that's all."

Sorla was about to lunge—but Markla moved first. She shouted and leaped at Sorla, grabbing onto her shoulder and clawing at her thick body. "Whoah!" Sorla said, and staggered backwards, obviously shocked—and that's when Markla jabbed a thumb into her eye. She didn't just poke her—she shoved it in hard, trying to blind her. She felt her thumb push through into the eyeball.

Sorla let out a shriek and then swore, seemingly stunned by the small girl's ferocity. She grabbed at Markla, trying to pry her loose, but Markla held on, biting into her neck—fast little bites that quickly tore through the flesh. Blood gushed down the front of Sorla's body. Sorla screamed again and whirled around, and Samantha swung an object at Markla's head but Markla let go and dropped to the floor—and Samantha ended up striking Sorla instead with something that looked like a rock. Sorla swore again and now Samantha turned fast but Markla darted past her on all fours, scurrying out of the cell.

Markla leaped to her feet and grabbed the door. Samantha stuck out her arm, trying to stop Markla from closing it, but this was a mistake. Markla swung the door as hard as she could and caught Samantha's wrist between the door and the door frame. Samantha howled as the metal door shattered her wrist and briefly pinned her in place. Then Markla opened the door fast and slammed it shut again, this time catching Samantha's fingers as she tried to pull them away. Samantha screeched in agony as three fingers were crushed. More blood spurted onto the floor. Markla finally closed the door again, leaving her attackers inside the cell.

But the door wasn't locked. The doors were opened and closed electronically, and they were open right now for the dinner hour—so they could come after her. Markla didn't care. *If I die, I die, but they'll know they've been in a fight.* They'd also never catch her because they were injured, and they were slow, and she was quick—like a wildcat.

The two injured women staggered out of the cell. Markla's eyes opened wide as she saw two more women coming toward her, running fast. She turned and ran the other way. One of the newcomers shouted, "Markla—wait! We're with you!"

Markla didn't wait. She didn't know these people. But she looked back and saw Sorla and Samatha take fighting stances—and watched as one of the newcomers leaped forward and stabbed Sorla in the stomach with a pointy object.

Sorla gasped and fell to the floor. Samantha held up her hands, including her crushed fingers—and both of the other women jumped forward, stabbing her in the chest. With a scream, Samatha fell to the ground. Then one of the attackers reached down and cut Sorla's throat. The other attacker walked slowly toward Markla, holding up her fist. It was a gesture of 20 Eyes.

Markla stopped running. She stared at them and took a few deep breaths.

The woman with the raised fist had long straight hair, black like a raven, and deep bronze skin. "Hi, I'm Rose," she said. "And this is Carla. Blu told us you needed some help." She reached out and touched Markla's shoulder. "How bad are you hurt? There's a lot of blood here."

Markla's head was spinning. "I'm okay," she said. "It's not

mine." Then she wiped her bloody mouth and face with her sleeve and looked down. The yellow jumpsuit was covered with blood.

The two women smiled. "Well, I guess you did fine without us," Rose said.

"Not really," Markla said. "I'm glad you came. Thanks… So, what happens now?"

"Now we go to dinner," Carla said. "And by the way, it's good to meet you."

"What about them?"

Sorla and Samatha were lying in a messy heap. Neither of them appeared to be alive.

"Don't worry about them," Rose said. "Someone will clean them up. We'll get rid of this jumpsuit and get you a new one, and then we can talk."

Chapter 10

Rune was thinking about his father as he headed to the bus stop. His mind was boiling with bad memories from the night before yet he also felt hopeful. If he did a great job at the Dream Prison, he could take a big step toward a future free of his father—and as a bonus, Blog would be infuriated. Rune quickened his pace. Things were looking good.

The glass beetle-bus didn't go directly to the prison but it stopped at a location that was a fifteen-minute walk away. This was also the same bus that carried kids to school, so Rune ran into Dimitri and Janna. They were sitting together this time, probably because Trilla wasn't here today and Dimitri had commandeered her usual spot. Dimitri motioned for Rune to come sit nearby.

Rune hesitated. Diana had announced Rune's new position as a writer of nightmares, but she hadn't mentioned Markla—and Rune was glad. He didn't want these people to know.

He sighed and headed toward them. Dimitri grinned as Rune sat down. "I'm surrounded by royalty," Dimitri said. "The dream master and the nightmare machine."

Janna laughed. "I'm glad you finally figured things out," she said. "Now bring me some strawberries. I expect you to scour the world. I don't want any small ones."

Dimitri's eyes got wide. "I'll fight an army to get you the biggest one. Or I'll go to a marketplace."

Janna laughed again. She seems happy, Rune thought. Well, she was the big winner—sort of. But what was going on with Dimitri? Maybe Janna was finally changing her mind about him. Then Dimitri said, "So, Rune, what's the story with this prison job? Are you a knobber now, like your dad?"

"I'm not a knobber," Rune said. "I'm a dream writer—and I'm nothing like my dad."

"That's true," Dimitri quipped. "His hair is neater. So, what are you doing? Are you going to write nightmares for Markla?"

Rune froze. "Who told you that?" he said.

"What? Nobody. I was joking. Why, is that what you're doing?"

"No. I don't know what I'm doing yet."

Janna eyed Rune and shrugged. "If you do write for her, I'm sure you'll do a great job. Make her suffer."

"What? Why?"

Janna hesitated and Dimitri jumped in. "How can you ask that?" he said. "We all saw the clip. She's a subversive! She joined a gang of murderers and cut somebody's throat. She's a psychopath, too—and she probably always was, right? I mean she punched Janna in the nose once."

Rune squinted at Dimitri. Meanwhile, Janna squirmed a bit and said, "I didn't mean that. I don't really want her to suffer. But we saw what she did, and no one should feel bad for her, either. If she's part of 20 Eyes, you never really knew her, Rune—none of us did. So just do what you have to do. After all, you're going to be a pro dream writer…just like me." She smiled and gave him a friendly punch on the shoulder.

Rune gave her a little smile in return.

Dimitri stopped looking jovial. "I don't think she should suffer!" he blurted. "Just do a good job, that's all, and don't worry about it."

Rune laughed to himself, and for an instant he felt sorry for Dimitri. Dimitri was obnoxious at times, but he really wasn't a bad guy, and his infatuation with Janna wasn't going well. When the bus came to the prison stop, Janna gave Rune another big grin and wished him luck.

"Tell me how it goes," she said.

"Yeah, tell me, too," Dimitri said. But he sounded less enthused. He gave Rune a quick wave and turned back to Janna who was still waving at Rune.

Rune pushed them both out of his mind as he left the bus. His heart was pumping fast as he headed down a gravel road surrounded by tall trees; his feet crunched through piles of leaves and acorns. He soon emerged at the edge of a clearing where he stopped and caught his breath. Rising from a field of tall grass was the Dream Prison, a sprawling gray fortress that looked like a beached whale—only this whale was wearing high walls, searchlights, and razor wire. Rune slowed his pace and approached the main gate.

The gate looked like the mouth of an ancient castle with two pointy towers on either side that resembled the fangs of a great monster. Rune fumbled to get his GoBug in place behind his ear. He tried to act casual as he signaled someone inside, and then the two gigantic doors of the gate swung open. As he walked through he saw no one, and when he got inside he had to stop and stare again.

He shivered. So Markla's in here? he thought. He shook his head.

The entire enclosure was square with an additional pointy tower at each corner. There were a series of stone buildings located a good distance away, across another grassy field, meaning the buildings were all surrounded by an area of open space. The low buildings were gray like the walls, except for a large number painted on the front wall of each, and they collectively formed a smaller fortress within a larger one. In the center of the buildings was a fenced yard. Overlooking the yard was a taller structure known as Building 6, and it seemed to be staring down like it was keeping watch on the others. This was where the Dream Center was located, and Rune hurried toward it.

As he arrived, a plain door slid open for him, and there was Diana Drogo. This wasn't a surprise, since this was a day when the academy students were at the regular academic school.

Diana wore a short dress that was blue like the ocean and

showed her bare legs. Her blond hair looked stylishly messy. Rune sometimes wondered about her age. He suspected she was about as old as his mother. She smiled at Rune, like she always did.

"Hello, Rune," she said, and her voice was warm and friendly. "Are you ready to write some nightmares?"

"Hi, Diana. I think I'm ready. I hope I can do it."

"You can. And you will. It's this way."

He followed her slender shape into a dim hallway. After a short walk, she opened a door and they walked into a spacious room where the lighting was low and there was little sound. The room was filled with dream stations. There were about a dozen people sitting at their glowing stations, apparently staring at nothing—but Rune knew they were seeing the images of LiveDreams in front of their eyes, dreams they were working on.

Diana smiled again. "This building is a major center of LiveDream creation. The dreams created here are mainly used in the prison, but sometimes LiveDreams are created for entertainment purposes as well. The broadcasts would come from the Dream Stations, of course. Like the one Markla attacked."

At the mention of Markla, Rune's heart jumped. After all, he was here to make her life miserable. He suddenly felt uneasy and shifted his weight a bit.

Diana was watching him. "Rune, everything is going to be fine. You've been a good student. I'm sure your mother is proud of you."

Rune didn't say anything but he guessed his mother was in the middle of a LiveDream right now. It would be her first of many today. He followed Diana to another door.

"This is Aldo's office. You know Aldo as the Director of the Dream Academy, but he actually works for the government and has an office here in the prison. You'll see him fairly often. Aldo is an amazing dream writer."

Once again, Rune didn't feel too enthused. Once again, Diana smiled and said, "Rune, this is going to be fun for you. It'll be more fun than that flyboard you're always riding. And by the way, you should be careful with that thing. You'll hurt yourself."

Rune gave a little laugh. How did she know he rode a flyboard? Well, everyone knew. Still it was strange to hear Diana mention it.

Finally they reached a modest office that also looked like a storage room. There were a few mops and buckets on the floor, and boxes stacked along the wall, and not much space. But there was also a desk in the corner that was equipped with a dream station.

"We're out of dream stations in the control room," Diana said. "So this is where you'll be for now."

Rune felt a surge of relief. He didn't want to be in the room with those others. In his head, he could hear Markla calling them all toads—and he grimly laughed to himself. She was a real character.

The dream station looked standard enough. It consisted of a controller with an electronic brain—an "EB"—that worked in conjunction with his GoBug and a local dreambank. There was also a screen, even though most of the imagery would be created inside his head. With the help of the GoBug, the images he created would appear a short distance from his eyes just like a standard mindstream.

Diana reached into the desk drawer, and Rune felt a spark of surprise when she retrieved a dagger in a simple sheath. The sheath could easily be attached to a belt. She pulled the weapon from the sheath and handed it to Rune.

"This is the actual weapon Markla used," Diana said. "Hold it in your hand. You've already seen the crime, but this can also be helpful. Imagine using it the way she did, and let it inspire your nightmares."

He took the dagger, and his heart skipped a beat as he imagined how this thing in his hand had killed someone. But then he studied it. The weapon was not ornate in any way. He gripped it and was impressed by how light it was—light yet solid. It was all black, including the blade, and it was made of hardened steel with a pommel and a short cross guard just above the grip. The blade was a bit longer than his palm, and it was razor sharp on both sides before tapering to a deadly point. Such a primitive weapon, Rune thought. He found it hard to believe Markla had owned it—and he could not picture himself ever using it the way she had.

Diana was eyeing him as she said, "I was the one who picked you for this job. It was my idea. I watched your nightmares, and I knew you'd be perfect—and I don't want you to hold anything back, okay?"

"I'll do the best I can."

"Good," she said. Then she blinked a few times, and her blue eyes got watery. When she spoke again, her voice was soft. "I shouldn't get personal about this, but I had a son, Rune—and he's dead because of 20 Eyes. He's dead because of people like Markla. Do you understand?"

Rune looked at her and said nothing.

Now her tone turned dark and vicious. "If she begs you to stop hurting her—don't. If she cries and pleads for mercy, think about her crime. These people always have excuses, things from their past or whatever, and it's all nonsense. She's a dirty little Basic, and always remember, you have a job to do—and it's an important one. Are you listening?"

Rune nodded his head.

She leaned closer to him and said, "We need information

from her. Normally, an interrogation gives us something—but not in this case. Not with most people from 20 Eyes. They're well-trained to resist, but we need the names of her co-conspirators. Unfortunately, she wouldn't talk, and it's against the law to use physical torture. But it's not against the law to punish her with nightmares—and if you make her experiences horrible enough, and then promise her a little leniency in exchange for some information, she might tell you something useful. If she does, it will impress the people who run things, and that will be good for you."

Rune hesitated. "You mean you want me to talk to her in the dream?"

"Yes. You know how it works, right?"

"I've practiced guided dreams, but I've never done a real one."

The Dream Prison used *guided dreams*. This meant the fundamental *dreamshell* was enhanced by a person who adjusted the dream as it progressed. In the case of commercial dreams, this was meant to enhance something pleasurable, and people paid large sums of money for famous Dream Guiders to supply those enhancements. In the case of nightmares, it was meant to provide a heightened experience of terror.

A LiveDream did not happen inside the GoBug or inside an EB or the dreambank connected to them. The dream only existed inside the mind of the dreamer. The GoBug placed the dreamshell someone had written into the dreamer's imagination and then allowed a Guider to enter that imagination and manipulate it. The dreamshell was a scripted backdrop. The blow-by-blow action of the dream could not be seen by anyone except the one guiding and the one dreaming—because there was no physical thing to see. The complete dream only existed inside the dreamer's imagination, and it was not yet possible to record someone's imagination.

This meant that anything Rune added to the dreamshell while guiding the dream could not be seen or heard by anyone but Rune and Markla. And apparently, Diana wanted him to communicate with her in this unseen place.

Rune's head was whirling. Could he do this? In his mind, he heard his father saying something about how he would fail. Then he heard Diana, who was still talking to him.

"The ones you practiced are exactly like the real ones," she said. "The only difference is that you're doing it with a purpose now. So get familiar with your dream station, and then look over the results of Markla's interrogation and psych profile. Like I said, there's not much there, and this is another important point." Diana gave a dramatic pause and then said, "The fact that she's had the 20 Eyes training means she's a hardcore member, Rune. She's not the girl you know from school. She's indoctrinated, and she's dangerous, and never forget it—and never trust her. Do you understand? *Never trust her!*"

"Yes," he said slowly. "I'm...ready to go."

Except that I'm totally not.

"Good," she said. "We'll need a new nightmare soon. In fact, as soon as you have a new one we'll use it." Then she flashed him a little smile. "Since you work here now, you have access to this place any time you like. The nightmares never stop, Rune. So start working on something. I'll be back in a little while."

Rune watched her walk away. She had a nice walk, and he usually thought she was pretty, but she seemed less pretty today. She wants me to speak to Markla, he thought. *I'm going to have to speak to her!*

His gaze jumped across the equipment in front of him. Some of this was new but most of it looked familiar. So he was really going to do this. He suddenly recalled Diana's words about Markla's profile, and he synced the EB at his station to his

GoBug. Images of Markla and her family appeared before his eyes while a friendly voice narrated inside his head:

Markla Flash. Adopted daughter of Sharli and Cramli Flash. Parents divorced. One step brother. Subject is intelligent and creative. Data from mind probe suggests history of serious physical and emotional abuse, as well as high levels of anger and strong violent tendencies. Subject shows exceptional resistance to interrogation— almost certainly the result of special training.

Abuse? The thought made him wince. And how had she been trained, and who had trained her? There were no images accompanying this piece of information, and it bothered him.

Maybe it's true, he thought. *Maybe I don't know her at all.*

He took a deep breath and loaded his dreamshell. He'd be ready soon.

Chapter 11

Markla took deep breaths. She felt her insides quivering now, recalling the recent violence, but she forced herself to look outwardly calm. She went with Rose and Carla to the dining hall.

It was a windowless room ringed by steel platforms where guards could look down and scrutinize prisoners lining up to receive food from automated dispensers. As Markla watched the sloppy-looking food splatter into her bowl, her mind flashed back to a food fight she'd experienced in school when she was twelve years old. Had that really only been four years ago? Her biggest worry that day had been her punishment for throwing some fried potatoes—and she hadn't been too worried. Now here she was in another cafeteria, thinking about two women who'd been slaughtered outside her prison cell. It wasn't the future she'd envisioned.

They sat at one of the rectangular tables along with three or four people Markla assumed were friends. Markla's stomach felt too queasy to eat, but Rose and Carla insisted she try.

Rose spoke to her in a low voice. "Nan told Blu that Sam and Sorla were offered a few perks by Dana to give you a good beating. They weren't supposed to kill you."

Markla noticed Nan sitting at a table with two other strange-looking people.

"How did Nan know?" Markla said.

"Nan hears everything," Rose said. "She's annoying but she finds out things. She's also crazy and dumb, and she likes to cause trouble. Sometimes she's useful but never trust her."

"Okay," Markla said. "You say they didn't want to kill me, but now they're both dead."

"You're one of us, and we can't let one of ours get abused like that."

"But won't they just come at me again? Won't it be worse now?"

"Probably not," Carla said. "After what just happened, they won't find too many prisoners who want to get involved. Sure, guards like Dana and Crolle can come at you directly, but they won't kill you for the same reason—because we'd get even. There are lots of us in here, and there are others who are friends. These guards walk the yard, walk the prison—we can get them. But they might want to rough you up a bit, so watch your back. And take this."

Carla was pushing something into Markla's lap. Markla glanced under the table and saw a knife. She raised her eyebrows. How had they gotten a knife in here?

Rose said, "We have connections, Markla, and that's why we're not running around stabbing people with pointy toothbrushes. It's all due to the corruption—but in this case it works in our favor. Just don't let them catch you with it. If they do, they'll really hurt you. Put it up your sleeve."

Markla didn't want the knife. Just touching the weapon gave her a sick feeling, and it also seemed stupid to give her a piece of contraband that would supply the guards with a perfect excuse to punish her. But she slipped it up her sleeve, anyway. At this point she was so far down the "stupid hole" it didn't matter.

Besides, she was sure someone would try to hurt her again. *My days in here are numbered.*

"Where do I hide it?" Markla said.

"We hide lots of weapons in common areas—like the shower, the library, the kitchen. That way if there's a cell search, they won't catch you with it. But you might put it inside your cell, if you can find a good spot. It's risky to have it—but it's riskier to not have it, believe me."

Markla wondered when there would be an inquiry over the fight. Certainly, she would be questioned. And here she was with a knife up her sleeve. But Carla wasn't too concerned. Carla said, "If they ask you anything, just say you came to dinner with us and you don't know what happened. We'll vouch for you. Hey, they're going to know what really happened—but since they initiated the whole thing, they won't want to investigate it too much. People get killed in here over all kinds of disputes. There's lots of corruption going on, and it's normal." Then Carla lowered her voice even more and said, "But you don't need to worry about this stuff because we're making our big move in a day or two, and I can see you're going to be a huge help."

"What?"

Carla raised an eyebrow. "Blu told you, right?"

Markla hesitated. "Not much," she said. "He said something was coming."

Rose and Carla smiled. "Yeah, it's coming—soon. You arrived at the right time, and when it happens a lot of these guards are going down—like Crolle and Dana. You can help us with that, right?"

Markla was quiet. She couldn't believe what she was hearing, and she didn't want to help with anything. But she was nodding her head.

"I'll help," she said. Because these people had just helped her, and she was part of 20 Eyes—and maybe she wouldn't need to do anything too drastic. Maybe it wouldn't work out that way.

"Good," Carla said. "We'll let you know."

Markla's head was whirling when she went back to her cell. I'm getting in deeper and deeper, she thought. But she felt trapped—because she was trapped. There were bars all around.

There was no sign of Sorla, Samantha, or the fight—incredible. She stared at the door, waiting for another attack, but nothing came. She slid the knife out of her sleeve and examined it more closely. It was a single piece of metal with a blade about the length of her palm. Her mind flashed with a picture of the weapon she'd used to commit her crime. When Dru had given it to her, she'd said it was pretty, but that had been a lie. Pink roses were pretty, and the breezy blue ocean was pretty, and a blazing sunrise in the summer sky was gorgeous. The dagger had not been pretty but it had felt powerful in her hand. It had made her feel less helpless, and for a moment that had been beautiful.

She cut a slit in her mattress and slid the knife inside. It wasn't a clever hiding place but it would have to do for now. Later the cells were locked and it was lights out. She doubted she'd get much sleep tonight but that was normal. She never slept much.

In the morning, the cells were opened, and Markla saw Dano and Crolle standing there. Her heart skipped a beat. She knew they weren't here to give her breakfast in bed.

Dano held up a pair of metal shackles and smiled. "Can you guess what time it is, honey?"

"What?" Markla sputtered. "But I just had a nightmare."

Dano laughed. "Oh, did they forget to tell you? The nightmares can happen anytime. We like to keep you guessing. Besides, you had an easy one last time. This one is more serious."

Easy? Her pulse was pounding as she glanced at the open door, and for an instant she considered trying to run—but where would she go? Even if she squeezed past these huge thunder lizards, she didn't know the layout of the place, and there was that long yard she'd have to cross, and she'd be shot down fast with a stun gun. Then she'd be whipped to shreds and have additional nightmares added to her sentence.

Her heart sank. I've got to be stronger than this, she thought.

"Get up," Crolle said. From her belt, she removed the black stick. "I'm not going to tell you again."

Markla leaped to her feet. She expected to feel the stick, but Crolle just laughed. Then the two guards escorted her to the dream room, and in a few moments she was once again chained to the ceiling.

Stay calm, she thought. But it was difficult. She remembered Rose and Carla's words and hoped they were right about the guards not intending to kill her, because they could do it in now very easily.

Dano looked her over and smiled. Then she hooked her index finger under Markla's chin, forcing her head upward, and stared into Markla's eyes. "So, Flash, you got lucky with those two who came to visit you, huh? Or maybe you're more dangerous than you look. Or maybe you have some good friends. Well, that's okay, because we have time—lots of time, and you'll just have to think about that. And while we're waiting and you're thinking, you have some nightmares coming. Lots of them."

Markla stayed quiet. There was no point in antagonizing them. Dano smiled again and released Markla from her grip. "They have a kid guiding your dream. He's good-looking, too—your age. They got him from your school. Maybe he could've been your boyfriend. Too bad you're busy for the next twenty years."

Now Markla perked up. "A kid?" she said. "What's his name?"

Dana didn't answer. Instead, she pulled the black stick from her belt and jabbed it into Markla's neck. Markla shrieked—the pain was unbelievable. Luckily, it only lasted for an instant.

Dano gave a satisfied grunt. "You're allowed to answer questions, but don't ask them. Do you understand?"

"Yes," Markla blurted. But inside, she felt rage rising like a geyser. She imagined plunging the knife Rose had given her into Dano's chest—and for an instant her fear was gone, and it felt good.

What's happening to me? she thought. *I'm becoming a monster.* I've got to get out of here any way I can.

Crolle put a GoBug behind Markla's ear. "Have a good

time," she said with a smirk. Then both guards left and the door slammed shut.

Markla was alone again. I've got to stay calm, she thought. But the real trouble was just starting. She heard a chime in her head. For an instant, her mind went blank, and then her cell vanished.

***

Where am I? Markla thought.

She was surrounded by darkness. It was totally black, like she was blind—but the air felt dank, and she sensed open space all around.

She took a deep breath. Slowly, she reached out her hands but felt nothing. She stood perfectly still and listened. A soft gurgling sound echoed in the distance, like rushing water. She got down on her knees and ran her hands over the ground. It was slippery and damp, like wet stone. Was she in a cave? Maybe, and that was fine. She would sit right here until the dream ended. But of course, she knew it wouldn't be that easy—and now there was another sound. It was a low growling noise somewhere in the darkness. It seemed to be far away, but as she strained her ears she could tell it was getting closer.

Obviously, it's going to find me, Markla thought. Well, she had no plans to move. She wasn't going to play this game. But then she envisioned a large black wolf, and it was leaping through the darkness, and its big paws were knocking her to the ground and holding her there, and it was snarling and drooling as it tore into her face with razor-sharp teeth. Okay, maybe she should move. Sure, it was pointless, but it might make her feel better.

So she took a careful step forward—and then she was shrieking. Two enormous hands were grabbing her and yanking her off the ground. A dim light shined down, and she saw a tall man staring into her face. His skin was white like porcelain, and his head was misshapen. He had no hair, and dull gray eyes, and a crooked grin filled with broken teeth.

Markla tried to kick him, but it was like kicking a tree. She felt his hands squeezing her body, almost caressing her, and she began to panic. *I can't be raped!* she thought. *Rape is not allowed!*

He didn't rape her. Instead, he carried her for a few long strides and slammed her up against a stone wall. And then his face changed, and he was no longer a hideous man. Markla now saw the face of a young woman.

She was pretty like a doll, but she had hatred in her eyes. "Do you know me, Markla?" she said. "I'm the wife of Edgardo, the man you murdered. And in six months, I'll be the mother of his unborn child."

Markla couldn't breathe. Was this true? She hadn't been told anything about a pregnant wife. But now the woman clamped a powerful hand around Markla's throat and pushed her harder against the wall. Markla started to gag as the woman kept her at arm's length and began slapping her in the face. Blood gushed from Markla's nose and mouth as the slaps continued, on and on like they would never stop—but then they did stop, and Markla's face felt battered and numb, and she was once again being carried into the darkness. She moaned and took deep breaths, trying to clear her head. And then she was staring into a chasm.

It stretched out before her as far as she could see, a deep gulf illuminated by eerie orange light. The light seemed to radiate from the floor of the chasm, burning in the way that hot coals burn. The entire space was also filled with jagged stalagmites, pointing up at her like knives.

"Are you ready to suffer?" the woman said. "It won't be quick."

"I'm sorry!" Markla blurted. "He was going to kill me! I couldn't breathe. I should've done something else!"

"Sorry won't help me or my baby. Do you see all the rocky spikes down there? There's a nice one, and that's where you're going. Right through your intestines, I think. It'll be agonizing, too—and you'll linger for a long time. And next time I'll do something even worse."

"No! Don't do it, please. I said I was sorry."

"My husband is dead and 'sorry' isn't good enough. Are you ready?"

Markla tried to kick her attacker again but it was still useless. So she shrieked once more—but this time she wasn't begging for mercy.

"I'm glad I killed him! I'd kill him again if I could! You're all puppets of evil and I don't care if I die!"

The woman froze. For an instant, she seemed surprised.

She stared into Markla's eyes, and Markla stared right back at her—and then Markla spit into her face.

"Do it!" Markla said. *"Go ahead and kill me!"*

The woman snarled and smacked Markla one last time across the mouth. Then she tossed her into the pit. Markla screamed again and braced herself for the impact—but it didn't come. Instead, it felt like she was rushing toward her doom, with the air whooshing past her—but she was actually moving very slowly. It was also obvious which stalagmite she was headed for.

It was especially tall and sharp, and then the point was against her flesh, and now it was cutting through her. It was ripping through the bones in her lower spine and pushing up through her insides. The movement was slow, so slow, and the pain was incredible; she was being skewered alive—and then suddenly it was fast. In an instant, she was yanked upward and quickly dropped back down. And now the pain was unreal.

Markla gasped. She couldn't feel her feet, or move them—and she hoped for death. Please let this end, she thought. *Please!* But she guessed it would not end soon. She would stay alive in this dream until the person guiding it decided to show some mercy. And then finally everything went black.

She opened her eyes. She was still in a cave but the spike was gone, and so was the pain. The walls seemed to be glowing with a ghostly white light.

She was panting, and her whole body was shaking. What did this mean? The first dream had been horrible, but it had ended quickly. Her understanding of these nightmares was that they were quick. Was she going to be put through more horror? But then she heard a sound, like someone breathing. She spun around, and saw a shadow on the wall. She heard a voice.

Chapter 12

Rune stared at the girl on the ground.

Markla was lying on the floor of a cave, and she couldn't see him. He was just a shadow, and that's how he wanted it. Despite Diana's words, Rune hadn't intended to do any guiding—or speaking. In fact, the thought had made him sick to his stomach. He'd written the basic dreamshell, but watching the dream happen and getting involved once it began were two different things.

But now he was involved, and who was this person quivering on the wet ground in front of him? She was someone he'd known his whole life, and yet she was mysterious. She was someone he'd just tortured. She was someone who'd spit into the face of his monster.

Why did I do such harsh things to her? he thought. *I hope she can forgive me.*

He had to get a grip on the situation. He needed to speak to her, yet his voice could still sound shaky inside a dream—if that's how he felt. But he couldn't let that happen. He had to be in control.

Rune took a deep breath. "Markla, are you all right? It's me—Rune."

She looked around like a dazed animal.

"What?"

"It's Rune Roko. I'm writing your nightmares."

There was a moment of silence.

"Rune," she finally whispered. "What's going on? Are you really talking to me?"

"Yeah, I am. No one can see what happens inside a guided dream, Markla. They can only see the dreamshell—the part you just did. By the way, I'm sorry about all that. I really am."

She hesitated—and then she spoke the way Markla often spoke, with that sarcastic tone Rune had first heard at the age of five.

"You're sorry?" she said. "Do you know how much it hurts to have a stone spike shoved through your body?"

"No," Rune sputtered. "But I wanted it to be convincing."

"Really? Congratulations—I'm convinced that you know how to hurt me." She shook her head. "I heard they got someone from our class to write nightmares. I guess it makes sense that it's you."

"Why do you say that?"

"Because you wrote the best nightmares."

"Oh," Rune said. "Well, thanks." When he heard his voice, it sounded sheepish and tinged with guilt. I didn't want to hurt you, he thought. *Not really!*

"Don't mention it," she said with a snort. "I wish they'd hired Dimitri. His stuff is so bad, I'd only be afraid of laughing to death." She paused, and then her body slumped. "I'm going to die in here, Rune—probably soon. Will that make you happy?"

"No! Of course not! You'll be okay. You need to stay positive."

"What are you talking about? You're my torturer."

"I'm not your torturer! I'm just doing my job. It was a chance to be a pro dream writer."

"Oh, is that why you're here? I'm glad to help with your career plan. I can't wait to be skinned alive or whatever."

"It's not like that."

"Really? You just impaled me on a stone spike. It's exactly like that... I thought we were friends."

"You did?"

"Well, yeah. I've known you forever, right? You used to talk to me, and I even showed you my LiveDreams. I always liked you."

"Did you really?"

She paused. "Yeah, I did. And I thought you liked me,

too—but you never said much, and now I'm in here and you're working for the toads."

Rune grimaced. Markla called everyone she didn't like a "toad"—especially conformists and authority figures.

"I'm not a toad, Markla."

"Of course you are, just like your dad. I'm sure he's real proud of you."

"I'm nothing like him!" Rune said. "And he's not proud of me at all."

"Ha, okay. Well, are you proud of yourself?"

"I'm proud that someone liked my nightmares."

"So why can't I see you?"

Rune felt a jolt of panic. He didn't want her to see him in the dream—no, not yet. But Markla understood dream writing, and if he tried to make up some phony technical excuse she'd know he was lying.

"I don't want to do that," he said. "I just don't."

She gave a snotty laugh. "Maybe you're not so proud. Maybe you're just another toad. Did they ask you to get information from me? Is that the real reason you're talking to me? How do I know you're really Rune?"

"I'm Rune," he insisted. Then he said, "When you were six, you made that monkey out of green clay, remember? You said her name was 'Trix'—but her friends called her 'Tricky.' "

Markla hesitated. "Yeah, I remember," she said. "I didn't realize my monkey made such an impression. I think you made a dinosaur, right? It was red, so you named him 'Red'—very clever. You said it was more powerful than my little monkey."

"Yeah," Rune said. "Red. But I was probably wrong about the power thing."

"Well, your dinosaur was bigger. But my little monkey could really maneuver. Okay, you're probably Rune, so I *will* tell you something. I'll tell you why I helped attack the dream station. Those new rules for LiveDreams and GoBugs, the ones coming up for a vote—that's all about controlling people, and we want to stop it."

"What?" Rune shook his head. "That's ridiculous. Getting rid of certain restrictions will make the LiveDreams better—and that's what people want. People voted for this stuff."

"Sure they did, but how did they decide? They get all their information through the same technology they're trying to control. It's all about power, Rune—and taking it away from us. This technology is a monster, and we need to cut off the head of the snake. It's the only way."

Rune squirmed a bit. "Markla, there's no snake. And besides, cutting off the head sounds like a messy way to fix things. No one's going back to the past. I love my GoBug, and I love LiveDreams. Besides, you're a dream writer."

"No, I'm not! I was just learning the language of the enemy. Did you watch my crime?"

The language of the enemy? Her tone was definitely unsettling.

"Yeah, I saw it," he said.

"I heard it was changed using the LiveDream tech. Since everyone uses GoBugs, it isn't necessary to show real recorded images anymore. They can easily create any scene or story the same way you create LiveDreams, and they can put those on mindstreams—and when people watch those streams on GoBugs, nobody knows the difference. You don't believe me?"

"Wouldn't that be against the law?"

Markla rolled her eyes. "Did they ask you to use the dreams to try and get information from me? Because that's against the law, too. You work in the Dream Prison, Rune. Go watch the real footage of my crime—see what it looked like before that toad Aldo changed it. We have spies, and we know he did it."

Then she paused and spoke in a softer voice. "I'm not saying I'm innocent—I'm not. But I'm sure it's not what you saw in your GoBug. So think about what that means."

"Markla, I think you believe a lot of propaganda. Diana said you were indoctrinated."

"Yeah, but Diana hates me. And why? Because of her son."

"Yeah, exactly! The one who was killed by 20 Eyes."

"Kalo was one of us! He was killed by the police—who knows, maybe even your dad. But does she blame them? No. She blames us because he joined the group. She's such a toad."

Rune found himself fighting to control his anger. How had this conversation gone so wrong? Maybe because he'd had no plan. After all, he was supposed to be getting information from her—but was that why he'd decided to talk? No, not really. So what was he doing?

"Rune, are you there?"

"Yeah, I'm here."

"Good. If the nightmare is done, go away. I don't want to talk to you anymore."

"What?"

"If you're going to hurt me again, go ahead. But if you're not, leave me alone. Until next time."

"I don't want to hurt you. It's not like that."

She made a look of disgust—and then she started shouting. *"Everyone's always telling me 'it's not like that' but it's exactly like that! You don't care about me and you never did! You're an evil person who tortures people—so just kill me another thousand times and go away!"*

Rune was stunned; he felt like he'd been slapped in the face. Then he was quiet. He was once again staring at her, this time noticing how small she was—small yet strong. Small yet fierce.

"I'll see you later," he said. He turned off the dream.

Chapter 13

Rune stayed at his dream station, staring at the blank wall. He imagined punching his fist through it. How could Markla scream at him like that? *I was trying to be nice to her, and she hates me!*

Her behavior made no sense. He had the power to make her life miserable—and yet, she didn't seem to care. Obviously, she had a terrible temper—or she really was crazy. Lots of kids had said that over the years. But maybe he shouldn't be so surprised by her attitude. After all, she'd stabbed somebody in the throat. She had a lot of nerve calling someone else 'evil'.

He thought about the things she'd said, and her ridiculous theories—and it was unnerving, because he knew Markla, and she definitely wasn't stupid. But *she's been indoctrinated*, he thought. Then his mind flashed with the memory of her impaled on the stalagmite, and a wave of nausea washed over him. It must have been agonizing. But it wasn't real, and everyone knew that—but to her, it had been real.

How could I do that to her? How?

Then Rune heard a chipper voice behind him.

"Rune, are you all right?"

Rune whipped his head around and saw Aldo peering at him through his InfoLenses. He was wearing his usual white lab coat, but he still reminded Rune of an insect that was vomiting curly red hair from the top of its head.

"Yeah," Rune said with a start. "I'm fine."

Aldo smiled. "Good. I watched your dreamshell, and it was excellent. I'm sure it was effective. Did you do any guiding?"

Rune froze. He guessed Aldo was going to ask if he'd gotten any information, and now he was in a sweat trying to remember a few things Markla had said—things about Diana's son, and wild theories about controlling people. *And she said she'd always liked me. She said that, too.*

"Yeah!" Rune blurted. "But I didn't get any information."

Aldo stopped smiling. "Why would you be trying to get information?"

"I thought I was supposed to try and get information about 20 Eyes."

Aldo's eyes narrowed. "Who told you that?" he said. "You're not supposed to be doing anything like that, do you hear me? It's against the law, and we never do that. Once a person is sentenced, they can no longer be interrogated. You're supposed to know this. Who told you differently?"

"I don't know—no one. Diana told me a few things, but maybe I misunderstood."

"Diana?" Aldo paused and gave a soft laugh. "Yes, you misunderstood her, Rune. Your job isn't to get information. Your job is to make your subject feel the same kind of pain her victim felt. Do you understand?"

"Yeah," Rune sputtered. "I'm sorry. I didn't realize that."

Aldo's expression softened. "It's not a problem. You did well for your first time, and Diana has a few issues that cause her to get a little too enthusiastic. If Markla happens to give you some information, do not pass it on to anyone but me. Do *not* give it to Diana; it will only upset her. I'll talk to her, and before your next dream you two will sit down and map out a plan to deal with this girl in the guided sections. Keep it simple."

"Okay, I'll do that."

"Good," Aldo said, and now he smiled once again. "With the school semester ending in a few days, you'll have a lot more time to work on this." Then he paused and pointed at the wall. "Look, there's a fly sitting there—in fact, there are two of them in this room, one male and one female. And there's a spider in the corner." He tapped the side of his InfoLenses and said, "I see everything."

Rune watched him walk away.

What an idiot, Rune thought. *Why would I care how many flies and spiders are in the room? And do these people know what they're doing? I was just following directions.* And come to think of it, Markla *had* told him a few things—but he clenched his jaw. He wasn't telling anyone.

He checked the time and realized he had a bus to catch. Luckily, none of his friends were on the bus, and he sat alone in the back where he kept recalling his conversation with Markla, and each time he imagined himself saying different things— things he wished he'd said. *I need to stop thinking about her,* he thought. But how could he do that when he also needed to write another nightmare? Besides, he liked thinking about Markla.

As he approached his house, he saw his father's car parked out front, and he was immediately seized by a sense of panic. He considered going somewhere else—but he didn't. For an instant, his mind flashed with a vision of Markla spitting into the face of that monster.

I'm going in.

Rune stepped inside, and there was Blog sitting on the living room sofa. Rune clenched his fist, ready to argue—but Blog didn't acknowledge him; he seemed to be staring at something far away. Blog was wearing his blue uniform, and in his big hand was a bottle of ale. Blog often sat on the sofa in his blue uniform and stared at nothing while drinking ale, but he never got drunk. Blog didn't need any help being difficult.

Rune hadn't spoken to Blog since Blog had knocked Rune's rice and beans to the floor, and Rune had no plans to speak to him now—at least not until he was done eating. But Blog had other ideas. He put down his bottle, and now he gave Rune a steely look.

"So, how was your first day?" he said.

"It was good," Rune replied. He wasn't going to elaborate.

Blog gave a grunt. "Was Aldo there?"

"Yeah," Rune said, surprised. "How well do you know him?"

"Well enough. Come here a minute."

Rune told himself to stay calm as he went to stand near his father. But he said nothing.

Blog took a long swig of ale and cocked his head. "Listen to me, Rune. Aldo is a LiveDream writer, and people like him are exactly why no one should learn how to do those things. He's a sneaky little runt, and he's not someone you can trust—so be careful. Do you hear me?"

Rune still said nothing. *He's just jealous*, Rune thought. Then he stared into his father's face and said, "Did you arrest someone named Kalo Drogo? My teacher's son."

His father stared right back, but then spoke in a surprisingly calm voice.

"You talked to that girl, didn't you? What did she say?"

"She says he was killed by the police." *Maybe even by you.*

Blog slowly nodded his head. "That's true. He attacked an officer, the same way that girl and her friends attacked the Dream Station, and he was killed. But it was self-defense—no one is murdered under my command, Rune. We're police, not executioners, despite what Markla Flash might have told you. And by the way, I looked up her psych profile. She's intelligent but she's got some serious issues. She's young and she made a big mistake. Don't be part of her next mistake."

At the mention of Markla's name, Rune's heart jumped. "Why would I do that?" he said.

"Because you're young, too. And because you like her."

Rune hesitated. "Why do you say that?"

"You told me, remember?"

Right. Come to think of it, he did recall yelling something like that before storming out of the house. But at the time, he'd just been trying to annoy his father. Well, maybe.

Blog sighed and rose from the sofa. "Your mother tells me you've always been interested in this girl. People do strange things for love, Rune, especially when they're inexperienced. Young love is a storm of confusion." He saw the way Rune was looking at him, and he gave a short laugh. "You think I'm too old to understand, the same way I thought my father didn't understand. But I was your age once, and it wasn't even that long ago, and I don't want to have to throw you in prison right next to her. That girl is a world of trouble—so be careful, okay?" Then he leaned his face a little closer and said, "I mean it."

He stalked out of the room, and Rune stood there for a second. He was usually angry at his father's never-ending advice but right now he felt stunned, like he'd been punched in the jaw. Love? Why was anyone talking about love? He wasn't in love. But then again, how would he know? He was supposed to be thinking about Markla—besides, she was interesting. And smart. And funny. And cute. And then his mother came out of the bedroom.

She was wearing her purple bathrobe, and she looked frazzled as usual. But she smiled. "Hi, Rune," she said. She had a GoBug behind her ear. She sat on the sofa where Blog had just been and started a LiveDream. Within a few seconds, she slid into a blissful trance.

"Yeah, my first day was good," Rune mumbled. "I talked to a girl I know about GoBugs and LiveDreams."

As expected, she didn't hear a word. Then he checked his own GoBug and saw a message from Janna.

He frowned. He didn't feel like talking—but then, why not? Maybe it would get his mind off Markla.

He stepped outside into the backyard where a strong breeze was blowing and the sky was being overrun by dark clouds. He sent a message, and in a few seconds a three-dimensional image of Janna was in front of his eyes. She was at home, lying on a soft-looking bed covered with red pillows. She was wearing a tight pink shirt and a pair of white shorts that nicely displayed her long bronze legs, and Rune couldn't deny a rush of excitement.

"Hi, Rune," she said with a smile. "So, how was it? How did it go?"

Rune smiled back. "Hi, Janna. It was okay. I did a nightmare."

"That's great! Did the prison people like it?"

"Yeah, I think so. It was my first one, so I need to improve."

"I'm sure it was fine. Was it guided? Did you do anything special?"

"Like what?"

"I don't know." Janna paused—but then she smiled again and said, "The semester ends in two days, but I guess you'll be working there over the break, right? Maybe we can get together and you can tell me about it. Maybe we can trade a few ideas."

"Yeah," Rune said. "That sounds great. But right now I need to go work on another nightmare. I have a deadline."

She gave an exaggerated pout, but then said, "Sure, I understand. I should go do something, too. I just wanted to see how things went."

"Thanks for calling. We'll talk soon."

"You're welcome. Call me tomorrow."

She smiled one last time and disconnected the stream.

Rune stood still for a few moments and stared at nothing in particular. Then he felt a gust of wind and heard the patter of raindrops on the trees. He wondered if Markla could hear the rain. Then he headed back into the house.

Chapter 14

Markla sat in her gloomy cell with her mind racing, replaying her conversation with Rune.

Who did he think he was, anyway? He was the guy writing her nightmares. So that's who he was.

He seems to feel guilty, she thought. *And he should! And maybe I can use that!* Then she frowned because being sneaky and manipulative wasn't her strongpoint. If Markla didn't like someone, she made it obvious. *But I never disliked Rune—not before today, anyway.*

She thought about all the years she'd known him, and how he was different from other kids. He was pensive, and he was good at lots of things. He also came from a different kind of family than she did, and he lived in a pretty little house, and his father was an important public official—but if she hadn't ended up in prison, could anything have ever happened between them? If she hadn't met Dru? But then, what had really happened with Dru? Not that much, and it was all so confusing, and why was she thinking about it now, anyway? Stupid.

I probably shouldn't have called him 'evil,' she thought. *I need to control my temper.*

She rubbed her bloodshot eyes and told herself to be strong. The chances of Rune or anyone else being able to help her now were slight, but she needed something hopeful to cling to. She felt like she was drowning, and she needed to grab at anything that looked like a life raft—like the mysterious escape attempt her instincts told her would be desperate and dangerous. *But what do I have to lose?* She wondered when she'd find out more details.

Her heart jumped as a guard rattled the door to her cell. "Flash, you have a visitor."

Markla braced herself for another attack—but instead, she

was taken to the same dreary room where she'd met with her mother, and she stopped dead in her tracks and stared. Sitting behind the glass window was her twelve-year-old stepbrother Tommi.

Tommi was the natural child of Sharli and her ex-husband Trono who'd been born four years after they'd adopted Markla. Trono had packed up and left about a year later. Markla guessed that two unwanted children had been more than he could handle.

Tommi was a great kid. He knew things about her that no one else ever would—but why was he here? He didn't follow her beliefs about the government, or about technology, or about other things, and she'd assumed he'd be ashamed of her. She assumed he'd leave her behind.

Tommi's hair was dark and tangled, much like Markla's, and his eyes were bright and soft like the eyes of a friendly dog. He looked happy to see her.

"Hi, Markla," he said. "I wasn't sure if they'd let me in. But they did."

Markla struggled to keep from crying. "Yeah, getting in is the easy part."

He smiled. "You'll get out eventually."

She was quiet.

"I brought you something," he said. "I gave it to the people at the desk. They had to inspect it but they said you could have it."

Markla hesitated. "What is it?"

"Some food. And your flute."

"Oh… Thanks. I don't know if there's a band in here."

"You never played in a band."

She laughed. "That's true. I was a solo act."

"But you were good. I'm sure you'll get real popular."

She laughed again, but this time her laugh was mixed with a few tears. "You have no idea," she said. Then she leaned a bit toward the glass. "Thanks for coming to see me. I thought you'd hate me."

"What? Why would I hate you? You always think everyone hates you. I feel bad that you're in here." Then he glanced around and said, "They came and asked us questions. But I didn't tell them anything."

"You don't know anything."

"I know more than you think." He lowered his voice. "Can they hear us?"

Markla felt her heart beating faster. "I don't know—why? Supposedly, this is all confidential but I wouldn't count on it."

He shrugged. "I read some of the things you wrote in your journal, and I've been thinking about stuff. And I think maybe you had some good ideas, that's all."

Markla's head started spinning. "What?" she said. Then she whispered in a fierce tone. "Tommi, don't get involved in anything, do you hear me? Do *not* make the mistake I made. This is the worst place *ever*. I'm going to die in here."

Tommi cocked his head and stared at her. "No, you're not."

"Yeah, I am, but it doesn't matter because that's not the point. Don't read the stuff I wrote—you shouldn't be reading my private thoughts, anyway. But most of all, don't talk to anyone like me… who's involved. Do you understand?"

"You'll get out of here, Markla. The *toads* won't win."

"Forget about the toads! Forget about everything I ever said! Please—promise me."

He shook his head. "I can't do that. It's great to see you, Markla. I'm glad you're my sister."

At this point, the guard gave the sign that their time was up. Tommi rose from his metal chair, and Markla was filled with an urge to reach through the glass and grab him, but of course she couldn't. As he walked away, she called out to him one last time.

"Tommi, remember what I said—please!"

"Don't worry, Markla," he said. "I'll do the right thing."

He smiled again, and he was gone. Markla swore and slammed her fists down on the window ledge.

What could she do? Tommi was probably the only person in the world who cared about her, and she wasn't going to let him mess up his life. Her mind flashed with thoughts of Dru—she had to get a message to him. *I don't want Tommi recruited!*

Supposedly, Blu had communicated with Dru. Markla looked at the clock and saw it was too early to go to the yard, so she ended up being escorted back to her cell. The guard also gave her the flute.

It was a wooden flute made by a local craftsman. She held it in her hands, and her heart flooded with emotion. It was something from the outside where she'd lived a few long days ago, and suddenly she wanted to play it. Markla had often played late at night or early in the morning because it had annoyed her mom. But she'd also played at those times because she was an insomniac—and looking back on it, wasn't that mostly her mom's fault?

Markla sat in her cell and played a soft melody. For an instant, she envied the notes as they drifted freely through the air. She didn't know many formal songs because she'd never wanted to learn any—she just liked improvising. Today the melodies were sad, and then they were angry. Come to think of it, she'd never played too many happy songs. Well, the flute was in a minor key so that could be her excuse.

Tommi had also brought her some high-protein bread, a bag of peanuts, some dark chocolate, and an assortment of fruit. This was great since now she wouldn't have to go anywhere to eat, at least not for the rest of the day. Markla was a light eater. But she had to go to the yard, and now it was time.

Nan caught up with her along the way. "So, you play the flute?" Nan said. She was out of breath as she spoke, seemingly excited to hear the obvious answer.

"Yeah," Markla said.

"People heard you playing."

Markla guessed Nan wanted her to ask whether this was good or bad, so she didn't. She wasn't in the mood.

"You have to be careful around here," Nan said.

Thanks, Markla thought. *I didn't notice.*

"So, what's happening with your friends?" Nan said. "They have a plan, right?"

"They didn't tell me much."

"Did they give you a weapon?"

"No."

"They always have weapons. They didn't give you one?"

"No. Nan, I have to talk to Blu, okay? I'll see you later." *I don't like to be rude but you don't leave me much choice.*

"Oh, okay."

They were in the yard now, on the paved section, and it was filled with prisoners gathered in groups of three or four. As Markla walked away from Nan, she almost felt like she was back in school, only today she was with the popular crowd—and it was unsettling. But then again, at least she had friends. She spotted Blu in a far corner of the yard, standing tall and looking formidable near a rack of iron dumbbells. He was talking to Rose, who was wearing a blood red headband that clashed nicely with her short-sleeve yellow jumpsuit. Blu grinned as Markla approached.

Rose also grinned, and for the first time Markla noticed how sinewy she was—obviously, she'd been hitting the weights quite a bit herself. "We were just talking about you," Rose said. "And here you are... Listen, it's all happening tomorrow. Everyone's got a job to do, but since you just got here you can help me. We're a little light in the women's zone so this will be good."

"I need to talk to Dru," Markla said. "I need to tell him something."

Blu and Rose looked at each other. "That's not a problem," Blu said. "Once we get out of here you can talk to him all day long, right?" He flashed her another grin.

"Right," Markla said.

"Great. So here's the plan."

Markla hoped the plan involved some kind of stealth, like wearing disguises and sneaking out in a garbage truck. But it didn't. The whole plan was about as stealthy as a fist in the face.

They were going to overpower the guards, and they definitely had a hit list. They also had lots of weapons the guards didn't know about, and while Markla guessed this was strange, she didn't ask for details. As for the guards themselves, Markla hated them—yet she still wanted no part of this. But how could she say no? She was a member of 20 Eyes, and they were leading the uprising. She couldn't just stand around and watch.

The rest of the plan was simple enough. The main gate and the fence around the yard would be opened, and everyone would run for the woods. Hidden in the woods at designated locations were clothes and supplies. There were also hideouts ready.

Blu said, "You're new here, Markla, but you come with us to Location Five." He looked away as he passed a small piece of paper to her, concealed in his palm. "Dru took care of everything there. We'll get you out of that jumpsuit and to a safe place."

At the mention of Dru's name, Markla felt a tingle of hope. He didn't forget about me, she thought. *He's still thinking about me.*

Blu said, "Standard procedure with that thing."

Markla nodded. He meant she should look at the map in her palm, memorize it, and then eat it. No problem.

Rose said, "At ten o'clock tomorrow, we go. Get your knife and meet me in the common area."

Markla felt a little dizzy but she heard herself say, "I'll be there."

Chapter 15

It was a dark night. The moon was like a smear of gold behind a blanket of clouds as Rune rode his flyboard to the Dream Prison. He couldn't sleep anyway, and he liked riding in the dark even though it wasn't the safest plan. But flyboards were the most fun when they were the worst idea.

Rune knew the Dream Prison was about twenty minutes away by bus, which meant ten minutes on a board, assuming he didn't crash into anything. Eight minutes later he was gliding to a stop in the grassy field between the prison and the forest. He stood in the moonlight and felt a chill go down his spine. The prison looked even more imposing at night, like a fortress dressed in shadows with cold lights glaring down. Rune signaled the main gate and a few minutes later he was inside.

He said hello to a guard who logged him in but the guard just nodded in return. Rune's stomach felt tight as he walked down a deserted hall in Building 6.

Markla's here in the prison, he thought. He wondered what she was doing, and how it felt to live in a cage. Maybe she deserved it—*but then, maybe not.* According to her, the original camera recording of her crime had been converted into a LiveDream that had then been modified by a dream writer's imagination. Then the LiveDream had been streamed to the public and passed off as a camera recording to be viewed via GoBug. Of course, Markla had neglected to mention that everyone was aware this could be done, and so the population had voted to restrict the use of LiveDreams to purely entertainment purposes. So if someone had done this it would be a crime. But who was the criminal?

Markla claimed that spies had named Aldo, so he was a good place to start. Rune gritted his teeth and tried to stay calm.

What he was about to do could get him into lots of trouble if he were wrong and even more trouble if he were right. But he had to know. The lights were low in the Dream Center, like moonlight, and the halls were deserted. Rune walked fast and finally reached Aldo's office.

He slipped inside the room. He didn't turn on any lights; there was just enough illumination from the hall to see shadowy shapes—a wide wooden desk, a few cushy chairs, a leafy fern in a pot, and a state-of-the-art dream station. Rune leaped toward the station and fired it up, and a bluish light sprang across the console. He moved his hand over the controls and found the dreambank called "Aldo X." As he touched the screen, his GoBug received a message in bright red letters that appeared to hang in the air in front of his face. The message was asking him to submit to a mind scan that would check his brain wave pattern and verify his identity. Rune took a deep breath and called up the special script in his GoBug that could supposedly solve this problem; it was a script he'd gotten late at night from a mysterious smasher on an obscure mindstream.

Jail breaker, he thought. *Connect to Aldo X.*

He could hear his heart pounding in the darkness. There was no way it would work—no way. But then it did, and Rune's mouth dropped open as red letters flashed with the message "Identity Verified. Welcome, Aldo."

In front of Rune's eyes were the names of a hundred LiveDreams. Rune grimaced because it could be anywhere—but luckily, Aldo was an organized guy, and all the LiveDreams were named the most obvious thing possible. Rune quickly scanned the list and saw one that said "Dream Station" along with the date the crime had happened.

He viewed it, and it showed exactly what he'd seen on the news broadcast. But Rune knew how to manipulate LiveDreams, and he knew how to reveal any previous versions. After all, isn't that why they'd hired him? Using mental commands, he went back, and back, and back—to the first version, the one that had presumably been converted from the raw camera file. He watched it, and he felt his blood turn cold.

Markla was telling the truth.

Maybe she wasn't completely innocent, but the images had definitely been changed—unbelievable! And they'd been changed by Aldo, the Director of the Dream Academy—and the person he was now working for. *That sneaky little toad.* Working fast, he used his GoBug to copy the LiveDream to his own dreambank. Then he started looking at some other scripts. One that caught his eye said "security: bunker." He took that one, too. He was about to turn off the dream station and head for home when he noticed something else—a separate file of LiveDreams called "Special Nightmares."

Rune had never seen any of Aldo's nightmares, and he was curious. He noticed the names of the nightmares seemed to be the names of people. Maybe he'd risk a few more minutes to copy them. Using his GoBug once again, he began copying the entire list to his personal dreambank—and while this was happening, he decided to watch one.

The one he selected was titled "Blu Baroke." He loaded it into his GoBug but kept it in monitor mode. This would allow him to watch the LiveDream in front of his eyes without actually being submerged in it; he couldn't risk being in a LiveDream right now. But he could get the idea. How scary would this be?

It didn't start out scary. He was in a restaurant, and on the table in front of him was a steaming plate of rice cooked with tomatoes, peppers, and onions. Rune guessed it would taste and smell wonderful if he were actually in the LiveDream. Now he was drinking red wine. Was this going to involve an agonizing death by poison? Would the rice turn into a pile of scorpions? No, nothing. Rune skipped ahead a bit—and now there was a woman, and Rune caught his breath. She was beautiful—statuesque, with eyes like big bright almonds, and black hair hanging down past her shoulders, and a short skirt that showed her long bare legs. Would there be a knife? Would she morph into a demon? It was a common nightmare trope. But no, that was not what she was here to do—not at all. Now the dream really started getting interesting, and the room started getting warm, and he heard a beep signaling the files were all copied so he skipped ahead again to—nothing.

The dream wasn't a nightmare. In fact, it was more like a party. And then he heard footsteps in the hall.

Oh no! He swore and fumbled to shut down the dream station and used his sleeve to frantically wipe his fingerprints from the console because the InfoLenses could see things like that. He spotted a closet in the corner and started to move, but he stopped—if he got caught in there he'd definitely look guilty of something. Maybe he should wait! Maybe he should step out into the hall. Maybe he should press himself against the wall and try to stay out of sight.

He turned fast toward the door—and there was Aldo.

Aldo looked startled; his eyes were unusually wide behind his InfoLenses. But he recovered fast.

"Rune," he said, and his voice was sharp. "What are you doing in my office?"

Rune's mind was racing. *Think, think, think!* "I'm sorry!" he blurted. "I came in to work on some stuff. I was walking by your office, and I started wondering about your dream station. It's...nice."

Aldo pushed his shoulders back and puffed out his chest, like he was trying to look bigger.

"If you wanted to see my station, you should've asked me. Did you turn it on?"

"No," Rune said. "I just looked at it."

Aldo switched on the light in his office and walked to the console. Rune held his breath. The smasher script should've erased the history of his activity, but could he be sure? But then Rune thought about Markla, and how Aldo had changed the footage of her crime—and suddenly he wasn't scared. Rune clenched his jaw as the fear was pushed aside by anger.

Aldo glanced at the console but didn't seem too concerned. "So, you're here at night? That's very dedicated." Then he sighed and said, "I'm only here because I've got nothing better to do. How are the nightmares going? Diana tells me you're doing a nice job."

Rune said nothing. Don't panic, he thought.

"Rune, are you all right?"

"Yeah. I'm glad Diana says that. She's a great teacher."

"Diana likes you," Aldo said. "And that's a good thing, isn't it? It's also not surprising—not at all." He paused, and for an instant he frowned. Then he added, "So, what does your father think about your job here?"

"He said it was fine."

"That's interesting. Did he tell you he knows me?"

Now he looked at Rune like he was studying his face.

Rune hesitated. "He mentioned it."

"And what did he say?"

"Not too much."

"Not too much—or not too much that was good?"

"Not too much...of anything."

Aldo chuckled. "Your father and I are on the same side, Rune. We're both fighting the people that threaten our world—even if our reasons are different. But I'm sure he appreciates what you're doing."

"I'm not like my dad!" Rune snapped. Then he softened his tone and said, "We appreciate different things."

"You're a dream writer," Aldo said, waving his hand. "Your father is old-fashioned. But the future always wins, Rune." He motioned toward his InfoLenses. "I see that your heart rate and blood pressure are higher than normal right now. It's getting late, and you should go home."

"Yeah," Rune said, once again restraining his tone. "I should."

Rune left the room and hurried down the hall toward his flyboard. He tried to look calm, but inside he was smoldering like a volcano. Had Aldo's lenses sensed how much he'd wanted to punch him in the face? I hope so, he thought.

He finally made it home and tried to sleep.

Chapter 16

Markla tossed and turned on her hard mattress but slept little. She stared into the darkness and felt her heart pounding. Finally, it was morning, but she skipped breakfast and stayed in her cell eating bread and peanuts while watching the clock. Then it was almost time for the escape—30 minutes to go. Then 25. Then 20. Then she heard a voice and almost jumped. Crolle and Dano were standing outside her cell.

Markla struggled to stay calm. Had they discovered the plot? Did they know about the knife?

Dano was laughing. "Are you okay, Markla? You seem a little nervous. It's not like you've never been to the dream room before. You're getting to be a veteran."

The dream room? *Now?* It took a few seconds for the implications to sink in.

Dano pointed at the flute on her bed. It was inside a soft case with a strap. "Bring that with you," she said.

Markla guessed this wasn't a positive development but she shrugged and slung it over her shoulder. They shackled her wrists and started walking her to the dream room—but the uprising was coming. It was going to happen while Rune was in the prison guiding her dream. They'll be breaking into the control room, she thought. *Will they hurt Rune?* For the first time she considered this possibility, and now she felt a jolt of panic. The dream writers and dream guiders were not popular here.

I should warn him! But then he would alert everyone—and besides, that toad tortured me!

When they got to the dream room, Dano took the flute from Markla, removed it from its case and tossed the case onto the floor. Meanwhile, Markla was quiet as Crolle chained her to the ceiling.

They raised her arms above her head, and then Dano blew into the flute, creating one warbly note. Markla wasn't surprised; Dano seemed about as musical as a car crash.

Dano frowned. "You were disturbing people with this thing yesterday." Then she swung the flute and smacked Markla in the face with it. A red welt appeared on Markla's cheek and both guards laughed.

Markla grunted but said nothing. In her mind, she saw an image of them both being slaughtered.

Dano smirked. "You don't like us, do you?" She dropped the flute onto the floor and pulled the black stick from her belt, flashing it in front of Markla's face. Then she turned it on and jammed it into Markla's stomach.

Markla screamed. She didn't want to but the pain was so intense—like a mix of lightening and fire searing every nerve in her body. She hung there, shaking in her chains.

Crolle and Dano laughed again. Then Dano leaned close to Markla's ear and whispered, "We don't like you, either. Do you think your friends can help you? Only to a point—and only for a while. Have a nice dream."

The guards turned and left the room, and Markla breathed a sigh of relief. Then she imagined snatching the stick away from Dano and jamming it into the woman's big mouth. It was just a fantasy—but then, what about the uprising? She knew certain guards were being targeted. Despite the rage she felt for Dano and Crolle, Markla wanted no part of the violence. *If I ever make it out of here, I'm going to disappear. I'll live in the woods like a Basic for the rest of my life. Well, maybe.*

It must be ten o'clock, she thought. No, maybe another ten minutes or so.

It was time for a nightmare, and her mind went blank. There was a moment of confusion, and she heard a chime, and the dream room vanished. In an instant, she was somewhere else—but where?

She blinked a few times as things came into focus.

It was dark, and the air was hot and heavy. There were scraggily trees all around, and they were draped with vines that hung down like snakes, and the continuous hum of insects filled her ears. So she was in a jungle, and she didn't care. She had bigger things on her mind—like warning Rune. *But I can't!* Because then he'd sound an alarm, and she would be a traitor—yet she opened her mouth, and she almost called out to him. But her voice died.

Don't do it, she thought. *He doesn't really know me, and he's not my friend!*

She was starting to sweat. Meanwhile, nothing was happening. She guessed Rune was trying to create terror through anticipation, and normally this would work—but things were not normal because the terror in this dream was trivial compared to the slaughter that was about to happen in the real world. Normally, she would be scared, but now she had different thoughts. How could Rune do this to her? She'd never realized he was such a toad—and his dad was a king toad. Then she thought about how Rune was fast, and he'd probably escape. In fact, the whole uprising could fail, and maybe no one would even go into the control room.

I'm rationalizing, she thought. Well, it was hardly the first time she'd rationalized bad behavior. Then with a rustling sound, something jumped out from under a fern. Markla leaped backwards—and there was a fat blackish-green toad. It was twice the size of her hand.

She laughed. Was Rune trying to be funny? But then there was another one—and another. They were jumping out all around her, and now she noticed they were not normal toads. These toads had red eyes and sharp little fangs.

So Rune was mad that she'd called him a toad, and she was going to be eaten by toads.

It was kind of clever, but it also made her angry. Yeah, this was Rune's job, but what harm had she ever done to him? This was her *life*, and he was trying to hurt her like others had hurt her, and maybe she'd warn him—but maybe not. Her suffering was a big joke. She felt her eyes filling with tears of rage—and sadness.

She ground her teeth. *Don't panic! Think!*

She wasn't going to stomp on these creatures, even if they were fake. No one was going to make her do that. But of course, she also didn't want to be eaten by them because it would be an agonizing death. She frowned and made a quick decision. She was going to climb a tree.

She leaped away from the toads and ran toward the closest tree, plowing her way through the high ferns and leafy plants. She was faster than the toads, but she knew they were coming, and she heard them leaping and croaking all around. She reached the tree and in one quick motion grabbed two lower branches and pulled herself up. She was a swift climber, but this wasn't a tall tree, and she could only go so far—and the toads were still after her because these toads could climb trees.

Markla wasn't surprised by this but she still made her way up to the highest branch she could reach and watched with wide eyes as the toads moved up the trunk. Soon they were just below her feet with their glowing red eyes and teeth like tiny ice picks, and she saw the ground below was now covered with them. The floor of the jungle seemed to be squirming like a mass of croaking jelly. She was breathing hard, waiting for them to overwhelm her. She guessed at some point she'd fall to the ground and be covered with toads, and they would rip her to shreds while she screamed and cried. Then a big one jumped up and nipped at her arm—but it missed and fell to the ground. More of them started leaping toward her but none of them bit her. Now they were leaping all around her—some up high, near her face—while others nipped at her ankles. But none of them touched her. And then they stopped.

It was dead quiet. Markla sat very still and felt the hair on the back of her neck rise. No doubt something worse was about to happen—and suddenly she wanted to warn Rune after all, because she'd killed someone, and maybe she deserved all of this, and maybe Rune was a decent guy she'd known for years who'd been indoctrinated—and she didn't want him to die, of course not! She was ready to shout to him—but then there was a sound, like someone beating a blanket, or maybe a huge bird flapping its wings, and then a monstrous black owl was flying out of nowhere. It had eyes like yellow saucers and razor-sharp claws. Markla sucked in her breath as the creature crash-landed on a branch just above her head, and then its own head changed. In place of the owl's head was Rune's face. She stared at it for a second, and then she was no longer in the tree or in the jungle. Everything vanished.

For an instant, Markla felt dizzy, and her vision was blurry. Then it was clear again, and she was sitting at a pretty wooden table that had a mushroom-like umbrella sprouting above it. It was still dark, and she was still outdoors, but the table was resting on a stone patio that was part of a quaint cafe with ornate green awnings and cherry-red shutters. The lights were on inside the cafe but through the wide windows she could see that no one was around—except for Rune, who was sitting across from her.

Chapter 17

Rune planned to tell Markla what he knew. He'd seen proof of the government's lie, and he was somehow going to help. And then he was going to tell her a lot more than that—maybe.

He was done kidding himself. He thought about Markla all the time, and every thought led to her name, and the sound of her name was electric. He wanted to talk about her and shout about her, and everything and everyone made him think of her—and he wanted her to know. But could he tell her? And if he did, would she care?

The question was burning in his head because why would she? Well, here she was, sitting across from him at a table outside a fairytale cafe inside a dream. He hadn't slept at all. His mind was still whirling with the last conversation they'd had, thinking about every word he should've said and imagining every word she might have said in return.

She looked cute in that messy Markla Flash kind of way. He was going to smile exactly the way he'd practiced smiling. He was going to speak exactly the way he'd practiced speaking. He wanted to seem nice—confident yet not overly aggressive, interested yet not overbearing. He stared at her and paused dramatically.

"Hi, Markla," he said.

She leaned toward him. "Rune, they're going to kill you. You have to end the dream and run."

Rune had anticipated many possible responses from Markla, but this had not been one of them.

"What?"

"The prison, Rune. There's going to be a revolt at ten—what time is it? They're going to take over, and dream writers are not popular. So you've got to go. Please don't tell anyone I told you. Please!"

"What?"

"Rune, you have to run! Do it now! You can torture people some other time!"

Rune paused, and he listened—and now he heard noise coming from somewhere in the building, a jumble of gunfire and shouting. He ended the dream and leaped from his chair.

He ran to the door, and he heard more shots and then an explosion. He stepped into the hall and stared out a window that faced the prison yard—and he saw prisoners running free. They had knives, and they had guns! His heart started pounding. He started to move in three different directions, but stopped short each time—and then he bolted back to his dream station, yanked open a drawer, and found the dagger Diana had shown him. He attached it to his belt. Then he ran back into the hall and raced down a flight of stairs that led to a network of underground passageways that connected the main prison to the Dream Center. He knew the dream rooms were down there, and at the bottom of the stairs he found a hallway with blueish light that led to a heavy wooden door bound by strips of metal. There were no guards around, and Rune guessed they'd gone to join the fight. With a grunt Rune unbolted the door and pulled it open—and there was Markla, chained to the ceiling like a helpless doll. His heart skipped a beat.

"Markla!" he said.

She gave him a quizzical look. "Rune, what are you doing here?"

His eyes scanned the shadowy room and found a switch. He pushed it and her arms were lowered. He fumbled around, helping her to free herself.

"Markla, are you all right?"

"Rune, why are you here?"

"I wanted to help you."

"I'm not the one in danger—you are. You need to get out of here or hide."

"Where am I going to hide?"

He strained his ears, listening, and now he heard nothing. But they were underground, in a room made of stone with no windows.

Markla ran to the doorway and looked down the hall. Then she whirled back around. "This might not be a bad place. There's no equipment in here to destroy—it's all upstairs. This is just a dungeon where they tortured me with a GoBug. But then again, someone might come down here, maybe to get me out. So you still need to go or maybe find a different room."

She pulled the GoBug from behind her ear, dropped it on the floor, and stomped on it. Markla was not heavy, and she wore soft moccasins. But she still made her point.

"Toad machine!" she spat, and then she stomped on it again.

Rune felt uneasy. What did I get myself into? he thought. But he blurted, "Okay, let's find a different room down here."

"I'm not coming with you, Rune." He watched as she picked up a wooden flute, placed it into a bag, and slung it across her back. "You need to hide alone."

"Why?"

"Because I'm going outside. I didn't plan this thing, but I don't want to stay in here for twenty years, do you understand?" She paused and cocked her head. "Thanks for helping me." Then she looked at his belt and said, "Hey, is that my dagger?"

"Yeah," he sputtered. He fumbled a bit and handed it to her—and then somebody was in the doorway, a muscular woman with a gun. She had wild black hair and frantic eyes, and a bloody slash on her arm. She stared at Markla and aimed the weapon at Rune.

"No!" Markla said, and she thrust her arm across Rune's chest. "He's okay, Carla. He helped me."

Carla kept looking at Rune as she spoke to Markla. "We heard they took you, so I came down. Things are going well but we need to hurry. Come on, let's go!"

Carla bolted down the hall toward the stairs with Markla close behind. She never looked back.

Rune hesitated—and then he ran after them. The two women reached the top of the landing, and Carla opened the door and slipped into the hall. Now Rune heard more shouting outside and more gunfire. He smelled acrid smoke and heard cheers—and a few screams. Markla put her hand on the doorknob but then turned to face him. They were only a footstep apart.

"Good-bye, Rune," she said.

She leaned forward, and before he knew what was happening, she gave him a kiss on the cheek and his whole body tingled. Then she opened the door and ran through—leaving Rune alone, surrounded by chaos and confusion.

Wait, don't go! he thought. He hated to see her leave. But he understood.

He tried to think of a plan. *Go back into the dungeon and hide!* These people were trashing the prison, but they would ultimately flee into the woods. There was no reason to go out there. But if he didn't go out there, he'd never see Markla again. He opened the door.

The hall was deserted, but he could see plumes of smoke pouring from the door of the control room just down the hall. There was a man lying in a pool of blood near the door—a guard Rune recognized. It looked like his throat had been slashed. Rune once again ran to the window overlooking the prison yard and saw a battlefield with bodies on the ground and buildings on fire. One of the high towers was engulfed in flames—and beyond the prison yard and across the green field, the main gate was open. He heard shouts and saw an anti-grav truck coming, heading for the iron fence around the yard. A group of prisoners was surrounding it, yelling and cheering. With a loud crash, the vehicle rammed the fence and smashed an opening between two bars. It didn't look big, but it was big enough. Some of the prisoners started running through it.

With a roar, gunfire blasted from one of the towers, and pock marks spread across the ground. Then more gunfire started coming from the ground, aimed at the tower—and Rune saw Markla! She was with a group of prisoners heading for the smashed fence when a few guards rushed from a building and opened fire with pistols. Some of the prisoners shouted and went down—but others charged at the guards. The guards shot several of them, but they were soon overwhelmed, and now the prisoners were beating the guards with clubs and stabbing them with knives. Some of the prisoners had guns. Rune watched Carla point her gun at the face of a downed female guard and pull the trigger. He felt sick—but he kept his eyes on Markla. She was not fighting—but then someone attacked her. It was another female guard.

Even from this distance, Rune could see the guard was huge. There was blood streaming down the side of her face, and she should've had a weapon but Rune guessed she'd lost it. She grabbed Markla and tossed her to the ground.

She'll be killed! Rune thought, and then he was running—down the hall and out the main door and then through the entrance to the yard. As he passed through the open gate there was an explosion, and the top of a tower burst into a ball of flame, and bits and pieces of it rained down. Rune saw that all the towers were burning now. He zig-zagged around bloody bodies, and dodged a few people with knives, and swore at the sound of random bullets whizzing by. He kept his eyes on Markla and the guard.

Markla was still on the ground. Her dagger was also on the ground a short distance away—somehow, she'd lost it. But the guard didn't go for it. Instead, she was kicking Markla hard, and Markla grabbed at her leg, and then the guard was on top of Markla, pummeling her with fists and elbows—and then Rune swooped in and grabbed the guard from behind.

Rune was not huge, but he wasn't weak, either. The guard swore as Rune wrapped his forearm around her throat and pulled. And then Markla jabbed the guard in the eye and scrambled to her feet. Rune and the guard were rolling around on the ground and then Rune tossed her away. A shot rang out—and the guard's head split open, cleaved by a bullet. Rune looked up and saw a tall guy with dark skin standing there.

Markla said, "Thanks, Blu."

Blu just fired at someone else and said, "Go! Go!"

Markla gave Rune a quick glance. Then she picked up her dagger and she was running again, heading for the hole in the fence. Rune was close behind as she slipped through the opening. Many prisoners had already gone through and were running across the grassy field, heading for the main gate.

Markla and Rune easily outran them all; most of them were lumbering in comparison to the swift pair. Rune knew he could pass Markla, but he didn't. A gust of wind ripped through his hair, blowing it back, and it felt good. He wanted to stay behind her—but his head was filled with a storm of thoughts.

What am I doing? And why am I doing it?

But he knew why. In his mind, he heard the echo of his father's words, something about being careful—but he didn't care. Now Markla was sprinting through the main gate.

Rune heard a roar, and he saw hover-ships up above. They were fast police transports, and they looked like big white horseshoe crabs dropping down all around. Some were landing inside the prison, and some were landing outside, near the woods. One of them landed right in front of two prisoners near the tree line. From inside the vehicle, officers fired shots but missed. Then the transport popped opened and a squad of police wearing black body armor emerged. They chased after the prisoners, firing as they ran. One prisoner was hit in the back but the other one made it into the woods. The police raced after him.

Rune followed Markla as she ran toward a different part of the tree line. As they reached it, he saw more hover-ships in the distance dropping down into the woods. He guessed Markla saw them, too. They waded into the forest, crashing through the undergrowth.

Rune tripped on a root and nearly fell but he regained his balance and kept going. Leaves and branches smacked him in the face, and he heard the sound of another hover-ship close by. He knew the troopers could see the forest from the air, so it was best to go where there was cover from the trees. But that was everywhere. These were untended woods, covered by a thick canopy of leaves.

They ran for another few minutes, and then Markla stopped. She turned to look at him. They were both breathing hard.

"Rune, I have to get the tracker out of my arm."

"What?"

"You say that a lot."

"What?"

She gave a short laugh and rolled her eyes. Then she pulled out her dagger and placed the point on her forearm, on a spot where there was a tiny mark, no doubt from when the thing had been inserted. The blade was razor sharp, and she was very deliberate as she sliced through her skin. Rune winced as he watched her, wondering how he could help. But he was no surgeon, and she deftly maneuvered the blade through the bloody slash she'd created—and then she had it. It looked like a little pill, and the tip of the blade was right underneath it. She picked it off the blade and squinted at it.

"Spy machine!" she spat. "I'd like to glue it to the back of an angry bear, but there's never a bear around when you need one. So I guess we'll just smash it."

Rune was busy tearing a piece of his shirt along the bottom, making a bandage.

"Wait," he said. "Hold still." He felt her eyes watching him as he tied the bandage around her arm as best he could. He had a feeling she wanted to say something but then changed her mind. Then she put the tracker on a flat stone and used another stone to smash it into pieces. She seemed to enjoy doing this.

In his head, Rune heard a beep, indicating he had a message—from Blog Roko. Rune felt a jolt. This was not good, and in fact, there were two messages. He decided not to play them.

Markla said, "They can track you through the GoBug."

Yeah, true—but he loved his GoBug.

"Not if there's no power," he blurted. He quickly pried it open and removed the tiny crystal that powered the device. He put the crystal in one pocket and the GoBug in another.

"Okay?" he said.

She frowned. He could tell she wanted to smash the GoBug, too—but she knew the science. Without a power source, it could not track. "Yeah, okay," she said. "Now I've got to get out of this jumpsuit. I look like a neon lemon. They can probably spot this thing from outer space. And there might be some kind of tracker embedded in it, too."

She quickly stripped it off, leaving her in just a bra and panties. Rune watched her, unsure what to do with his eyes. He'd seen Markla in skimpy clothing before—the Run Team uniforms weren't much less revealing than her undergarments, and her undergarments weren't any more revealing than a typical bathing suit. But for some reason, he felt a little embarrassed. So he looked away.

"Mosquitoes," Markla said. "That's my main concern now." She tilted her head and looked at Rune.

His heart started beating fast. *What is she thinking?*

"Rune, are you wearing two shirts?"

"What? Oh, yeah. I am."

He was wearing a stylish brown pullover shirt with a v-neck collar. It was made from a tough material, something that simulated animal skin, and he thought it gave him a rugged look—but underneath, he was also wearing a white cotton shirt because he didn't want to sweat and ruin his style on top.

"Well, can you lend me one of them? Unless you want to keep me in my underwear."

"Sure! Of course," he said, and he fumbled to get the shirt off and handed it to her.

"Thanks."

It was meant to be worn untucked, and it was long on her small body, so it looked like a short dress that went well with her dark hair and her moccasin-style shoes. Rune vaguely considered how he'd never seen Markla in a dress—she always wore pants. This particular outfit made her look like some ancient tribal person, which seemed to suit her.

Markla rolled up the jumpsuit and buried it under a bush. Rune started to help her, but she was quick and before he could do anything she'd used her hands to dig the soil and then pile some leaves over it. Then she started walking fast through the woods. He followed by her side.

"Listen," she said. "Thanks for helping me back at the prison. You saved my life, and I appreciate it."

Rune shrugged. "I didn't want you to get hurt. But you probably would've done fine without me."

"I doubt it. I'm not a skilled fighter, Rune—all I've got is rage and desperation. And that guard didn't like me."

"You knew her?"

"Yeah, I make enemies fast. Her name was Dano… But you shouldn't have gotten involved. I'm a criminal—at least as far as the toads are concerned, and your father is the law around here. Do you see how that might cause trouble between us?"

Between us? Somehow, he liked the sound of that phrase.

"I'm not my father."

She didn't respond. Instead, she stopped walking and listened—and there was a whooshing sound not far off. A hover-ship was coming!

"Over here!" Markla said, scrambling to get under some thick bushes. The police vehicle passed overhead but then landed in the woods close by.

Markla watched and said, "I think they're going to the last spot where they got a signal from my tracker. They'll probably come after me with an H-dog. Luckily, it's a windy day—that'll help."

Markla started running again, and once again Rune followed.

He swore to himself as he ran. He wanted to tell her about Aldo and the LiveDream but this whole prison revolt situation was getting in the way.

Rune knew an "H-dog" was a device that could track someone by scent. Long ago, people had used real dogs to do this, but the H-dog was a hovering beast that could do it much faster. The police just needed a sample of Markla's scent—and they had one, from a memory bank of information created about Markla when she'd been admitted to the prison. Rune knew all this from hearing his father talk. He guessed it wouldn't take long for the H-dog to be on Markla's trail.

Markla seemed to know where she was going, but this didn't

surprise Rune. He knew she liked the outdoors, and she could very well be familiar with this section of forest.

Rune also knew the outdoors was part of the 20 Eyes lifestyle.

The organization claimed to largely reject technology, and the idea of 'primitive survival' was part of their mantra. How many of those skills did Markla know? She'd never mentioned anything about it, but she'd always seemed a bit like a creature from a forest. Supposedly, 20 Eyes held meetings in the woods, and they had items stashed there as well—like weapons.

Rune knew the police wouldn't walk along with the H-dog; they'd turn it loose and let it chase her down. The H-dog was equipped with cameras that would allow the troopers to sit in the hover-ship and watch what was happening. The device could fire rubber bullets and tranquilizer shots as well. It would be a formidable opponent.

They came to a shallow stream surrounded by a dense clot of trees, bushes, and undergrowth. The water was clear like glass and not much higher than an ankle, and the bank to reach it wasn't steep. Markla scanned the scene and said, "Wait here." Then she went to a spot on the bank near a tree with low hanging branches. She walked down the bank of the steam and put her toes into the water. Then she carefully retraced her steps back up the bank—moving backwards. When she reached the top, she leaped toward the tree, landing in a spot just behind it. It was a long leap for such a tiny person, but she could jump like a rabbit. Then she started climbing the tree.

She was a great climber, of course. Maybe there was a reason she'd liked monkeys at the age of six. She didn't go too high, but she was high enough and in a spot surrounded by leaves, and no one would probably notice her unless they were directly looking there.

Rune wasn't sure what to do. He started to come near the

tree but she called down and said, "Rune—no. It's not looking for you. Hide behind a bush or something. Or if you really want to be smart, go home."

Her last remark stung him a bit, though it wasn't completely unexpected. Rune wasn't sure what to say, but then he heard a sound in the distance. It was soft and heading his way. He scurried behind a wide tree trunk, and less than ten seconds later he saw the H-dog. He held his breath—had it seen him? No, it seemed to be focused on the ground, using powerful sensors to pick up Markla's scent. Rune looked at the thing and felt a chill go down his spine.

It was black and about the size and shape of a fireplace log with a bulb-like head on one end. The cameras, sensors, and antennas sprouting from different places made it look more like a giant insect than a dog. It floated a short distance above the ground and moved about as fast as Rune walked. But he knew it could move much faster.

It came so close to Rune's hiding spot he could've leaped out and touched it—but it passed on by. Then it started moving along the bank of the stream. It went down the bank, reached the water and hovered, almost like it was thinking. A strong breeze was blowing, and this was fortunate since it would curtail the ability of the device to pick up scents in the air. Another breeze rustled in the trees, and the H-dog floated up the bank on the other side and started scanning the bushes and undergrowth. Soon it was out of sight.

The stream wasn't deep but the camera would spot anyone walking in the middle of it, so the knobbers were probably thinking Markla had crossed the stream—but they couldn't know how far she might have walked in the water first. That's why the device was scanning along the bank, looking to pick up her trail on the ground where she'd presumably left the stream.

Unfortunately for the tracker, she could have gone upstream or downstream, and she could have emerged on either side. So it might have to scan both sides in both directions, and there was a lot of tangled foliage in the way—but sooner or later the troopers probably figured they'd find the spot. She could only have gone so far.

Markla dropped down from the tree and started walking back the way she'd come. Rune noticed she was quite precise about where she stepped.

He walked with her. "Markla, that thing is going to come back."

"Yeah, I know. And next time, I might not be so lucky. But it already knows I walked this way, and it might just think this is the same scent. So anyway, why are you still here?"

"I can help you get out of the forest and go wherever you need to go. You saved me back at the prison. If you hadn't told me to run, I'd probably be dead."

"Maybe. But you helped me, too. So we're even."

She turned her head, staring at him. It looked like she was going to say something harsh—but then she didn't. Instead, she scanned the ground and said, "Stop. Wait."

There were leaves all around. She walked across the leaves in a different direction now—a direction that no longer retraced her original path. She had a light step, and when combined with her soft shoes she made very little sound. When she was about twenty steps away she said, "Move the leaves where I just walked. Scatter them around."

Rune understood. Using his feet and sometimes his hands, he scattered the leaves between where he was standing and where Markla now stood, dispersing the scent trail the H-dog might use if it came back this way. He was severing the link from where she'd been to where she was now. Rune was sure the device would pick up the trail again, but this would buy them a little time. He ended up a step or two away from her.

"Thanks," she said and started walking again. "Now I think you need to go home, Rune. I'm sure your parents are worried about you."

"They'll be fine."

"Won't your dad be looking for you? How will they feel?"

Rune shrugged. "My dad told me not to take the job. So he'll be glad to know he was right. My mother won't even notice I'm gone. She spends all her time watching LiveDreams… Where will you go?"

"I don't know. Maybe to Narna. But I have to get out of this forest first."

Narna was the country next to Sparkla. But it was a long way from here.

"Maybe I can help you get there."

"I don't want you getting into trouble because of me."

She stopped walking and stared at him once again. She tossed back her jumble of hair, and Rune noticed there were bits of leaves stuck in it. There were also streaks of dirt on her face, along with some bruises and a tiny scar on the side of her forehead, like a dent—but she looked nice, in a Markla kind of way.

"Rune, you know I'm part of 20 Eyes, right?"

Of course he knew. But her words still shook him.

"Yeah," he said slowly. "I know. Does that mean I can't trust you?"

"No. But don't think I'm some poor misguided girl you're going to change because that's not how it is. You don't really know me, and your father is a Centurion, and I've done things I can't fix. You should leave me here and go live your life." Then she glanced across the forest. "If you had any sense, you'd turn me in and collect a reward or whatever."

Rune gave a snort. "I'd never do that—and why do you say I don't know you? I've known you forever."

She laughed. "Yeah, but not really. If you saw what was inside my head, you'd run."

"No, I wouldn't," he insisted. "And I'm sorry for what I did to you in the dream. I never should've taken that job—but maybe it was a good thing." Then his voice rose with excitement and he said, "I broke into Aldo's dreambank. I stole a copy of the real footage from the dream station raid. You were right—they changed it! That guy was going to kill you, and I want to help you get away. I can help you get to Narna."

Markla's mouth dropped open. "You broke into Aldo's dreambank?" She paused, and then she looked away. "You did that for me, Rune? That was really nice of you... I'm not surprised they changed it, but two people died in that raid, and I'm not innocent. I need a place to hide, at least until I can contact some friends."

"I have a place!" Rune blurted.

"You do? Where?"

Rune puffed out his chest a bit. "Don't worry—it's a place no one will look. Let's start walking and I'll explain."

"Okay. But I think we better run."

Chapter 18

Aldo gave a grim smile at the reports streaming through his GoBug. The prison had been overrun, and now his brother, the President of Sparkla, was concerned about the casualties. Apparently, fifteen guards were dead and sixty convicts were still missing—and why was this a problem? His big strong brother worried too much. Sacrifices had to be made, and the plan was proceeding nicely, and his brother would still go home to his pretty wife tonight.

Of course, Aldo hadn't been at the prison during the uprising, and neither had several other key prison personnel. Meanwhile, Diana had been busy teaching at the Dream Academy, and now she was sitting across from him in his office there. She looked lovely in a weary kind of way, like a rose that had just survived a thunderstorm. She was wiping a tear from her eye, and his InfoLenses told him certain protein levels in her blood were elevated—an indication of extreme sadness.

"Rune is missing," she said. "He's just a kid, and I put him in there. Now he's missing, and it's all my fault."

"Don't be so hard on yourself," Aldo said, trying to sound sympathetic. "You didn't know there would be a revolt. Besides, I have a feeling he's fine, and he'll turn up soon. The prisoners destroyed the security cameras, but we have a witness who saw Rune running into the woods."

"Really?" she said, and her eyes lit up. "That would be great news. But why hasn't he contacted anyone?"

"Because he's with Markla Flash."

Aldo's InfoLenses showed an immediate spike in her heart rate. "How do you know this, Aldo?"

"A prisoner told us. She's one of our craziest informants but she notices things. She says Rune helped Markla fight off a guard and then ran with her into the woods."

"I knew it!"

"You knew what?"

"Something terrible," Diana said, shaking her head. "I've been their teacher all year, and I knew he liked her—I mean he *liked* her. It was painfully obvious. But Rune's nightmares were perfect, and he's a great kid, and I thought he'd earned the opportunity. I told him to keep things in focus. I told him she was indoctrinated."

Aldo laughed. "There's never been any indoctrination stronger than a boy in love."

"How stupid! I was hoping he'd see the truth about her. It's such a waste."

"It might not be a waste," Aldo said, and he lowered his voice to a more comforting level. "He probably won't stay with her, so let's wait and see what happens; he might end up back here with some useful information. I have a good feeling about the whole situation."

"A good feeling? He could be in danger! I've seen Markla's LiveDreams, and she's disturbed. She's also violent, and he's broken the law because of her, and he's getting in deeper every minute. His father is the Centurion."

Aldo waved his hand. "I know, and that's why I didn't want Rune interrogating Markla during her nightmares, even though we do it with other prisoners. Rune's father is a law-and-order imbecile who can't see the big picture. But he also doesn't know exactly what happened here, and we're not going to tell him. We'll wait and see where Rune turns up. Rune made a mistake, but nobody has to know about it, especially if he fixes it. I'm a forgiving person."

"Are you? I wish I could be that way."

Aldo wondered who she couldn't forgive. Her handsome ex-husband? The man had been an idiot. The police who'd killed her son? Her son had been a moron. Either way, there were limits to the information his InfoLenses could supply. But she's so pretty, he thought, *pretty and sweet and broken.*

"It's not always easy," he said. "But I try. I try to forgive people all the time—if they're worthy." Then he smiled, and he thought about how few were worthy, and he said, "Please stop stressing yourself. I can help."

"Can you really?"

For one instant, she looked happy, and now Aldo felt his own heart beating faster. "Yes," he said. "And by the way, are you doing anything later? Maybe we could have dinner."

He held his breath.

She smiled. "That sounds nice. What time?"

"Any time that's good for you," he said. His head felt light.

Chapter 19

Markla had no intention of going to Narna now. Yeah, she'd mentioned it to Rune, but that had just been a spontaneous thought. Still, it wasn't a terrible thing to say. Certainly, it worked better than the truth.

She was staying right here in Sparkla where she could fight the toads. She just had to make it out of these woods and connect with Dru. If Rune could help with that, great. She would hate for anything bad to happen to him—*but I told him who I am, and he knows he's at risk!*

Can he really like me this much? she thought. The idea was flattering, and it made her flush with a strange kind of warmth. *But in the end, he has to leave me.* And for an instant she felt empty inside, and sad, too—but she shrugged it off. People had left her before. At least with Rune, it wouldn't be a surprise.

They ran for a while. Eventually, they stopped and started walking fast, heading through a dense stretch of forest and up a steep hill. The leaves on the trees were changing colors, and the forest was a fiery mix of yellow, rust, and orange, and the sky was a timeless shade of blue. Under normal circumstances, it would have been fun—even romantic. Markla loved the outdoors, and she'd often slept in the woods, especially when her mom had an inebriated boyfriend staying over. She wondered if Rune had ever slept outside. She gave him a sideways glance.

"So, Rune, you were going to tell me your plan."

He glanced back at her, and he grinned.

"You can stay at my house."

"What?"

Rune laughed. "You say that a lot."

"No, I don't. Only when I hear something ridiculous."

"It's not ridiculous. If we keep walking this way, we'll come to the woods behind my house. I have a shed in the backyard—way in the backyard, partly in the trees. No one ever goes in there, but it's not bad. You'll have to sleep with a bunch of drums, though."

"Your dad is the Centurion."

"Yeah, I know. Who's going to suspect you'll be hiding in the Centurion's shed?"

He gave her a sly look, obviously pleased with his plan.

She shook her head. "Maybe someone who knows you helped me escape. Maybe someone who knows we were together in the woods—at least until my tracker and your GoBug went off."

"What?" Rune sputtered. "Didn't they destroy the surveillance stuff?"

"Yeah, supposedly, but we don't know if that actually happened, right? Besides, even though personal GoBugs aren't part of the surveillance system, I'm sure someone turned on their eye-capture. Also, there could've been witnesses—guards and prisoners. Someone's bound to say something. I need to get out of here, and you need to come up with a story about where you've been."

Suddenly, Rune was frowning. He seemed to be brooding.

She didn't tell him about Location Five, where she was supposed to find clothing and other helpful items. But that's because she didn't plan to go there. It seemed like way too many hover-ships had appeared over the woods too fast, so she hadn't run in that direction. There was something about the whole escape that felt wrong. But still, she was free—and that felt right. She had her own plan.

"Rune, don't get me wrong," she said in a rush. "Your idea is, uh, bold—maybe even clever. But I have a different idea. Put the crystal back in your GoBug and call your father. Tell him to come pick you up. Tell him you ran from the prison, and tell him you saw me. Tell him you talked to me, but then we went our separate ways."

"Why?"

"Because it's pretty close to the truth, and it'll be harder to disprove. Tell him you fought with me, hand-to-hand combat—but I was too powerful, and I ran off with your shirt."

"Yeah, my dad would love that—losing a fight to a girl who weighs less than a sack of oatmeal."

Markla laughed. "Hey, I know I'm not big, but I resent having my body compared to a 'sack.' "

Now Rune laughed—and then he stopped. There was a sound in the distance—more hover-ships.

"Get down!" Markla said.

They dove for cover in a patch of tangled foliage. Then they peered upward through the branches and leaves as three police hover-ships passed overhead. They resembled flying crabs hanging above the forest, and they were making a sound like a wind storm. Then the pitch of the engines changed to a screechy whine, and it was obvious they were decelerating.

"Come on!" Markla said. She scrambled through the woods to the top of the hill with Rune right behind her. At the bottom of the hill on the other side there was a clearing, and the hover-ships were dropping down. Markla and Rune both got down on their stomachs, crawling through the leaves and viewing the scene below.

The ships landed, and doors popped open, and heavily armed people in black body armor started leaping out. There were also a bunch of H-dogs, at least six of them. Then a tall man wearing a gold sash got out of the lead vehicle, and Rune felt his blood run cold—it was Blog Roko.

"Wow, look at that king toad," Markla said. Then she paused. "Oh, is that your father?"

"Yeah," Rune said.

"Sorry. These H-dogs he brought are probably programmed

to find my scent and the scent of other prisoners—but now maybe your scent, too."

"Why do you think that?"

"Because your dad might be looking for you. That would be normal, right? I mean since you're missing. So forget my plan about calling him because he's right here, and it won't be good for you if we get caught together."

Down below, the police were fiddling with the H-dogs, getting ready to turn them loose. Blog was barking a few orders.

"Yeah, I know," Rune said, and he scrunched up some leaves with his hand. "So what do we do? We can't outrun those things forever. And I don't think we're going to lose a whole pack of them."

"We split up."

"No."

"It's the best way! You don't want to get caught with me. At least put some distance between us."

"I'm not leaving you, Markla. Forget it."

Markla stared at him. She wanted to stare longer but there wasn't time.

What's wrong with this guy?

She made a quick decision. "Okay, let's go!" she said.

She turned and bolted down the hill with Rune right behind her.

"Where are we going?"

"To a place I shouldn't take you. It's close."

"But won't they track us there?"

"Rune, I'm making this up as I go, okay?"

It was only partly true, but he seemed agreeable. She turned a bit, heading in a different direction.

She went deeper into the woods, wading through undergrowth even more dense while ducking and dodging thorny branches and finally reaching an area where the towering trees formed a thick canopy that blocked out most of the sun. Can he keep up? she thought. Rune was definitely faster than her on an open field, but they were in a forest, and she heard him crashing around behind her, probably slowing down to keep from stumbling over roots or getting poked in the eye. She glanced back over her shoulder and saw he was still back there but losing ground.

"Come on!" she said.

"I'm trying!" Rune said. "I can't glide over the ground like you."

She laughed and then abruptly stopped running. They'd reached a small clearing—and a crooked little house. The house seemed ancient, and it was covered with faded red shingles and wrapped in leafy vines, and it looked like it was being devoured by the forest. She watched as Rune stomped through a clump of vegetation and then stood by her side.

They were both huffing and puffing a bit, but not too much. He looked at the house and then back at Markla.

"Oh, good," he said. "You found us a place to stay. I hope they have a shower. I'm pretty sweaty."

"Shh!" she said, and she spoke in a low voice. "Rune, I hate to keep saying this, but you should probably leave me here."

He hesitated. "Why? What are you going to do?"

"Nothing. But if you get caught with me, it won't look too good on your resume."

"Markla, I'm staying."

She took a deep breath. "Okay," she said. But why am I asking? she thought. If she followed her plan, they'd have to separate in a few minutes, anyway. "Come on," she said and hurried toward the house.

In the back of her mind, she knew those knobbers would be on their trail soon. They had to be quick, and they had to be careful.

Markla had registered this place as a 20 Eyes hideout, as required—so another member could be here, and that person probably wouldn't like that Rune was with her. But hey, there were extenuating circumstances. He'd helped her escape from prison, and she could always claim she was trying to recruit him.

She almost stopped walking. *Now there's an idea!* It was an electric thought, like a bolt of lightening—and it was both wonderful and terrible. But it was there. *Don't try it! Leave him alone!* Well, she'd be leaving him alone very soon. She walked up a few broken steps, pushed open the creaky front door, and then crept inside.

She was in a living room that was dimly lit by tall windows covered by moldy green curtains. The air was dank and smelled like wood still wet from the last rainstorm that had poured through the broken roof. She had one hand on her dagger, and her heart was beating fast, and now she was glad Rune was with her. But there was no one here.

The room was empty, except for cobwebs and spiders and a sofa covered with a smelly old blanket. Markla ran to it. She reached underneath and pulled out something wrapped in cloth—a lighting orb. She touched it, and the room filled with gold light and shadows. She saw Rune watching her with wide eyes. What was he thinking?

Should she take him into the basement? It's not like she hadn't warned him. But would he turn on her when he discovered what was down there? She was definitely breaking 20 Eyes protocol—but yeah, she was going to do it and hope for the best.

The basement door was narrow, just like the wooden staircase that led downward. It was stuffy and dark at the bottom, and the ceiling was low, and the basement was filled with junk—dishes, clothes, boxes, old furniture, and other random items. For an instant, Markla felt trapped and smothered, but she shook off her sense of panic and quickly moved through the clutter and across the damp stone floor to what looked like a pile of wood. But it wasn't. It was pieces of wood hammered into a frame that made it resemble a pile. She swung it aside and then removed a piece of tattered tarp—and yes, it was all here.

Rune was staring over her shoulder.

"What's this?" he said.

She picked up the knapsack first. It was packed with survival gear and other helpful items. She dropped it at her feet and peered back into the dark. The other stuff—the bombs, the guns, the ammunition—she didn't touch it. Not yet.

Rune reached for a gun but she smacked his hand.

"Don't leave fingerprints," she said.

"There are weapons here."

"Yeah, I know. Pretend you didn't see them, okay? It's just a dream—like one of your nightmares. Only in this one, I'm not going to be torn apart by killer toads."

She was surprised by her sharp tone, and she could tell Rune was a little hurt. But when he spoke, he was calm.

"Markla, I had to make the dreamshell look like a nightmare. I was going to tell Diana you died in the guided section and hope she believed me. I didn't know all this would happen." He gestured with his arms. "I'm sorry for torturing you. I am."

She sighed. "I'm sorry for bringing it up. I didn't know you had such a grand plan… You've helped me a lot."

"So, are you planning to fight the police?"

"Do you really think I'd bring you here to shoot at your own father? I've never blown up anything. I've never fired a gun in my life—well, not too many times."

She reached back into her stash, into a burlap bag, and pulled out some clothes. She also stuffed the flute that was still slung across her back into the knapsack. Then she stripped off Rune's shirt and handed it to him.

"Thanks," she said.

She saw he was staring at her, and then he looked away.

"Rune, are you checking me out?" she said with a laugh. "In the middle of all this? I look like a mess, right?"

"No!" he blurted. "You look great! And I wasn't looking." Then he shrugged and gave her a little smile. "I'm just making sure no one's sneaking up behind you."

"That's what I like about you, Rune—you're always looking out for me."

She hesitated and considered making a joke about how they could check each other out later—but she didn't because there wasn't going to be a later. And then there was a pang of sadness, but that's how it had to be. She turned away from him and pulled on a pair of blue denim pants and a dark green shirt. Then she once again looked into the depths of her supplies and said, "I really came here to get this…"

She pulled off another tarp, and there was a flyboard.

Rune's eyebrows shot upward with excitement.

"They can't track me on a flyboard," she said quickly. "It doesn't touch the ground! And I can go fast. So that's the plan. But I only have one, so now you need to make that call to your dad."

He looked at her—and then beyond her. "You have two," he said.

"What? No, I don't."

He laughed. "You do say 'what' Markla—and you do have two boards." He pointed, and now she caught her breath. There was a second board, a glossy black one with red flames painted on it. She hadn't put it there, but of course she recognized it. It belonged to Tommi.

Her head started swimming. No! she thought. Sure, Tommi knew about this place because they'd come here many times as kids. But he didn't know anything about 20 Eyes—or maybe he did. *No!*

Meanwhile, in the back of her brain, she heard Rune talking.

"Markla? Markla, are you all right? What's wrong?"

"Nothing, I'm fine," she stammered. "You can't have that board, Rune."

"Oh, so you're going to leave me here? I don't want the police to catch me, remember?"

"Okay—whatever. I don't have time to argue. Take it." Then she reached down near the floor and grabbed something else. "But wear this."

It was a mask. It was plain red and would fit over the front of his face. It was the kind of mask worn by someone in 20 Eyes.

"I can't do that," Rune said.

"But if you don't, you might be identified."

"But they can do that anyway, if the tracker matches my scent."

"Yeah, but it's not the same as a visual ID. Just because your scent and mine are both in the woods doesn't mean we were there together. But if someone gets you on a camera while we actually *are* together, it's over."

"Who's going to do that out here?"

As he spoke, he heard a sound coming through one of the broken windows in the basement—hover-bikes. The police had arrived.

Chapter 20

Rune kept staring at the mask in his hand. He had to decide fast.

"Please, Rune," Markla said with pleading eyes. "If things go wrong for you, I'll never forgive myself."

She's a sweet girl, he thought. He put it on. Then he watched as she grabbed something else from her stash—one of the pistols.

"Markla—"

"It's okay. I'm not going to hurt anyone."

She also seized a magazine marked in red. She popped it into the gun and then attached the weapon to her thigh with a leg holster. She tossed a few extra magazines into her knapsack.

Rune started sweating a bit. Markla said, "Come on!"

She maneuvered through the basement to a short stairway leading to a pair of rusty metal doors that opened to the outside. Then she put on a blue mask of her own. Rune followed as she swung the doors open.

This was the back of the house, and the police were on the other side. She fired up the flyboard and jumped onto it. Rune did the same with his. He felt the board grip his feet and they were off.

Markla pointed to a spot in the nearby trees and flew toward it. He was right behind her. And then he heard the sound of someone shouting.

"Hey, there they are!"

The troopers were still on their hover-bikes. There were only two of them, but Rune knew they'd be calling their friends. He also guessed the hover-ships would get involved soon enough—but right now, they had to lose these two.

Rune got down into a low stance with one hand forward and one stretched out behind him. It was a stylish look, for sure, and he zoomed between the two troopers, zig-zagging in front of one and then swerving in front of the other. He heard them swear as he darted into the forest.

Bushes and plants whizzed by. The flyboard worked fine in the woods, hovering just above the low foliage and plowing through the undergrowth. The main thing was to keep from slamming into anything that would knock him off the board. So he swerved around a tree and then smashed into some bushes and barely avoided another tree and then—yeah! He was flying! He glanced back and saw the two knobbers were still there. *Too bad they can't see the grin on my face!* The hover-bikes were plenty fast but they couldn't maneuver as well, or maybe the knobbers were just a bit more cautious—or maybe they just wanted to get close enough to fire a few good shots.

Rune swore as the sound of gunfire ripped through the air. He moved left, and he moved right, and a bullet hit a tree just as he swung around it. A few more shots ripped through the leaves. Then the troopers started broadcasting through speakers in their helmets.

"Stop or we'll shoot! Stop or we'll shoot!"

But you're already shooting, Rune thought. *What a couple of toads!*

Markla was still up ahead but he saw her swing her board to a dead stop behind a tree. It was a sweet move that showed some fine control but then he had a bad feeling, and there was a whooshing sound, and something whizzed past his head—and there was an explosion not far behind him.

He heard the troopers swear again as one of them sideswiped a tree. The bike bounced off another tree and slammed sideways into a bigger one. It hit the ground with a loud thud and skidded into a nearby boulder.

Markla had fired something at their pursuers. It wasn't an

ordinary bullet, though—she'd loaded the pistol with some kind of exploding cartridges.

The other trooper fired a few wild shots in Markla's general direction and then circled back to his fallen comrade. Rune swung his board around in a wide arc to get a better look. He peered through the forest and saw that the guy who'd hit the ground was shaken but seemed okay. Rune breathed a sigh of relief. The other one was talking into a GoBug.

Rune knew more knobbers were on the way. Markla was watching him as he pulled up beside her. He noticed she'd lost her mask.

"Markla, what are you doing?" he snapped. "You could've killed that guy!"

In an instant, her eyes got fierce. "Rune, he was shooting at you! Besides, I didn't come close to hitting him. I'm just trying to survive, okay? I told you who I am! *Go back to your pretty little life and leave me alone!*"

She spun around on her board and took off through the woods.

"Markla, wait!"

He took off after her. In the distance, he heard the sound of more hover-bikes. But he suddenly didn't care about them—and now he was plowing through all kinds of plants and ducking under branches. She was moving faster now, too fast. *She's going to crash into something for sure!* Up above, he heard the sound of a hover-ship. It was dropping down somewhere in the distance, probably trying to cut them off. And then he saw two more troopers on bikes up ahead, coming toward him at an angle. He swerved off in a different direction, and now he had four knobbers behind him and no clue where he was going.

He heard the sound of more gunfire, and something struck a tree right near him—and it bounced off the bark, and Rune guessed it had not been a kill shot! These people were firing rubber bullets, and they wanted him alive. Two more shots whistled over his head.

Rune tried to stay low on his board. Where was Markla? He'd lost her. Then he heard a crash, and he swung the board around a towering tree and came to a dead stop.

Whoah! He almost fell off the flyboard—but he kept his balance. One of the troopers had hit a tree and Rune was getting a lucky break. Great! Another trooper, a tall female, stopped to help her comrade, but the other two were still coming toward him. Rune snarled and gunned the board right at them.

Rune laughed at the look of surprise on their faces as he came plowing through some branches, heading right for a collision. The first trooper gave a yelp and turned sharply to the side. Meanwhile, Rune swerved a bit the other way and passed right beside his bike—just as the other trooper fired a wild shot at him. The rubber bullet hit the other trooper's bike, causing it to wobble and then smash into a thorny bush. There was a shout as the bike skidded sideways before slamming into a tree. Both knobbers swore. Rune kicked the board up into a high arc as the shooter came to a stop. Look at this move! Rune thought, and he spun around a few times. Then he zoomed off through the trees.

Under his mask, Rune was laughing. Hey, this was fun. Then he thought about where that hover-ship had gone and how he should go the opposite way—but no! That ship had passed right over Markla's head. That ship was after her. It would land and more police would come charging out.

He headed in that direction, moving quickly once again. In his head, he heard the echo of his father's words, telling him to be careful. He grimaced and pushed his father out of his mind. Then he heard an explosion—and there was Markla.

She was in trouble. She was moving fast, and she had the

pistol in her hand—but two troopers on bikes were close behind, swerving around trees and firing guns of their own. Rune ground his teeth and prepared to attack, or maybe just distract them and make them crash—but one of them fired a shot, and Markla lurched as she was hit, and then she smashed into a tree. With a shout she tumbled from the board.

No! Rune thought. *No!*

Both troopers came to a quick stop, and the first one pounced, keeping her on the ground while trying to cuff her. But she was fighting hard—and the trooper didn't see Rune come blasting out of nowhere.

Rune gave a shout, and he angled the flyboard up high and struck the trooper in the face with it. The trooper swore, and Rune swung around quick and tried to hit him again. This time the guy ducked under the board. But now the other knobber was aiming a pistol at Rune. Rune saw it, and for one second he thought it was over—but Markla was on her feet, grabbing the barrel of the gun. She swiped the pistol from the guy's hand and it flew into the woods—but the trooper swung his fist and hit her in the jaw. She staggered backwards but did not go down. Rune flew at the trooper and got the board to go high, higher than it should be able to go, almost at the trooper's head. The trooper leaped back and in that instant Markla took off and ran to her flyboard.

In a flash, she was back on the board. Rune noticed she still had the knapsack on her back, but she no longer had the gun. She looked at Rune and said, "Come on!" She took off once again through the trees.

They were once again tearing recklessly through the woods. As Rune swerved around a large tree, his mask flew off and disappeared. He didn't care. I am who I am, he thought, *just stay behind Markla!* But did she know where she was going? They stayed in the deepest part of the forest, and he knew it was to gain cover from the trees. But he also knew the forest wasn't that big. Sooner or later, every patch of woods led to water, and then people, and then the ocean. But they weren't going to see the ocean. Instead, they burst through the trees, and there it was—the Rainy Wish River. On the other side was a stretch of forest and then the town of Turnaround.

Markla slowed down while Rune looked up at the sky. It was clear now, but there were hover-ships around. Sooner or later they would be spotted—probably sooner. But Markla seemed to be looking for something, and then she stopped.

Rune pulled up beside her. He glanced at her and saw there was a purple bruise on her chin where the trooper had punched her. There was an angry-looking splotch on her forehead from the crash with the tree. There was blood on her arm, coming through the makeshift bandage where she'd cut out the tracking device.

"Markla, are you all right?"

"Yeah, except for the injuries. You lost your mask."

"I know. But I don't like masks, anyway."

"Neither do I... Look over there."

She pointed across the wide river, and Rune saw a fat metal pipe emerging from the opposite bank. It was a storm drain coming from the town beyond.

She said, "Can we get into that pipe without being seen?"

Rune felt a quake in his stomach. He wasn't thrilled with this plan. There was lots of room to maneuver out here, and they could get trapped in a pipe. Then again, the police were all around, and maneuvering meant constant fighting, and sooner or later they were going to lose.

"We'll have to cross the river," Rune said.

"Right. I see that."

"Have you ever crossed a river on a board?"

"Yeah. It's tricky. Have you?"

"Yeah. Tricky."

Using a flyboard over water was always a risk. The flyboard used an anti-gravity generator that constantly calculated the distance from the ground, but water was less solid than ground, and the calculation was less precise—so the board tended to oscillate, and it was harder to maintain balance. While the board would still grip the rider's feet, that didn't mean it couldn't tip over, and tipping over meant going into the water, falling off the board, and not being able to get back on.

Plus, the Rainy Wish was broad and deep. They couldn't stand in the middle of it, no way. So falling off the board would be a disaster. Also, there was no cover over the river, so they'd need to cross it fast before they were spotted. Hopefully, the hover-ships were all on the ground dealing with wrecked hover-bikes and injured police officers.

"Rune, you should head back into the woods and—"

"I'm going with you."

She stared at him. "I'm sorry I yelled at you back there," she said. "I'm sorry for saying those things. I have a bad temper." Then she gave him a little smile. "Thanks for saving me." She turned away and tapped the board with her heel. In an instant, she was over the water.

"No problem," Rune said. He was right behind her.

They both crouched down on their boards, gliding at a moderate speed. Right away, Rune felt the flyboard wobbling more than usual. *Whoah—whoah!* But he kept his balance, and he kept his eyes on Markla. She was wobbling, too. She also had the knapsack on her back. But she kept it steady, steady, steady—and just as she reached the opposite bank, she stumbled.

She let out a whoop as the flyboard shot out from under her feet and crashed into a bunch of tall weeds. But she didn't fall off—she just stepped hard to the ground. Rune slid to a stop beside her.

Markla picked up her board and grinned at Rune. "Nice riding," she said.

He grinned back.

She scanned the sky. "We need to hurry."

Looking at the pipe up close, Rune was even less enthused. Sure, it was big for a pipe but not for a person. Meanwhile, Markla was taking something out of her knapsack—a lighting stick. Then she was pushing her board and the lighting stick into the pipe ahead of her and sliding herself inside. She was tiny, but she was still on her hands and knees. Rune wasn't a huge guy, but he wasn't Markla-sized either, and he was going to have a harder time.

He squeezed in behind her. Okay, not too bad. It smelled like dampness and rust, and they were crawling along now, and Rune guessed Markla could see where she was going, but he didn't see much.

She was moving fast and he was glad. He felt cramped, and trapped, and crawling on the metal hurt his knees. But the town of Turnaround was probably a good half hour away. Could they crawl for that long through this pipe? Would the police figure out where they were and be waiting for them when they got there? Then again, if no one had seen them cross the river and enter the pipe, this could be a perfect plan.

The pipe went on and on. Rune had never considered himself to be claustrophobic, but he'd also never spent too much time crawling through an endless metal pipe, either. The farther they went, the more he was filled with dread. What if it suddenly started raining and the pipe filled with water? They would never get out in time, and who would ever find them? Who would ever know that he, Rune Roko, dream writer extraordinaire, had been drowned in a storm drain?

Get a grip, he thought. Markla wasn't thinking about any of this—she was totally fearless, and anyway, there wasn't a cloud in the sky.

Suddenly, Markla stopped crawling. For a moment there was silence. Then Rune heard her breathing, and of course it was heavy because crawling through a pipe was harder than it looked—but it was worse than that. It sounded like she was hyperventilating.

"Markla, are you all right?" he blurted. "Markla!"

She was gasping. "I can't breathe!" she said. "I have to get out of here."

"We're close to the end!" he said. "You'll be okay—just stay calm! You'll be okay."

"Rune—I'm trying."

There was more heavy breathing, and Rune's heart was racing, and he felt so helpless. *I've got to do something!* He put his hand on her calf and gave it a light squeeze. "We're going to make it, Markla! We will!"

There was a long pause—and then her breathing got more even. "I'm okay," she said. "I can do this, I can... I'm okay now."

"Good," Rune said, and he sighed with relief.

Then she said, "Hey, I was also thinking, if it starts raining we're in big trouble."

Rune gave a soft laugh. "Markla, you worry too much. There's not a cloud in the sky. We'll be fine."

She hesitated and took several more deep breaths. "Right," she finally said. "That's true. Let's go."

They started crawling again.

How much time had gone by? He wasn't sure, but just when he thought his knees couldn't take any more pounding on the cold metal, Markla stopped—and she turned around. The lighting stick was now between them, and in the shadowy darkness

Rune could see another pipe above her head, leading upward. It had a much larger opening than the pipe they were in, and there was also a ladder mounted along the side.

"We made it," Markla said, and she smiled.

Rune looked her over. Even in the dim light, he could see she was pale. Then he glanced upward. "Yeah, but where does this go?" he said. "Are we going to end up in the middle of a street?"

"It's not a street. We're behind a building, close to a street."

"You know where we're going?"

"I never went through the pipe before, but I was told it could be done."

"Oh," Rune said. "Who told you?" Then his voice got a little harsh, and he added, "Someone in your group?"

He instantly regretted the snotty tone.

"Yeah, my group, Rune. The group that wants to save people like you from their own stupidity. This isn't the best place to talk about it."

"I'm sorry," he said. "I shouldn't have said that."

"No, I'm fine talking about it. In fact, I'd like to talk about it—later. But right now I need to get out of here."

Rune hesitated. *So, there's going to be a 'later'?*

"That sounds good," he said. "I'll go first."

"No!" she said, and she started scrambling up the ladder. "I need to get out." She left the flyboard in the pipe.

Rune watched her climb up and then push aside the metal cover at the top. Then he followed her and poked his head out of the hole.

They were in the middle of a paved area behind a building with no windows—nice. Then he saw the trees. They were right at the border of the woods, near a building on the edge of town. It was an inconspicuous place for them to be, and maybe that's why someone in 20 Eyes had told Markla about it.

Then Rune saw Markla, down on her hands and knees with her head near the ground.

"Markla!"

He ran to her. He knelt down and put his hand on her back. "Are you okay?" Obviously, the pipe had been a bad experience for her.

"Yeah," she said as she once again took some deep breaths. "Whose stupid idea was it to go through that thing, anyway?" She gasped a few more times. "Rune, I'll be fine. I'm just a little claustrophobic, that's all. But it had to be done, and we did it—thanks. Did you get our stuff?"

He went back and retrieved the flyboards. But he kept a close watch on Markla as he did it. He also wondered, how long until someone from 20 Eyes showed up?

20 Eyes—the thought of her being in that cult made him crazy. How long had she been a member? *How many people does she know?* From what he understood, there were more guys in the group than girls, and he didn't like the idea of Markla being in a group with lots of guys. Also, they were known to be killers and murderers, so there was that, too.

As he climbed out of the hole with the second flyboard, he saw that Markla was now standing. Once again he sighed with relief and put the cover back on the hole. Then he followed her into the nearby woods, presumably to plan their next move.

Chapter 21

Dru Nava swore at the news stream coming through his GoBug. Then he started pacing the floor of an office that resembled a tool shed. The room was attached to a greenhouse, and it was filled with blinking gadgets, primitive gardening implements, and containers of fertilizer that gave the room an acrid smell.

He cursed again. The prison revolt hadn't been too successful, and while none of that was his fault it still gave him stuff to worry about. He paused to check his reflection in a small mirror nailed to the wall and wondered if he needed a haircut. The cropped style made him look more athletic, and girls always thought he was sexier that way.

Meanwhile, Dru's friend Stono wore a grim expression while sitting on a nearby sofa surrounded by various clay pots. Stono was short and stocky and had dark hair similar to Dru's but he seemed less concerned about the styling.

"We better get moving," Dru said. "A lot of them have been captured already."

"Yeah, I see," Stono said. "It should've gone better, considering all the weapons they had. I still don't understand how Blu smuggled all that stuff inside."

Dru laughed. "It was easy. He used the money we gave him to pay off the main guy who checks packages—a guy who resigned two weeks ago. He was sitting at home today counting his cash while his friends were busy getting killed. These government people have no sense of loyalty."

"Yeah, but what good did it do us?" Stono said. "Most of our people never made it to the drop points, and the ones who did got caught real fast. Makes me think someone talked."

Dru was quiet for a second, staring through a window that

overlooked a leafy forest of hydroponic tomato plants. "No one talked," he said. "If there'd been a leak, the whole thing would've been squashed before it started."

"Yeah, true. So maybe the whole plan was bad."

Dru shrugged. "It could've gone better, but some of our people will make it out of there. Besides, we're not done yet—and we're in the news. That's always a big part of the plan."

It was true. Publicity was important, and they were getting lots of it. The story of the prison uprising was the only story in the news today, and the towns of Cooly Strip and Turnaround were filled with fearful people on the lookout for escaped prisoners. In fact, the whole nation of Sparkla was on alert.

"What about your little savage?" Stono said with a laugh. "Sorry—I mean your girlfriend. Still nothing?"

Dru grinned and puffed out his chest. "They didn't get her yet, and they won't. Say what you want about Markla, but she's smart, and she knows those woods. She's going to make it."

"That's a good thing, I guess. But you know how I feel."

Now Dru felt the blood rushing to his face. "She's one of us, Stono! I'm not going to tell you again. Other people in the group have been arrested, and it's no different."

"It is different! She's a girl. She's sixteen. She'll talk and identify us all!"

"She didn't talk! She got her sentence and they're done interrogating her. How many questions did the police ask you? *None!* They didn't come around here once, even though she's worked here for years. What does that tell you? Markla's as tough as anybody."

Stono gave a heavy sigh. "Yeah, she's tough… I'll never forget her initiation. That was brutal, and she took it all, and then she almost killed Sklog—I think he's still recovering. But you can't deny she's always been a little crazy—and it might be more than a little. And you know they'll keep coming at her in the dreams, even though they're not supposed to, and I don't want to end up in a cell right next to her."

Dru crossed his arms. Was Stono out of his mind? The idea of hurting Markla was ridiculous. Sure, Stono had been his best friend since they were small, and that was the only reason he thought he could broach the topic—but he was sadly misjudging the situation. Markla was one of them *and you don't turn against your own!* Besides, she'd been close to letting him into her pants when that whole disaster had come crashing down, and if she did manage to escape he intended to pick up where he'd left off. It wasn't the main thing on his mind but it was there. He'd put some time and effort into that little savage.

Dru gave Stono a hard stare. "She doesn't worry me," he said. "I'd be more worried if you got arrested, Stono."

"I'd never talk!" Stono snapped. "You know that. We've known each other forever."

"I've known Markla a long time, too. If she finds her way over here, you watch your step—you hear me?"

Stono hesitated. "Yeah, okay, Dru. But I think you should know, it's not just me. The others who went that night feel the same way. They're worried."

Dru whirled around and yanked open a drawer. He pulled out a black dagger and pointed the blade at Stono's face. "See this?" he said. "Markla put one of these into somebody's throat—for us! That's more than any of them ever did—and if anything happens to her they'll answer to me. So you tell them that. You hear me?"

"Yeah," Stono drawled. "I hear you. I hear you fine."

"Good. Make sure everyone else hears what I'm saying, too. But then again, I'll tell them myself. Now pack up your stuff and let's roll. We've got a few things to destroy."

He opened the door to the office and stormed out.

He stomped into the greenhouse. His chest was heaving with rage but then as he paced up and down the rows of bushy tomato plants he started to calm down. For some reason, the greenhouse usually had this effect. Markla always said there was something about plants that made people calm, and she was right. In some ways, these plants were better than most of the people he knew.

Hopefully, he'd see Markla soon.

Chapter 22

Markla found a spot in the woods where they could peer through the trees and watch the vacant area behind the building. She dropped her knapsack on a pile of leaves next to her flyboard and plopped down hard. She was tired.

Rune sat down across from her, and she glanced at him. Strands of black hair were strewn around his face, and his shirt was ripped where he'd made a bandage for her, and his eyes, usually bright like the eyes of a deer, seemed a little tired—but overall, he looked sexy. Rune always looked sexy, but he never seemed pompous about it. He was low-key and modest, making him even more attractive. All the girls lusted after Rune, and it was one more reason she'd never really thought he'd go for her.

What am I going to do with him? she thought. She couldn't deny it was nice having him around, but they had to separate soon—because she was a convicted murderer on the run, and he was a guy in school with a future. Exactly why he couldn't figure this out was beyond her. But then again, he probably *had* figured it out, and he was just putting off the inevitable, and that was sweet of him. It gave her a good feeling inside—something exciting and magnetic. It would be hard to walk away from him. Maybe she wouldn't mind putting it off a little longer, too.

"What time is it?" she said.

"I don't know but I'm thirsty. Escaping from prison is a real workout."

"You weren't in prison."

"Not yet."

"Rune, that's not funny. I don't want you going to prison."

He laughed. "So what happens now? Can you believe it's only afternoon? This has been a busy day."

She opened her knapsack and found a bottle of water. She

drank a few swallows and handed him the rest. "Here," she said. "My gift to you for all you've done. It's not much, but I'll try to do better next time."

"Thanks. I love water. This is my favorite kind, too."

"You mean the kind that's wet?"

"Yeah, exactly. I love wet water."

"Rune, I have to go find my friends now."

He put down the water and stared at her. "I'm your friend, Markla."

"Yeah, I know. But I have to go find other friends."

"You mean people in your group?"

"Yes."

Why did he have that look on his face? Maybe he hadn't figured this out after all.

He leaned toward her a bit. "Do you have a way to contact these friends? You don't use a GoBug, and everyone is looking for you."

"I know, but don't worry about it. I have a plan. It's an old-fashioned method."

Rune shook his head. "The whole country is looking for you. Not just you, but everyone who escaped. I'm sure there are pictures on every news stream, including some special ones dedicated to finding you—and people look at those streams. Old people stare at them all day long, and it's still early. None of them have gone to bed yet."

Markla squirmed a bit. She had a plan, but she didn't want Rune to know the details because it was a 20 Eyes secret.

"I can wait until dark," she said.

"That's better, but it's not like you'll be invisible. You need to hide out for a while. You need a place that's not connected to your friends." Then he paused and said, "Like my shed."

She rolled her eyes. "I will never be in your shed, Rune. We will never share a GoBug in your shed."

Instantly, she regretted her words. He was looking at her like he'd been stung by a wasp.

"I'm joking!" she blurted. "I don't want to go to your house, that's all. I don't think it's safe... If I weren't in trouble, I'd be happy to visit your shed—I mean, in a friendly way...or whatever. Or nothing! What am I talking about?"

She took a breath and tried to regain her composure. This was so stupid. She had bigger things on her mind than rolling around with Rune on the floor of his shed—*what? Why am I thinking this? Get a grip, Markla!*

Meanwhile, Rune was quiet. And yeah, this was another thing she liked about him. He knew when to shut up.

Finally, he said, "Why do you hate GoBugs so much? Technology is great. I love the stuff my GoBug can do. I don't want to go back to the past. I don't want to live like a Basic."

"I'm not a Basic," she said, feeling relieved at the turn in the conversation. "I know everyone jokes about me because I'm not too fashionable, but that doesn't mean I live in a cave and spend my day scrounging for acorns. And I don't hate technology. I just don't want it controlling my life. But you should hate the GoBugs because they track everything you do. If you put the power crystal back in that thing, the knobbers would be here in a minute."

"Yeah, but that's because of the circumstances. Under normal conditions, no one is tracked."

Markla laughed. "Everyone is tracked all the time, and the 'circumstances' happen pretty often. And every mind stream you look at is recorded somewhere."

Rune shrugged. "Everyone knows about this stuff, Markla, and most people support it. It's not some big conspiracy. People know what they voted for."

"Do they?" Markla said. "LiveDreams make it easy to create any kind of image or scene, since the scenes are created in someone's imagination. They don't need actors or a film crew. Then that stuff can be streamed out like it's real, and no one can tell what's true from what's made up."

"I can see that now," Rune said. "But I don't think violence is the answer. That's my dad's way, and his way is usually wrong— for everything."

"We don't want to hurt people. But some people are just no good."

"Yeah, but who decides who's 'no good'? How do you know you're the one who's right?"

"I don't always know," she said, and her voice got louder. "But if someone was beating up a kitten or a little kid, you'd know it was wrong, wouldn't you? Because there are people like that. There are people even worse."

"Well, yeah. In that case, I would know."

She paused. "Rune, I respect your attitude about non-violence, but I'm not as nice as you, okay? I also don't think I'm a mean, heartless person—at least, I hope not." She paused again and felt a wave of grief rising inside her, and she felt her eyes filling with tears. "I'll always remember that night at the dream station, and I'll always think about that guy's pregnant wife, and I'll feel terrible about it for the rest of my life." She stopped again to wipe a tear away—and then her eyes shined with anger. "But do I need to be tortured to death a thousand times? Do I need to have that hanging over my head every minute? If someone kills me, I don't want them to get that kind of punishment, and it's one of the things we want to stop—any way we can."

She glanced at Rune. He seemed uncomfortable, like he was sitting on a nail. He must think I'm a real mess, she thought. *Crying and raving—a high maintenance girl for sure.*

But Rune was calm. "Markla, you're not a mean person. You made a mistake, that's all." Then he shifted his position on the ground and added, "Anyway, that guy didn't have a pregnant wife; he wasn't even married. I made all that up. I was just trying to make the nightmare more powerful."

Now Markla's mouth dropped open. For an instant, she couldn't speak. Then some words came to her.

"Rune, you're such a toad!"

"It was my job!"

"Yeah, but you didn't have to be so fanatical! It was your first time. Couldn't you have started me off with something less...hurtful?"

He waved his hands. "I'm sorry! I was planning to make the nightmares easier next time. But I didn't want to quit, because I knew they'd just get someone else to do it. Besides, I wanted to talk to you again."

"You mean after the torture?"

"Well, yeah."

"They have visiting hours at the prison, you know."

Rune gave a soft laugh. "I didn't think of that. But really, I thought I might be able to help you somehow if I kept the job. That was my plan."

"Do you think it's right to use nightmares to torture people?"

"No," he said, and his voice was firm. "I'm against it now. You're right about that."

"Do you think it's right for them to use LiveDreams the way they do? Do you think people like Aldo and your father are doing something good?"

"No. I don't."

His words sang inside her head. "Okay," she said. "So we agree on some things. Anyway, I do have a plan, but I have to do it alone." She paused. "I think we've reached the end of our adventure." *Maybe.*

Rune frowned. "Why?"

"Because you have a future and I don't. Not in this world. Not now, after what's happened."

Rune hesitated. "I don't want you to go. I want to see you again."

This is crazy, she thought. *Don't do it!* But as she gazed into Rune's eyes, she knew what she was going to do—and it felt awful and thrilling at the same time. She leaned toward him a bit and lowered her voice.

"Rune, do you want to meet my friends?"

He hesitated again. Then he said, "Yeah."

I'm a horrible person, she thought. *I'm a monster! But I don't want him to disappear from my life.*

"All right," she said. "But you can't do it today. Everyone in the Eyes looks like a normal citizen; we're all pretending to live ordinary lives, but we all have this other secret life, and you can't know who else is a member until you've been checked out and you pass a few tests—and even then, you'll only know a limited number of people, the ones in your 'pod.' So right now you need to go back to your house, and I need to find my friends. But someone will contact you. And then...maybe we can see each other sometime."

His eyes were bright. "Good," he said. "When does all this happen?"

"I have to wait for my ride. After dark, like I said."

"I'll stay with you until they come. I can help."

"Help me how? I'm just planning to sit here. I know how to sit." Then she paused and considered how she didn't really want him to go. "If you want to stay a little while, that's okay," she said. "I suppose you could get some rest. Hanging around with me involves a lot of running."

"I'm not tired."

Markla sighed. "Maybe you should get some sleep, Rune,"

she said. "There's a good spot over there, by that tree. I have to go back into the woods for a few minutes."

"What? Why?"

"I need some privacy. It's not like we have restrooms out here."

"Oh—sure. No problem."

"I'm glad you approve."

"Yell if you get into trouble."

"Sure," she said with a laugh. "If I forget what to do, I'll give you a shout. Thanks."

She couldn't help but laugh again as she moved farther back into the trees. But then a wave of guilt washed over her, and it felt like a tidal wave. She swore to herself. Why was she getting Rune involved? He was a normal, happy kid, and she should leave him that way—but then, he could be a great ally. His father was a Centurion, and he was an amazing LiveDream writer. He could really help the cause. If she recruited someone useful, everyone in the group would love it. They would love her, too.

She knelt down and pulled out a little square object. Maybe someday Rune would have one of these but right now he couldn't see it.

It was a transmitter, but it was unlike any GoBug or modern transmission device. It was only capable of broadcasting beeps she would key in manually. By making the beeps longer or shorter, she could create codes for letters of the alphabet. The beeps were sent out on a primitive radio frequency that no one monitored—no one except 20 Eyes.

Somewhere nearby, in this very town of Turnaround, a device would turn on when she started broadcasting. It would begin recording the beeps, and it would even translate them for the listener so no one had to sit there and figure out the letters. It would also sound an alarm in the house, telling anyone nearby that a message was coming through.

She could receive signals as well, and she could set the device to show them as tiny flashes rather than sound off as beeps. A tiny screen would translate the beeps into words and display them. She started sending her message. She received a response right away.

Chapter 23

Aldo clutched a package shaped like a coconut and stopped walking. So this was Diana's house. He stood on the street and studied it. It was normal for him to study things before making a move. Then he felt something like butterflies in his stomach, and that was normal, too—at least when it came to women.

The house was snow white with solar tiles on the roof that matched the blue trim. From a distance it resembled a doll house, yet the magnified images he saw through his InfoLenses showed it hadn't been painted in a while, and the paint and shingles were chipped and cracked, and while the thorny holly trees had obviously been pruned at one time, they were now on the verge of growing out of control. But not just yet.

Aldo ran a few fingers through the curly red hair that fell to his shoulders. Why had he gone bald so young? It wasn't fair. He'd never been the best-looking guy—"rat face" was a common insult he'd heard as a teenager—but couldn't he at least have been allowed one beautiful thing? Well, he'd taken control of the situation. He'd gotten this snazzy hair replacement, and the InfoLenses made his face look more like an owl than a rodent. But did any of it help? No, because girls were always interested in the worst guys. Tall, handsome, and dumb would always be preferred over short, clever, and radically fashionable.

But not today. This one I can get, he thought. *This one is mine!*

He rang the bell and Diana opened the door, and his heart started pounding. She looked sleek and sexy in a loose grey top and black tights. Her blonde hair shined like gold, but her eyes were the same as always—blue, with a hint of sorrow.

For an instant, Aldo couldn't speak. Then he managed to say, "Diana, hello. It's nice to see you. I brought you something." He shoved the package toward her.

She smiled. "Hi, Aldo—thank you. Come in."

He entered the living room and glanced around fast. The decor was sparse yet cozy, with a small sofa covered by a knitted blanket, and a few paintings of the ocean hanging on the cream-colored walls, and a woven rug on the hardwood floor. There was also a fireplace with a mantel, and scattered across the mantel were pictures of a young man. In many of the pictures the man was in the woods along with a dog. That must be Kalo, Aldo thought. *That dumb kid of hers who got himself killed.*

"My son, Kalo," Diana said.

"That's nice," Aldo said, and then regretted not saying something smarter. Then he blurted, "I guess he loved the outdoors."

"Yes, he did," Diana said, and she was still smiling. "He loved being outside. He also loved animals."

Aldo tried not to wrinkle his nose—but had he done it anyway? *Ugh! I'm such a fool!*

Diana just laughed. "You don't like camping, Aldo?"

"Oh, I love it!" he said, but then as he looked at her, he also laughed. "Well, not really, Diana… I prefer LiveDreams to animals and the wilderness. Animals are so unpredictable—you never can tell what they might do."

She laughed again. "Well, that's why you need to treat them nicely and know which ones are dangerous… Anyway, thanks for coming."

"I was happy to come over," he said, and he puffed out his chest, trying to look as tall as possible. "It's not good for you to be alone—not with this situation going on."

"I'll be all right," she said and placed the package on the mantel. "What did you find out? The news is saying there are still twenty convicts out there, including ten from 20 Eyes."

"Don't worry, they'll all be captured."

"But these explosions… It's nerve wracking."

All afternoon, 20 Eyes had been staging attacks, setting off bombs obviously designed to keep the police occupied.

"It's trivial stuff, Diana. We know how to prioritize. It won't do them any good."

"What about Rune? There was nothing in the news about him."

Rune, Rune, Rune! She's always talking about that stupid kid!

He forced himself to smile. "Rune isn't a convict, so I made sure we kept him out of the media. He still hasn't been found and neither has Markla Flash. But Rune's father is personally looking for them."

"Is that good or bad?"

Aldo shrugged. "Blog Roko is a neanderthal who's a little too attached to his club, but now and then he has a good moment. Unfortunately, his dinosaur style of police work is a problem. We have so many devices that can be used—DNA trackers, tooth scanners, facial recognition scanners—but we need to be able to implement them on a large scale. Most people lack the intelligence to make informed decisions about these issues, but there are more votes coming up soon, and I think they're starting to realize why we need to have this equipment in use all the time. This prison escape might help people see it more clearly."

"The way you talk about the escape it almost sounds like a good thing."

"In disaster there's opportunity."

He was about to say something else when there was an especially loud explosion outside. It shook the room and resonated like a thump in the chest.

"What was that?" Diana said.

Aldo didn't know, but he put his arm around Diana's shoulder. "It's nothing," he said. "It's just a lot of noise." He gave her a little squeeze and hoped for another blast—but then his GoBug started making a low hooting sound. He swore to himself, and he reluctantly pulled away from her.

"What?" he said. Then he cursed again with even more disgust because someone had blown up the North Central Streaming Station—and that was a little more disaster than he'd expected.

Meanwhile, Diana had turned on her wall screen, and it was showing a two-dimensional version of the news while Aldo was looking at a three-dimensional image of Blog Roko. Blog's big jughead was in front of his eyes.

"It's another attack from 20 Eyes," Blog said. He wasn't just talking to Aldo; there were others on the stream as well. "This looks like the worst one so far... This is going to cause a disruption in some of our GoBug communication. Not all of it, obviously—but definitely with some of the officers in that area."

Aldo frowned. "Why are so many of them still out there? This wouldn't be a problem if we'd captured everyone."

Blog snorted. "I didn't see you chasing anyone in the woods, Aldo."

"It's not my job to chase people, Blog. But it's my job to find out how they escaped, and who helped them do it."

"We don't know who helped anyone!" Blog snapped. "And if we catch anyone who aided the escape of a prisoner, they'll get what they deserve."

At this point, someone else broke in—Gin Xantha, the President of Sparkla and Aldo's brother. His voice was peppy and bubbled like water from a mountain spring. "This arguing is a waste of time," he said. "We're doing fine. Let's capture the rest of the escaped prisoners and get the security gear back up and running."

There was a murmur of agreement. Then there were a few questions about logistics and the stream ended.

Diana was still watching the wall screen. Aldo's GoBug

conversation had all happened inside his head, so he knew she hadn't heard any of it, but based on the news report he was sure she understood the general idea.

"I hate 20 Eyes," she said, and her voice was bitter. "I hate every one of them."

Aldo took a quick step toward her and grabbed her hand. "I know you do," he said, and the butterflies in his stomach grew into a swarm. "But that's why we're going to capture them all. You'll see."

"I hope Rune doesn't get hurt because of that awful girl. I've seen it happen before."

"I know you have, and it won't happen this time. Don't worry, she's just a kid. She's just a girl."

"The one who tricked my son—she's one of the people who escaped. Did you know that?" Then Diana shook her head and said, "I hope she dies—her and Markla. I hate to say it, but it's what I feel." She wiped a tear from her eye and whispered, "It's what they deserve."

"You're right, Diana. I'm sure we can make that happen."

"We can?"

"Yes. I can do that—for you. I can control everything… Open the package."

She eyed him for a second and then walked to the mantel to retrieve it. She unwrapped the plain silver paper, opened the tiny container, and removed something that looked like a metal coin.

"What is it?" she said. Aldo reached out and touched it—and a three-dimensional image of a shimmering red rose sprang from the object.

She laughed once again. "You and your tricks."

"You can sync it to your GoBug," he said. "Watch this." She stared as the rose got longer, and then shorter, and then cycled through a variety of shapes and colors. "It's so much better than a real one, Diana. And it will last forever." Then he looked into her eyes and said, "Let's forget about the news right now."

"All right," she said. "I'll try." She hesitated, and then she leaned forward and gave him a kiss.

Chapter 24

Rune opened his eyes with a start. Where was he? Was that an explosion? What was going on?

Then he saw Markla, and everything came back into focus. She was sitting under a nearby tree with her legs crossed, like a kid around a campfire. It was getting cool outside, and she was now wearing a flannel shirt over her brown cotton shirt, along with a necklace made of pebbles. She also wore her usual moccasins, and she looked right at home on the outskirts of a forest.

"Rune, you're awake—good."

"I guess I fell asleep."

"Yeah, you were really sleeping. But get ready to go. Things should be easier now."

"Oh, yeah? Why?"

"Because the North Point Streaming Station was just destroyed, and a lot of the toad machines aren't working. Also, the knobbers are busy doing other things. There's a lot going on—small attacks."

Rune rubbed his eyes. "Did a war start while I was asleep?"

Markla laughed. "It started a long time ago. But it just got a lot noisier."

"I noticed. So, how do you know about this stuff?"

"I just know."

She's communicated with people, Rune thought. *But really, it should be expected.*

"Did anyone get hurt?" he said.

"I don't think so. Are you worried about your father?"

"No," Rune said, and he was surprised at how sure he sounded. But it wasn't because he didn't care; it was because he couldn't picture anything happening to Blog. The guy was like a slab of granite. "Now that you mention it," Rune said, "he's probably going to be in a bad mood." Then he gave a snort. "He's always in a bad mood."

"Yeah, I understand. My mom's like that, but I guess I never helped much."

"I'm sure you weren't the problem."

Markla shrugged. "I could've done better. Sharli adopted me, and I guess she wanted me more than my 'real mom' did. But then my adopted father left, and she turned into a monster—and I wasn't the greatest daughter, either. It's been a bad situation." She paused. "I don't like to talk about this stuff."

"You can tell me. I like when you tell me things."

Markla laughed again. "Well, that makes you different from most people, Rune."

"Did you ever want to find your biological parents? Maybe I shouldn't ask that, right?"

"No, it's fine, and I don't want to find them. Not at all. They didn't want me."

"But there were probably circumstances."

"I don't care about their circumstances. They gave me away to Sharli, and that was a terrible thing, and I don't care about any excuses—and I don't care about the 'father' who left us, either." She sighed. "I know it sounds cold, but I will never forgive any of them. No chance." She shook her head and smiled. "This girl who's sitting in the woods with you, Rune—she's unforgiving in a nasty way. So, what are your parents like?"

For an instant, Rune thought about some of the things in Markla's psych profile—but no, he wasn't going to ask too much. Instead, he said, "I don't think you're nasty, Markla... My mom's nice, but she's too busy watching LiveDreams to really care about what I'm doing. My dad asks me what I'm doing all the time, and no matter what I tell him, it's wrong." Rune deepened his voice a bit and snarled as he imitated his father. "Life is full of choices, Rune… You need to be tougher… Someday, you'll come to a crossroads… You need to be strong… You need to eat steel bolts for breakfast and boulders for lunch… Most of all, you need to stay away from girls like Markla Flash."

"What?" Markla said. She stopped smiling now. "Your father said that?"

"No," Rune sputtered. "I mean—yeah. When you were arrested. He asked if I knew you."

"Oh. What did you tell him?"

"I told him I did. I told him…I liked you."

"Really?" Her eyes went wide with excitement. She banged the ground with her hand and laughed. "And what did he say?"

Rune grinned. "He said my chances of becoming a Centurion were slipping away. My future was grim."

Markla's smile faded, and she slumped a bit. "He probably knows we're together. I don't know what you're going to tell him."

"No problem. I'll tell him we got married."

Ugh! Why did I say that?

"That was a joke," he said.

"Yeah, I know," she replied, and she laughed a little. But she looked away from him, and he sensed she was uncomfortable.

"Markla, I'm just kidding. For all I know, you got engaged in prison."

Her face was blank. Then she looked down at her palm because something was flashing.

"I need to go," she said. Then she paused. "You're not supposed to be here with me. You need to go back into the woods."

"Okay," Rune said. But he didn't move.

"I mean now." Then she frowned and said, "Rune, there are some things you don't know, and some things I'm not sure about. But right now, you need to go into the woods, okay?"

What was she talking about? She seemed frazzled and angry

now, and he didn't understand why. Of course, she was under lots of stress but he didn't want to leave with a bad vibe. He got up to walk farther into the woods, but he paused, waiting to see if she would stand up as well.

She was still sitting cross-legged on the ground. She glanced up at him, and he wondered if she was about to snap at him—but she didn't. Instead, her frown vanished and she leaped to her feet.

"Leave the flyboard with me," she said. "The knobbers are looking for a guy on a flyboard, so there's no sense trying to ride home. Wait a bit, and then use the GoBug to call for a self-car. When you get home, tell your father you were scared, and you hid in the woods, and you turned off the GoBug because you were afraid 20 Eyes could track you. You were scared and paranoid, okay? Because he knows you're not the kind of guy who eats boulders for breakfast—even though you are."

I am? And hey, that might work. He nodded his head.

She took a quick step forward and hugged him. He was surprised, but he hugged her back, and he wrapped his arms around her, and she squeezed him hard. But then she tore herself away and stepped back.

"Go!" she said.

"Okay," he said. But he had to wait a few seconds, because he wanted to stare at her one last time. Finally, he walked into the woods, moving backwards, so he could still see her—and she was watching him. He smiled at her, and he waved. She rolled her eyes and laughed again. She waved back and then turned around.

He wondered what things he didn't know. She's part of a radical cult that fights the government. She killed someone... Was there bigger news? It didn't matter.

He didn't go far into the woods. Instead, he crouched down behind a small bushy tree and watched. Markla was rummaging around in her knapsack once again, and now she was putting on a hooded jacket and pulling the hood over her hair. Within a minute, he saw an anti-grav car coming around the corner of the building. It was dark now, but the car had no lights on. It was white like a tooth, and it was moving slowly, and it reminded Rune of a shark gliding through shallow water. Markla walked toward the vehicle.

She had the knapsack on her back and she was carrying both flyboards. The car stopped moving.

Rune's heart was beating fast. Yes, there was fear—but there was also excitement. He was hiding in the dark, watching people from the most dreaded outlaw organization in the nation, and he knew one of them. The trunk of the vehicle popped open. He could see the silhouette of the driver as he got out of the vehicle. He was tall, and he took Markla's knapsack and put it on the back seat of the car. She tossed the flyboards into the trunk and closed it—and then they kissed. And it was like a bomb exploded inside Rune's head.

What?

It was not a quick peck on the cheek. It was not the affectionate kiss someone might give to a friend. The guy held her shoulders and kissed her on the lips. It was a serious kiss. It was the kind of kiss that said *we are together.*

Rune's head started whirling. He couldn't breathe, and he was sure he was having a stroke.

It couldn't be—but it was. Markla had a boyfriend.

She never looked toward the woods again. She quickly slid into the car and it drove back around the corner of the building.

Chapter 25

Rune knew he couldn't stay in the woods for the rest of his life. But he wanted to. He wanted to stand right here until he was covered with leaves, and then snow, and then he finally dissolved into the earth.

His mind was screaming in two different directions. The first direction was filled with rage toward Markla, and the second direction was filled with hope and desperation—and the thought that maybe somehow it would all work out, and she'd end up in his arms.

She'd never mentioned a boyfriend. Why not? And what about the magnetic feeling he'd felt toward her all morning? It had seemed mutual, there was no doubt in his mind—but now there was doubt. No, there was no way, she'd seemed to feel it, too. She'd said things to him, and she'd hugged him, and she'd even kissed him at the prison. Why had she done those things, and what had she been thinking at the time? Rune's head rattled like it was filled with loose marbles.

Maybe it's not too serious, Markla and this guy. And now there was a spark of hope. After all, he was a guy she'd known before this morning and before the last few days. Maybe she'd kissed him because he was expecting it. *Maybe she's really thinking about me.*

And now he wanted to shout until his lungs exploded. What an idiotic idea! She's not thinking about me! She's thinking about him, and she's probably going to wake up in his bed tomorrow morning—and the thought made Rune want to vomit.

He pulled the GoBug out of his pocket and replaced the power crystal. He knew his dad would now be able to track him, but he didn't care since he planned to go home, anyway. He put the device behind his ear and connected himself to all the mindstreams of the world, and it was like turning on a city of lights. How had he gone without this for so long? Then he realized it hadn't even been one whole day, and he gave a grim laugh and thought about how Markla would've laughed, too. Then he ordered a self-car. The self-car had no driver, just an EB, and it arrived within a few minutes. Rune could use his GoBug to enter an address into the EB and it would take him there.

He didn't have much money in his bank account but he had enough for a ride home. Rune never used any cash, although it still existed. He knew it was one of the many things certain people wanted to do away with, since cash supposedly aided crime. People like Markla would have a hard time being fugitives if there was no cash because everything they purchased would be tracked by a GoBug. He vaguely wondered if he still had a job at the prison now that Markla had escaped.

He gritted his teeth and pictured her, and she looked so nice. But he was numb inside; he felt dead like a rock.

He settled into the front seat of the car as it started to move. Then he used a special script on his GoBug to tune the communications monitor to a police stream. Instantly, he heard something that made him jump.

"Watching a white Seacrest on Bluebird Drive. He came from behind that empty building on Storm Street."

Rune caught his breath. Then he swore and called up another script.

Start smashcar.

This was another script he'd never tried, but like the one he'd used to break into Aldo's dreambank it worked perfectly—and now he could drive the car himself. He grabbed the wheel and stomped on the accelerator.

Bluebird Drive was a main street in the town of Turnaround, a place that sat on the same bay as Cooly Strip but on the opposite side of the river that emptied into it. As Rune headed fast up Bluebird Drive, he hardly noticed the glowing streetlights and storefronts.

He knew Markla and her friend were in that white car. He kept listening to the reports and drove faster.

She might be in trouble! Maybe I can help.

Chapter 26

Markla wondered how they looked sitting together. She and Dru were supposed to be a couple of innocent kids having fun, but then she opened the glove compartment and saw a pair of grenades. I might have fun again, she thought, *but the innocent part is over.*

"Nice job with the escape," Dru said. "I knew they'd never catch you."

"Yeah, I used a flyboard that was stashed in the house—and why did I find Tommi's flyboard there, too?"

Dru hesitated. "Tommi's a good kid," he finally said. "He wants to help. We can talk about it later."

"We can talk about it now. I don't want him getting mixed up with us."

"Did you ever think about what he wants? It's not your decision."

"He's only twelve! I was fourteen and that was still too young."

"Yeah, you did start kind of young—at least with that."

Markla almost hit him. But she clenched her jaw instead. *Is that what's really on his mind?* Stay calm, she thought. They both had bigger things to worry about.

"Dru, I woke up this morning in a prison cell. Don't start."

He laughed. "I'm joking, Markla. And Tommi hasn't done anything, not yet. I don't know if you'll get a chance to talk to him much. You might need to get out of the area, maybe head south or something. Maybe wait until things cool off up here."

"But you're up here. You want to send me away?"

"No, it's not like that. I'm just thinking about what's best for you."

She didn't reply. If Dru was telling the truth about Tommi's lack of involvement with the group, that was good news. She still had time, and she'd convince him to stay out. She pressed herself down into the seat and said nothing.

Markla knew she should be asking about everyone in her pod, and who else had escaped, and what was happening with the attacks. But instead, she found herself thinking about Rune. Did he see me kiss Dru? she thought. *Of course he did!* Her plan had been to get into the car as fast as possible, but then he'd kissed her, and how could she refuse? Dru was her boyfriend—sort of—and Rune was someone she couldn't have that kind of relationship with, not really. So there was no reason to feel guilty. But there was guilt, and it felt like a stain she wanted to wash away.

Meanwhile, Dru was talking about the immediate situation. "Blu and Rose are still free. They're going to split up and head south." Then he grinned. "The knobbers are running around like blind people. What a bunch of dummies."

"I know someone we can recruit," Markla said. "He was working at the prison—and he's old enough. He helped me escape."

"Oh, yeah? Who?"

"A guy I know from school. He was working there as a LiveDream writer."

"You mean a torturer?"

"Yeah, but I'm the only one he tortured, and only once. Anyway, he'll probably still be working there, so that could be useful, right?"

Dru shook his head. "Why did he help you? You must have made a big impression on him."

She could hear the tone in his voice—the instant jealousy thing.

"It wasn't like that at all, Dru."

"Really? Is that what he thinks?"

"Hey, the guy saved my life! Stop jumping to conclusions, okay?"

Dru gave a sarcastic laugh. "Okay, whatever, but we can't be too trusting. A LiveDream writer? That's the last thing we need."

"Dru, I'm a LiveDream writer—because that was the plan, right? Infiltrate the school and see what I could find out about Diana and Aldo. Well, I didn't find out much because I'm a terrible spy. But this guy could do better. Not only is he in the school—he's inside the Dream Center. Think about it."

Dru seemed to be thinking, or trying to. "What's his name?"

"Rune Roko—yeah, he's the Centurion's son. But that could also be a big plus; he could find out all kinds of stuff."

Dru rolled his eyes. "Blog's kid? Are you crazy? That's risky. I think you should leave the strategy to people who know better." Then he turned his head to look at her. "I also think you should forget about him right now and hide in the greenhouse for a few days. I've got that room out back. You could even help me with the crop."

"Yeah, sure," she said. "That sounds great."

But it didn't—because she didn't want to forget about Rune, and she knew Dru wanted her to do more than water some tomato plants, and there was no real reason for her to say no, other than the reason she'd been giving him for two months. "I'm not ready," she'd said, and that had worked fine, and then she'd gone to prison which had worked even better. Well, now she was out, and was she ready? Maybe. She wasn't the first girl for Dru, she knew that—but where were the others? Had he cared about them? They didn't seem to be around.

Dru said, "Hey, we might have a problem. There's a knobber behind us."

Markla glanced back and grimaced. Yeah, there was a police car back there.

"It might be nothing," Markla said. "Don't panic."

But she knew he was going to panic.

"What if they identify you?" he said in a shaky voice. "Then I'm going to be tagged, too. My cover will be gone, and they might link me to all kinds of stuff."

"Dru, he hasn't even pulled us over. And if he does, I have fake identification. We're just two people driving around. We're looking for a place to eat, okay?" She reached out and gripped his arm. "Stay calm. We'll get through it."

But her heart sank as a siren whooped and the police car flashed its colored lights.

Dru cursed again and pulled the car to the side of the road. They were in downtown Turnaround, right near a shop called Fly Away that sold the best flyboards and accessories. Markla vaguely recalled the day she'd saved up enough money to buy her first board, and the guy in the store had asked about her age because she'd looked so small. She took a deep breath and reached for the fake identification chip in her knapsack. Meanwhile, the trooper was getting out of his car. He was tall like a lamp post, and he started lumbering toward them—and when he was a few steps away Dru slammed his foot down on the accelerator.

"We're out of here!" he said.

Markla swore. So stupid! she thought. Meanwhile, the trooper gave a shout and scrambled toward his vehicle. Dru laughed, and Markla's head banged back against the seat—obviously, this car was fast. There was a whooshing sound, and in a few seconds the trooper was out of site and they were racing out of town, hurtling down a dark road surrounded by scraggy trees.

"He was going to tag us," Dru said. "I know it!"

Markla shook her head. *Maybe—but maybe not. And now we're definitely in trouble.*

She gripped the armrest, and she thought about how Dru had probably panicked and left her at the dream station to be arrested—and how it didn't surprise her. Maybe he could've stayed, she thought. *Maybe he could've gotten me out of there.*

"Don't go straight down this road!" she said. "They'll just be waiting for us in the next town—double back on another road and make sure you lose him. "

"Markla, I know what I'm doing," Dru said. Then he paused and added, "We'll double back," and he swerved the car into a hard left turn, and then another—heading back but on a parallel road.

Markla was tossed against the door while listening to the sound of a siren in the distance. The knobber was far behind and not visible. But Dru was still snarling and wrestling with the steering wheel.

"Slow down!" Markla said. "I don't see anybody. Take the car off the road. We can park it somewhere and hide."

"We don't need to park anywhere. They're not going to catch us."

"But they have other cars around! We need to hide."

He ignored her and kept driving.

The woods were set farther back from the road now, across an area of tall grass. There were a few houses but they were spaced far apart and close to the tree line. Markla could tell Dru was feeling pretty self-satisfied, but then another car appeared, coming toward them in the opposite lane. It looked like an ordinary car—but as it drove past it made a sudden turn and pulled up behind them—and a light on the dash burst into bright shades of red and blue. A voice boomed through a loudspeaker.

"Pull over!"

Dru cursed and jammed his foot down on the accelerator. But the pursuer stayed with them.

"Pull over!" the voice said again.

"We're not going to outrun this guy!" Markla said.

Dru frowned. "Yeah, I can see that. That's why we need a new plan."

Markla's heart sank. Dru's plans were rarely good. Then Dru grunted and slammed on the brakes while veering left into the oncoming lane. For an instant, the police car shot closer, right along the passenger side—and Dru gave a shout and muscled the wheel hard to the right, trying to run the trooper off the road.

Markla grabbed the bottom of the seat. The car shuddered as it collided with the other vehicle. Dru swore again and rammed the other car once more, and it swerved off the road and shot across the grassy clearing—and smashed head-on into a tree. Dru let out a whoop—and then his car was off the road, too, heading for another tree. Markla screamed.

The impact rattled her skull even as the inside of the car exploded with foam. But the foam kept her face from going through the windshield. Then it was quiet.

With a hissing sound, the foam receded, and Markla tried to get her bearings. Okay, her hands and feet could move, and there was no blood or serious pain.

"Are you all right?" Dru said.

"I think so. But I can't open the door."

Dru had his door open, and he was jumping out. He turned to help Markla who was now crawling out fast on her own. She had her knapsack with her, and she quickly scanned the scene and saw that both cars had traveled farther from the highway than she'd expected. She stared at the wrecked police car but didn't see anyone moving. She knew they didn't have much time.

"Can you pop the trunk?" she said. But Dru didn't answer because he was busy running toward the other car. What now? Markla thought. She lunged back into the car and hit a button, opening the trunk. Then she grabbed the two grenades from the glove compartment and shoved them into her knapsack before scrambling out of the vehicle. She ran to the trunk and retrieved the two flyboards. Unfortunately, Dru did not know how to ride a flyboard, and Markla considered how she could be halfway to Narna by the time he figured out a way to get home.

Dru was peering inside the other car. "Hey!" he said. "It's Blog Roko!"

"Really?" Markla said, and now she felt queasy.

"Yeah! He must've been listening to the trooper chatter and decided to get involved. Bad day for Blog!"

Markla whipped her head around and scanned the dark highway—still no one coming. But that wouldn't last.

She ran toward Dru. "How is he?" she said. "Is he dead?"

"He's not moving, but I think he'll be okay. The foam probably saved him. But we can take care of that."

"What do you mean?"

Now Blog was starting to move. Dru yanked open the door of the car and pulled him out. He dragged Blog by the armpits for a short distance, dropped him on the grass, and stripped away his pistol and GoBug. He took a pair of handcuffs from Blog's belt and cuffed the big man's hands behind his back. Then he ran back to the police car and grabbed something from inside—a rifle.

Blog was face down on the ground, and Dru pointed the rifle at Blog's head. "Can you hear me, Centurion? This is 20 Eyes talking to you."

His words blasted through Markla's head. "No!" she yelled, and her hand shot out and grabbed the barrel of the gun, lurching it away. "Are you crazy? Don't do that."

Dru scowled at her. "Markla, I'm getting tired of you telling me what to do."

"And I'm getting tired of you acting like a moron."

"This is our chance to make a statement! This guy is one of the government's main stooges."

Suddenly, Blog opened his eyes and turned his head. He seemed dazed.

Markla looked at Dru. "That's not the way to do it," she said—and she pulled out her dagger. After all, it was the official weapon of 20 Eyes.

She dropped down fast next to Blog. Dru watched with wide eyes as she knelt close to him. But she didn't use the weapon. Instead, she fumbled around and found what she was searching for—a red button on the shoulder of his uniform. She pressed it hard.

Dru's mouth dropped open.

"You pushed his distress signal!" he yelled. "They'll be here in a few minutes!"

"Yeah, I know."

"But this guy can identify me!"

"It's dark, and he can't see you from where he is—and do you really care about me?"

Dru gave her a quizzical look. "What are you talking about?" he said, waving his hand. "Of course I do. What does that have to do with this?"

"I don't want him dead. I'm asking you to do this for me."

"That's ridiculous!"

"We don't have time to argue. Are you going to back off or not?"

He opened his mouth again, but he said nothing. He just glared at her, and she glared back—but he didn't make any more hostile moves.

"Help me move him away from the car," she said.

"Why?"

"Just do it!" she hissed. Then she shook her head. "They already know *me*—I'm trying to protect *you!* Fingerprints, DNA—evidence. We need to destroy as much as possible." She pointed to a spot on the ground. "Put him over there."

Dru cursed and grabbed Blog's feet, dragging him across the grass to a spot away from the police car. Meanwhile, Markla pulled a rag from her knapsack and wiped Dru's fingerprints from the handcuffs locked around Blog's wrists. She grabbed Blog's gun and GoBug from the ground where Dru had flung them and raced to the police car and threw them inside. Then she pulled a grenade from her knapsack, set the timer, and tossed it into the car. She bolted to the other car and did the same with the second bomb. Then she looked at Dru and said, "Get down!"

They both dove to the ground as the grenades exploded. Both cars were instantly engulfed in flames—and now Markla saw two headlights coming down the road.

"Here they come," she said. "We need to run!"

Blog moved his head a bit but then seemed to slump back into unconsciousness. Meanwhile, the other car was slowly coming toward them. The lights of the vehicle went off but not before Markla saw who was driving.

She gasped—it was Rune! Would he never go home? But at the same time, her heart leaped. He's got great timing, she thought. *Well, he is a drummer.* And he might provide a faster option than running into the woods and signaling one of the Eyes.

She whirled toward Dru. "This is the guy I was talking about," she said. "He's okay." Dru had another bewildered look on his face as she ran toward the car. Rune was getting out.

She was out of breath when she reached him. "Rune, what are you doing here?" she said. "Don't come over here."

Rune peered over her shoulder at the burning cars and the dark shape on the ground.

"Hi, Markla. I heard they were looking for a white car, so I decided to try coming down this road. They'll be here in about a minute... Did you blow up these cars?"

"Yeah. Can you give us a ride? It's not far. We'll be good—I promise."

"Is somebody hurt over there?"

"He's fine. I pulled his distress signal—really, I did. But we need to go."

Rune stared at her, and at Dru—and then he said, "All right. Hurry up."

Markla waved at Dru, who came walking over. But Rune eyed the rifle and shook his head. "You can't bring that," he said.

Dru stared in disbelief and then laughed. He pointed the gun at Rune and said, "I think I can."

"Dru, he's right," Markla said. "If we get caught, this is evidence. Think about it." She leaned toward him and said, "Think."

Dru's jaw clamped shut, and his face was a mask of rage—but he also looked confused.

"Give me the gun and get in the car," Markla said. She didn't wait for his reply. She yanked the rifle from his hands and ran toward the flaming wreck of Blog's car. She tossed the gun into the flames.

Markla knew that if they got stopped, the gun wouldn't matter much, except that Dru might start shooting and get them all killed. But as evidence, it was trivial. There was no bigger evidence of Dru's crime than Markla herself—a real live member of 20 Eyes who'd escaped from prison that morning. But she knew Dru didn't think well under pressure. In fact, he didn't think too well ever. And she didn't want him to have that gun while he was with Rune.

Markla came running back toward Rune's car. Rune was behind the wheel now but Dru was still standing outside the vehicle.

"Let's go," she said as she slid into the back seat.

Dru paused long enough to sneer and then he got into the

front seat next to Rune. He looked more baffled now than angry, and Markla thought that was fine. It was the less dangerous option.

Rune eased the car back onto the road. Markla noted with satisfaction how he didn't drive too fast. She also sank down into the back seat and stayed out of sight.

"Where are we going?" Rune said.

"Just keep going straight," Dru barked. "It's about ten minutes away."

Chapter 27

Rune snuck a glance at the guy sitting next to him. So this is what Markla likes, he thought. Okay, the guy was handsome—at least to someone who thought a chiseled statue of an ancient god was appealing. But could he ride a flyboard? Did he know that Markla had once boycotted school over a kitten?

Rune kept his eyes on the road and said nothing. I've got to stay focused, he thought. This was no time to sulk, and this was no time to think about whatever crime Markla and this guy might have committed back there. In a few minutes, Markla would be gone, maybe forever—but maybe not. So he had to make a positive impression right now. He had to show her he was better than this guy, and he took some solace in the way he'd told the guy not to bring the rifle—and the guy had backed down. *Of course, that was right after Markla stopped him from shooting me.* But still, Rune had shown he was no pushover.

In his head, he heard the words of his father: *One of the reasons your mother liked me was because I was not weak.*

Suddenly, Markla jumped up in the back seat. "Rune, is your GoBug on?" she said.

"What? Oh, yeah. Sorry, I didn't think about it. I was using it to listen to the knobbers. Then I was busy rescuing you."

The guy next to him made a look of disgust. "I knew we shouldn't have come with him, Markla. We need to get out right now."

"It's probably okay," Markla said in a rush. "He's not an escaped prisoner. If he turns up with a believable story, no one will check the car's history. We're getting off soon, right?"

"Yeah, right," the guy said. "We have a new hideout—Underground 3."

Markla looked at him but said nothing. Then he said, "We'll get out here. That would be the best way."

Rune scanned the dark tree-lined highway and said, "Sure." Then he drove the anti-grav car off the road and maneuvered it into the black woods, finally dropping the landing gear behind a group of shaggy evergreens. "There's not much out here," Rune said. "Are you sure it's safe?"

The guy scowled. "It would be perfectly safe if I had that gun. But we'll be okay. I told you, we have a place nearby."

He got out of the car, and Markla followed. Then she reached back to get her knapsack. She handed the flyboards to her companion.

There was no reason for Rune to get out of the car, but he did. He was pretending to help unload things, but he really wanted to talk to Markla one last time. He could see it probably wasn't going to happen, and his hopes dimmed. And then she turned to the guy and said, "I want to talk to Rune for a minute. Go on ahead. I'll be right with you."

In the darkness, Rune could see him scowl again. "But you don't even know where we're going," he said.

"Just go into the trees and wait for me, okay? I'll be right there."

Rune could see he was thinking about not going—but then his expression changed. Suddenly, he looked smug, and he said, "Sure. There's no rush." He stared at Rune. "We'll be the only ones there, anyway. We'll have a great time... Hey, thanks for the ride."

"Don't mention it," Rune said, but he felt his face getting hot.

The guy stomped away, and Markla turned toward Rune. Then she tossed back her hair that was so ragged and ruffled, and she was quiet. Was she waiting for him to speak? That was fine—he had some questions.

"Who is that guy, Markla? Is he your boyfriend?"

She hesitated, like she'd expected him to say something else. "I'm not sure," she said. "It's complicated."

"But who does he think he is? And is he really a good guy for you to be hanging around with?"

"I'm not as pure as you, Rune," she said with a sigh. "I keep telling you that."

"I'm not pure. But that guy's going to get you into lots of trouble."

"I'm already in lots of trouble. I'm pretty sure you've noticed."

"Okay, but you're just going to run off with him? Just you and him—alone tonight?"

Instantly, he was sorry he'd said it. Even in the moonlight, he could see her face flush with that anger he'd seen before.

"Yeah, that's what I'm going to do!" she snapped. "And it's none of your business, okay?" She paused and took a deep breath. "I appreciate all your help, Rune, and I wanted this to end in a good way—but now you just need to go home and figure it out." Then she paused again, and she was almost calm. "I have to go now."

She whirled and walked off into the woods. Rune was stunned, like he'd been punched in the face. How many times was he going to watch her disappear from his life? It seemed like this was the second or third time today. He followed her silhouette with his eyes, and he watched her walk through the trees toward the tall guy from 20 Eyes—again. But this time Rune wasn't filled with surprise. This time he was filled with longing. This time his heart was breaking.

He wasn't done yet. "Hey, Markla!" he shouted. "Come see me! Come see me about that thing we discussed. I'm interested!"

He saw her stop walking and turn around. He couldn't see her face—but she waved, and now his heart jumped with hope. Then she turned back around, and once again she disappeared.

After a long moment he got back into the car and headed home.

Chapter 28

Markla stood in the shadows of the forest and watched Rune drive away. She felt like something was being torn from her, and despite all that she'd just said, she wondered if she'd ever see him again.

Meanwhile, she heard Dru laugh. "Do you think he really believes there's an underground hideout here? What a fool."

"You don't know what he believes," Markla said, and she thought about the last thing Rune had said—about coming to see him.

"So, Dru, what do we do now?"

She had a good guess what he was going to say, but she figured he'd like to brag about his obvious plan.

"We signal Stono and get a ride to the greenhouse," Dru said, sounding smug. "I had your friend take us a bit down the road just to get us away from the troopers. But they're not going to come looking through these woods. They'll figure we stayed in the car we used to escape. Pretty smart, right?"

"Sure. What about the car you crashed into the tree? Whose car was that?"

He grinned. "It was a stolen self-car. It's totally untraceable, and we've been using it all day to run missions—and that was lucky. Plus we burned it, so I'd say everything is fine."

Yeah, that was lucky, she thought. In many ways, Dru was often lucky, and maybe she shouldn't underestimate that quality in him. Luck was often the best thing to have.

Dru pulled out a signal device and started tapping into it, and Markla walked a bit farther into the woods. A cool breeze blew through the trees and scattered some leaves around her feet. Her mind was racing with thoughts about Rune and his father, and she hoped Blog wasn't seriously hurt. At some point,

Rune would find out his dad had been the dark shape on the ground—and would Rune hate her for not telling him? At the time it would've been a bad idea—just like joining 20 Eyes might be a bad idea, at least for Rune. Joining the group was something that had to be done for a good reason.

But am I not a good reason?

Dru was walking over to her now, and he had that look on his face, like he had a headache. Markla guessed he'd been thinking.

"Hey, Markla, we need to talk about your friend—because he can identify me."

An alarm shrieked through Markla's brain. "He's not a threat!" she blurted. "He wants to join. Why else would I let him give me a ride?"

Dru was quiet, studying her. "This is the guy from your school, right? The LiveDream writer who was torturing you, and then helped you escape? The guy who doesn't know we almost killed his father?"

"*You* almost killed his father—not me. But yeah, this is the guy."

Dru stood up tall and crossed his brawny arms. Markla knew he liked to look powerful when he was contemplating a decision. She also knew he'd judge Rune's worthiness mostly on how he compared Rune to himself. He wouldn't want Rune around if he thought he was a threat to his intelligence and good looks—and this was unfortunate because Markla felt Rune had him beat in both categories. But on the upside, Dru was probably too conceited to believe it.

He paused and gave a dramatic sigh. "Maybe we can use him," he said. "It's a little risky but it might be worth it. After all, I get judged by the people I can recruit, and recruiting the Centurion's son will make me look amazing. But what's the real story between you two?"

"Dru, I've known him since we were five, and there's no story. He's a friend."

"Is that what he thinks?" Dru said with a laugh. "But hey, he seriously broke the law to help you, and that's a good sign. Maybe he can be one of us. Look, our ride is here."

Markla watched as a car glided to a stop near the side of the road. Then Dru's signal device flashed a few times and he grinned.

"It's been a good day," he said. Let's go celebrate."

Chapter 29

Rune took his time getting home.

Along the way, his thoughts became more and more hopeful. After all, Markla had waved to him, and she hadn't actually said "good-bye." So maybe she'd be back. Maybe. But right now he had work to do.

Rune ordered his GoBug to activate a script called "ride scrambler" and erase the car's history. From listening to his father, Rune knew that every self-car had a history that could be accessed by law enforcement. Rune came across many interesting scripts when he GoBugged with smashers, and this one had looked too good to pass up. He hadn't mentioned it to Markla because he'd never tried it before, but he tried it now and it seemed to work perfectly. So now if someone started investigating the car, the lack of a history would look suspicious—but it would be much better than someone seeing how he'd stopped the vehicle by the side of the road at the exact location where there'd been a crash.

He used another script to scramble any tracking information from his GoBug—just in case Markla's paranoia was correct. Yeah, it would've been better to remove the power crystal, but this would probably work fine, and there were many such scripts available because Markla wasn't the only paranoid person in Sparkla. In fact, it was common.

He used one final script to erase the history of every command he'd used to initiate every other script, and he smiled as it did its work. Then he turned the car's auto-drive system back on so he'd be free to sit and think, but he discovered his brain was tired, and he didn't want to think about anything—yet everything was there, screaming at him.

He had several new messages on his GoBug. In addition to the two he'd ignored from Blog, there was one from his mother, which was rare, along with one from Dimitri, and one from Janna—and also a message from Diana.

He crinkled his forehead at that one. Diana had never contacted him before outside of school. Her message was short, but she spoke in a shaky voice and asked if he was all right. Well, that was sweet of her, and he considered sending her a quick reply—but then he recalled how she'd told him to hurt Markla as much as possible, and so he sent nothing. That part of his life was over. He was done writing nightmares in the Dream Prison.

The car pulled up to the house, and Rune stepped out, and then he stopped and stared. His mother was running out to meet him, and her hair was like a windblown mop, and her face was streaked from tears. A wave of guilt washed over him.

Maya lunged at Rune, hugging him hard. "Rune, where have you been? Why didn't you answer me? Your father is in the hospital."

"What?"

"He was chasing someone, and his car crashed! He's lucky to be alive. They said he's going to be all right but we need to get over there now."

Rune jumped back into the car with his mom and they headed to the hospital at top speed.

Maya was crying, and Rune tried to console her, and his mind was racing because how could Blog be hurt? The guy was made of rocks. And then he had another thought—had that been his father lying near the side of the road? Yeah, of course! It all made sense—the way Markla had told him not to walk over there, and now he felt a flush of rage. *How could she not tell me?* But she'd also claimed to have triggered his distress beacon, so what had really happened?

Rune ground his teeth. If he'd discovered his father lying there, it might have complicated things for Markla. It might have interfered with her plan to escape in Rune's car with her smug-looking lover-boy—but Rune might never know for sure because he might never see her again, and that thought hurt more than anything, and now he felt even more guilt that he was more concerned about Markla than he was about his own father. His thoughts were interrupted by his mother's voice.

"Rune, what happened today? Why didn't you answer? We were so worried."

"I ran into the woods and hid. When it looked safe, I came out."

"But we didn't hear from you all day."

"It's a long story," he said. "I'll explain it when we see Dad."

They saw him soon enough, lying in a hospital bed. He was in a private room surrounded by monitors and blinking machines, and he had two black eyes and a swollen face, and Rune's jaw dropped. He'd never seen his father look so mortal. But he was also awake, and it was quickly obvious he wasn't seriously injured—and then Rune breathed a sigh of relief and instantly felt less anger toward Markla. Then Blog narrowed his eyes and focused them on Rune, and Rune felt his pulse pounding. He knew what was coming—but Maya spoke first.

"Blog, what happened?" she blurted, and she wiped her eyes. "You could've been killed."

Blog gave a snort. "Don't worry, I'm fine" he said, and his voice was strong. "But they'll regret not killing me before this is over." He was still staring at Rune. "Where were you all day?"

Stay calm, Rune thought. "I was in the woods," Rune said. "I was hiding."

"You didn't answer your messages, and you took your GoBug off the stream."

"I was worried people from 20 Eyes could find me if I left it on. I heard they don't like dream writers."

"They don't," Blog said. "But they were too busy running from the prison to be hunting for you, and the GoBug would've let us know you were okay. You didn't think of that?"

"I did. But I didn't want to take any chances."

"Is that so? And where's your flyboard?"

Rune's heart skipped a beat. *He knows! He knows everything!*

"It's at home," Rune said. "I didn't take it to the prison today." Then he quickly added, "I wish I had. I would've been home a lot sooner."

"Your girlfriend is good with a flyboard. Did you know that?"

Rune hesitated. "Are you talking about Markla?" he said. "She's not my girlfriend—and yeah, she's real good. Why does it matter?"

"We tracked her to a house in the woods. In that house we found guns, explosives, bombs—things designed to murder people. That's who she is, Rune, and that's why it matters."

In his head, Rune heard Markla's words, telling him to keep things as close to the truth as possible.

"I told you, she's not my girlfriend," Rune said.

And that's the truth, he thought. *And why do I feel so bitter and angry about it?*

Maya glanced back and forth between her husband and son. "He just got home, Blog. He took a self-car, and I'm just glad he's all right. I'm glad you're both all right."

"Yeah, I'm fine," Blog said, "It's just a minor concussion." Then he eyed Rune and said, "We'll talk more about this later. Right now I need to get out of here."

Rune felt a dark cloud settle over him, like a storm gathering strength. It was obvious Blog was suspicious, to say the least. But what could he prove?

Blog was released from the hospital but he didn't ride home with them. Instead, he said a car would be coming to take him to police headquarters.

Maya frowned. "The doctor said you need to rest."

Blog shook his head. "There's too much going on, and I'm not good at sitting around. The medication is working fine. I'll be home soon." Then he looked at Rune and said, "I have criminals to catch and a country to save. I'll see you both later."

On the way home, his mother said, "Rune, why is your father asking you questions about Markla Flash? She was one of the people who escaped, right? Did something happen between you two?"

For a long moment, Rune was quiet and stared out the window. Then he finally said, "Nothing happened. Nothing at all."

Maya sighed and put her hand on Rune's leg. "You say that like it's a bad thing. Forget about her, Rune—that's the smart thing to do. You'll see her on a news stream, and it won't be for anything good. And by the way, Diana Drogo called me. She wanted to know if I'd heard anything."

Diana—again. She was being awfully persistent. "I guess she's concerned about me," Rune said. "She got me the job there. Maybe I'll send her a message."

"She said she felt terrible, and she hoped you were all right—and that you should contact her immediately. They have a new job for you."

A job? Rune wanted no part of any new job at the Dream Center. But now he was curious. Maybe he'd send her a message.

Chapter 30

Markla loved greenhouses. They didn't have the wild flavor of the woods but they were still filled with plants, and no plant had ever hurt her. She'd been working at greenhouses owned by Dru's family since she was twelve years old, strictly cash and off the books. But she'd never worked at this one. This wasn't one of the giant greenhouses owned by the Navas—this was a smaller one they let Dru run by himself.

She followed Dru into a small room in the back of the building. In the room was a desk along with some shelves filled with basic gardening tools—and a bed. She dropped down onto it with a satisfied-sounding plop. She was exhausted.

"How many others are still out there?" she asked.

"Not many," Dru said. "Just you and a few more. We didn't do too well with the escape, but we did cause lots of fear and we got lots of publicity."

"Yeah, but it's bad publicity."

He sat down beside her and grinned. "It's fun to be bad, Markla." Then he put his arm around her and kissed her.

She saw him coming too late to move away—but she kissed him back. Then she did pull away and said, "It's late Dru, and I'm really tired. I'm also filthy and sweaty. Do you have a garden hose around here?"

He laughed. "I don't care if you're filthy." He kept his arm around her shoulders. "I'm so happy you escaped, Markla, and I'm so glad to see you. I was afraid I'd never see you again."

She hesitated. "I need to clean up. And probably sleep for a few days."

"There's a shower in the bathroom. Maybe I'll join you."

"I can work my own soap."

He sighed. "Okay. There's a robe over there... But I'll be here when you get out." Then he smiled and said, "I know you've had a crazy day. But if you're in the mood to finally take our relationship to a better place, I have these."

He held up a little box filled with spherical black pills. Markla had never used them before but she knew they would prevent pregnancy in women. There was another version for men but those pills were blue.

Markla studied the box. "There are about thirty pills here, Dru. I told you I was tired."

He laughed. "We won't use them all tonight," he said, and then he put the box on a nearby shelf.

She didn't undress in front of him. Instead, she took the robe into the bathroom, planning to wear it when she came out.

It was a compact shower, and for a moment she felt trapped—but the moment passed quickly, and then the water felt amazing, and she let it pour down on her, hoping it could wash away the world. What should she do? With all the stuff she'd been through today, the last thing she wanted was another fight. In fact, the last thing she wanted was anything at all. She just wanted to empty her head and forget everything but unfortunately Dru had other plans. Dru hadn't spent the morning hanging from a ceiling, wrestling with a prison guard, fighting with police, and crawling through a storm drain. All he'd done was crash one little car.

Why is he so interested in me, anyway? He could find a better-looking girl, for sure. I suppose I should be flattered, she thought. *And maybe I'll do it.* After all, it's not like they'd never touched in an intimate way, because they had. She'd just drawn a certain line, and she'd come close to crossing it, and he'd handled her resistance in a respectful manner—and yeah, what if she were captured tomorrow, or even killed? This might be her last chance to not die a virgin. And certainly, plenty of girls would jump at the chance to be with Dru. So why didn't she want to do this?

She dried herself off and stared at her reflection in a grimy mirror hanging over a stained little sink. The dirt was gone but she had welts and scratches on her face, and more bruises on her arms, and a cut where she'd stuck a blade to remove a tracking device, and a purple bump on her forehead from a flyboard crash with a tree. Then she put on the robe and discovered it was far too big, and it hung on her like a heavy blanket she didn't want to wear. She clenched her fists and walked out of the bathroom.

Dru was sitting on the bed with his shirt off. The muscles in his arms and chest seemed to ripple with a life of their own, and she could tell he'd combed his hair. For an instant, she stopped and admired him—and despite her exhaustion, she did tingle a bit. In fact, she suddenly didn't feel so tired. Then he smiled at her, and while the room was somewhat dark, his smile was bright.

"You look great," he said.

She was quiet for a few seconds, and then said, "Dru, I haven't slept for three days, and my hair looks like a wet mop, and I do not look great."

"You're a cute little mop, Markla. I don't think you realize how cute you can be."

He was laying it on thick, she thought. But she couldn't deny a primitive attraction—so again, why not? What was holding her back? She suddenly realized her heart was pounding. She wanted to tell him something. It was something inside, something buried, bubbling up from below—and suddenly she was sure. Suddenly, she was certain of exactly what she wanted to say. She looked into his eyes.

"Dru, why did you leave me at the dream station?"

He maintained his smile, but it cracked a little.

"Markla, I didn't leave you."

"I was still there with a guy trying to kill me. You were gone. You left."

"It wasn't like that!" he sputtered. "The alarm was ringing. We had to get out of there. Besides, I thought you were already outside."

"Why would you think that?"

"Because you were downstairs, near the front door."

"But when you went outside, did you see me? Did you look for me?"

He leaped to his feet and threw up his hands. "I can't believe you're talking about this now," he said, and she knew he wanted to sound indignant but he just sounded desperate. "I went and picked you up tonight, didn't I?"

"Yeah—thanks. Thanks for doing that. I appreciate it. But that had nothing to do with the dream station."

His eyes flashed with anger. "I always stick up for you, Markla," he said, and he pointed a finger at her. "You don't know what other people say."

"What people? What do they say?"

He turned away. "It doesn't matter. Forget it." Then he whirled back around, and the veins in his neck bulged as he spoke. "What happens if you get discovered here?" he said. "What happens if I get caught with you? The police are going to connect us, and they'll connect me to that night, and then I'm going to prison. Do you think everybody in the group would take that risk? Sure, they're supposed to—but if you think they all would, you'd be wrong. You have no idea what some people think."

He snatched his shirt from the bed and stomped toward the door. As he grabbed the doorknob, he glared at her. "I'll come and see how you're doing in the morning," he said. Then he paused, like he was waiting for her to stop him. But she didn't. So he went through the door and slammed it behind him.

Markla stared at the door for a few long seconds. Then she plopped down onto the bed and put her head in her hands. She wanted to sleep but now her mind was whirling.

Had she been too hard on him? After all, he was helping her—and maybe it hadn't been so simple at the dream station. It had been chaos that night, and everyone ran. But would she have left Dru the way he'd left her? No. And would Rune have left her? *I scream at him to leave me, and he sticks like glue—at least so far.* And now she did not feel guilty about her words to Dru. In fact, her heart felt light. I need to see Rune, she thought. *It won't be tonight but it'll be soon.*

She started gathering her things. She took off the robe, put on her other clothes, and packed everything neatly into her knapsack. Then she reached for the flyboard—and for her dagger. She wasn't going to sleep in this room tonight. She'd stay nearby, but not here.

Chapter 31

The prison was back under control. There were bombed out rooms and smashed pieces of equipment to be repaired but the building was once again operational—and downstairs in the Dream Room, someone was chained to the high ceiling with a GoBug behind her ear and a gag in her mouth.

Aldo was at the prison, and he was bursting with energy. He'd come to work early and headed for his office inside the Dream Center. He was enthused by the results of yesterday's vote, and he sat behind his dream station as Diana entered the room, and he smiled. *Will she like the gift I have for her? Will she love it?*

He noted Diana looked tired as always, but she still looked pretty in black tights and a white cotton shirt. He peeked at his reflection in the glass of the console. He'd washed his hair this morning, and the red strands were unruly like kinky wires. But he was hoping it made him seem wild and adventurous. Women love adventurous men, he thought. *Especially if they're smart enough to wear InfoLenses.*

Diana turned to Aldo, and now her face lit up. "Did you see the report?" she said. "Rune Roko wasn't injured, and he wasn't involved in the escape of any prisoners. The witness you mentioned was lying."

"Yes, I saw the report," Aldo said. "But I also wrote it, so it says what we need it to say."

She hesitated. "What do you mean?" she said.

"I mean that Rune's just a kid who made a mistake, and his ability to write LiveDreams is more valuable than his infatuation with an insignificant girl. He could help influence lots of teenagers with this new project."

"So what you wrote was a lie?"

"Yes—and if there's any GoBug footage that shows differently,

I'll handle that, too. A lie that contributes to something good isn't a bad thing, Diana. In fact, that's what this whole project is about."

She hesitated once again, and then she reached out and put her hand on top of his. "That's nice of you to help Rune."

Aldo's heart fluttered. "I'm glad you're happy about it. I thought you would be."

"You're right—he just made a silly mistake. Did I ever tell you he reminds me of my son?"

"I'm sorry about your son, Diana. That was a terrible tragedy."

For an instant her eyes got watery but then she seemed to compose herself. "I sent Rune a message," she said. "I offered him the job but he hasn't answered yet. I also offered a job to two of his friends. You know one of them—Janna Krolla, our Dream Project winner. Her style is predictable but her execution is excellent."

"She's perfect, and I predict the population will love her."

"Right. And the other one, Dimitri, isn't the best LiveDream writer but he could still appeal to a certain demographic. I asked him because he's friends with Rune, and I think it might inspire Rune to come along. I'm so glad Rune wasn't hurt. It was lucky, the way so many prisoners were captured so fast."

"Yes," Aldo said. "We were lucky."

It was almost like we knew they would escape.

"Most of them were caught right away."

"That's true. Apparently, there were stashes of supplies in the woods. Most of them were caught right after they reached them."

It was almost like we knew where the stashes would be. It was almost like the items were embedded with tracking devices.

"So how many are still out there?" Diana said.

"As of this morning, there are only two prisoners still free. One of them is Markla Flash, but she'll be found along with the other one—and there's no rush. When the public is worried and scared they're easier to control. They also vote the right way."

Diana raised her eyebrows. "Did you see the results from last night? A lot of restrictions were removed on the use of LiveDreams. We can use them to a fuller potential now."

"Exactly," he said. "And we can test out the results today—with this person."

As he spoke Diana's GoBug came to life, and there in front of her eyes was the image of Carla Rosette hanging from her wrists in the Dream Room. She was in a yellow jumpsuit, and she was chained and gagged. But her dark eyes were still filled with fury and defiance.

Diana's mouth dropped open. "How did you do this, Aldo?"

"I had her case transferred to the Dream Center. Go ahead and talk to her."

For a few seconds, Diana was quiet. Then she used her mind to issue a command that allowed Carla to see and hear her. When Diana spoke, her voice was shaking with rage.

"Hello, Carla. Do you recognize me? I'm Kalo's mother. I'm the one who lost a son because of you. But I guess you can't answer, and that's fine. I don't need to hear any of your lies."

Aldo nodded with approval. "I had her gagged so she'd feel more powerless," he said. "Of course, she can still talk inside the dream unless she's gagged there as well—that's a decision for the guider. I've created a basic nightmare shell, but with these new protocols the guided section can be much more brutal. We can legally interrogate someone in the dream and ask them anything—and we can do almost anything to them if they don't respond. Democracy is a wonderful thing." He stood up. "I thought you might want to do the guiding."

Diana stared at him for a moment, like she was in a daze. Then she slowly sat down at the controls.

"I'll do it," she said. "Thank you."

"You're welcome," he said with a grin. Then he reached over and manipulated one final control. "By the way, Diana, are you doing anything later?"

"No. Call me."

Aldo felt his heart swell. Then Diana touched the screen in front of her, and Carla was hurled into a nightmare. Aldo could tell it was going to be a long one.

Chapter 32

Rune blinked and sat up fast in his bed. How long had he slept? He remembered lying down, and now the morning light was spilling into his room. He grabbed his GoBug and checked the news alerts and saw nothing about Markla being captured. He breathed a sigh of relief, and soon enough he was in the kitchen eating oatmeal and bananas. I guess I'll contact Diana, he thought. *I'll see what she wants—maybe she'll tell me something useful about Aldo and the plan to capture the escaped prisoners.* He sent her a message and she immediately appeared on his GoBug stream.

For an instant, he was startled. Her eyes were rimmed with red and she looked shaken, like someone had been strangling her just a few seconds before. But she managed to smile.

"Hello, Rune," she said. "How are you?"

"I'm fine." He hesitated and then said, "How is everything with you?"

"Good—good. So, what happened yesterday? I heard different stories."

"I was in the woods. Then I came out."

She stared at him, obviously wanting to hear more, but he said nothing. "I'm glad you weren't hurt," she finally said. "I'm sure it's a day you'd like to forget. At least most of the prisoners have been captured."

"Yeah, I see. That's great."

There was more silence, and then she said, "Rune, have you talked to Janna or Dimitri?"

"No."

"Oh. Well, I'd like to offer you a new job in the Dream Center. It's got nothing to do with nightmares or prisoners. We're hiring three students for a special project, and they're the other two."

Now Rune raised his eyebrows. "What's the job?"

"Creating LiveDreams for mindstreams that are popular with teenagers. These are 'public service announcements' that we want told in a subtle and entertaining way. There's certain content you'll need to include but you'll still have some creative freedom."

So it was toad propaganda. It made sense that Janna was involved because she was a top-notch dream writer—but Dimitri? He was a hack. For one angry second, Rune realized he'd hate to see Dimitri gain any professional advantage over him. And what would Markla say? He imagined a conversation with her, and she was making a joke about Dimitri's juvenile dream writing skills—and it was funny and totally true.

"Rune? Rune, are you listening?"

"Yeah. Thanks, Diana. So, what do I need to do?"

"Come to the Dream Prison. They need about two more days to complete a few repairs, but I'll send you a message when we're ready."

"Okay. Thanks."

"You're welcome."

She disappeared without saying goodbye, and this felt strange to Rune. Obviously, Diana was upset about something, but this news about "teenage propaganda streams" was excellent information—Markla would like to know this, and he could probably get even more information if he took the job. But he'd have to wait two days. And two days from now, Markla would have spent two more days and nights with that guy.

It doesn't matter, he thought. *She'll be back—I know it. I'll see her again, and I'll get another chance.* Then he heard a beep and saw another call coming in on his GoBug. It was Janna.

He switched on the stream, and there she was lying on a bed in a pair of black shorts and a dark maroon shirt. The shirt was tight, the shorts were minimal, and her bare legs were long and sexy. Was she posing? It was hard to say. Janna always looked like this, and Rune instinctively wished he'd combed his hair before taking the call.

"Rune!" she said, and her voice bubbled. "Where have you been? I sent you messages. We've all been watching the news streams."

"I was having an adventure. It was crazy."

"I'm sure it was, and I'm so glad you're okay! So what happened?"

Rune tried to sound casual. "I fought my way out of there," he said. "Just me and my fists against guns and knives. But when the smoke cleared, I was the last one standing."

She laughed. "Was it really that dramatic?"

"No. I ran into the woods and hid behind a rock until they were all done killing each other."

Now she laughed harder. "That was the best thing to do. You're a clever guy... It looks like almost everyone's been captured, so that's good."

"Yeah, it is."

Of course, they both knew who had not been captured, but neither of them mentioned it. Then Rune heard another beep, and he said, "Hey, Dimitri is calling. He wants to join us."

Janna rolled her eyes. "I just talked to him. He keeps calling me."

"Yeah, but he'll get mad if I don't let him in. Besides, I haven't returned his messages."

"Okay, let him in," she said with a sigh. "But I'll see you at the Dream Center, right?"

"Maybe."

"Rune, you have to do it. I don't want to be stuck there with Dimitri." Then she stared at him with her big brown eyes, and when she spoke her voice was sweet with a hint of pleading. "Please do it—please. I really want you there."

For an instant, Rune realized he wasn't breathing.

"I'll do it," he said, and he found himself smiling.

Janna smiled back. "Great!" she said, and then she paused. "I guess you better let Dimitri in before he has a nervous breakdown."

In his head, Rune voiced a command and Dimitri appeared for both Rune and Janna to see.

He was lying on an unmade bed, grinning. All around him was the wreckage of his room, with clothes strewn around like the aftermath of a riot. "Hi, Janna," he said. "Didn't I just talk to you? Hey, Rune, you're back. We were worried about you but I knew you'd be all right. So, did you marry Markla in prison? I hear she's still on the loose. Is she under your bed?"

"Hi, Dimitri," Rune said, barely concealing his annoyance. "Hey, I'm sorry but I need to go. I hear my dad calling."

"Oh, that's too bad. I guess I'll just stay on with Janna."

Janna frowned and shook her head. "Sorry, Dimitri. I need to go, too."

Rune shook his head and ended the stream. He guessed Janna was busy doing the same.

Chapter 33

Markla awoke with a start before dawn. For an instant she couldn't breathe—but then things came into focus. This was a common way for Markla to wake up.

It had been a typical night filled with black dreams, dreams that had mauled her mind like something made of teeth and tentacles. Now a new day was here, and she was lying in the cool grass on a blanket near a thorny bush covered with purple flowers. She was still free, and it felt wonderful, but could she stay that way? She reached for the dagger that was lying nearby. She held it up to the lavender sky and wondered if she had the nerve to kill herself if necessary—because there was no way she was going back to prison. No way.

She imagined plunging the blade into her abdomen—a rare form of suicide, and for good reason. With a grunt she put the weapon down; it was hard to know before the moment came. I'll probably be dead soon, she thought. *One way or another, that's probably how it's going to go. And who will care?* Then she thought about Rune and realized he was the one person she wanted to care.

I need to stop thinking about him. Or maybe just do something about it—something we both might regret.

At the sound of a soft hum, she turned her head and saw a sporty black car parking by the greenhouse. She narrowed her eyes as the landing struts descended and the anti-grav engine shut off. Dru was back. He was alone, and he was walking into the other building where he was probably expecting to find her. She was impressed he was here so early, but he knew her habits, and of course there was a crazy situation going on. She imagined him searching for her, and maybe thinking she'd left—and why not leave? Why not get out of here? Well, it might be tough to travel right now without being seen. She needed to lay low until things calmed down. Also, she wasn't ready to go—not yet.

She slid the dagger into the sheath on her belt, concealing it beneath a fleece-lined flannel shirt she wore like a jacket. She left the flyboard and her knapsack in the high grass and headed toward the squat building.

Dru looked up as she entered, and he smiled. He was dressed all in black with a sleeveless shirt that seemed flimsy for the cool morning, but it showed off his muscular arms.

"There you are," he said. "I thought you ran off."

"I was outside."

She saw no need to tell him she'd slept there.

"Oh. Well, I was thinking about where you should go, and what you should do."

"I'm staying here."

He studied her a bit, and then he grinned. "Okay, I understand that."

"No, you don't," she said, trying to keep her voice even. "I don't want to be your girlfriend anymore, Dru. So that's not why I'm staying."

His face twisted up a bit. "Markla, is this about last night? I should've known you were tired—"

"It's not about last night. Things have changed. That's all."

He hesitated and then threw up his hands. "I'm sorry I didn't go back into the dream station, okay? I thought you escaped—I did, and that's the truth!"

"I believe you," she said, even though she did not. "But that's not the reason, either, and I don't want to argue."

"We're not arguing. We're talking."

"Yeah, we're talking. But I just said everything I have to say, and now I'm done."

He looked confused. "So you're really breaking up with

me?" He gave a little laugh. "I think you can at least give me an explanation, Markla. If it's not about last night, and it's not about that other thing—then why?"

She knew the truth was a bad idea. Dru would never believe she just wasn't that into him—and that was only part of the truth. There was that other big part where she was constantly thinking about someone else.

"There is no 'why.' It's just the way I feel."

He sat down on the bed and eyed her for a few seconds. "Okay, fine," he said, and he slapped his hand down on the mattress. "If that's what you want, that's great. No problem." Then he smirked and added, "Until you change your mind."

Markla was quiet—but in her head, she laughed. She'd expected more resistance, and did she feel a smidge insulted? No, because his pomposity explained it. He was certain she'd be kneeling at his feet by nightfall.

"Thanks for picking me up last night," she said. "But I don't think I can stay here anymore."

Dru rolled his eyes. "Just because you're not sleeping in my bed doesn't mean you have to leave."

"It's not about being in your bed, Dru. The problem is that people know I'm here."

"But they're our people."

"I don't want anyone to know where I am. Like you said, if I get caught with anyone, that person will be connected to the group."

He stared at her and said nothing. Of course it was on his mind, and who could blame him?

"But where will you go?"

"I don't know. But even if I did, I wouldn't tell you. As long as we can signal, it should be okay. I'll be nearby... So, what's happening?"

She studied his face, wondering if he could keep their personal business out of the bigger plan.

He shrugged. "Everyone's been captured except for you and Blu, so it looks like we lost big. But I just found out that the government has a new plan to try and influence people. They're going to hire kids to create LiveDreams that target other kids, and those LiveDreams are going to be filled with propaganda. So guess what? We're going to destroy the Dream Center inside the prison. I'm supposed to figure out some way to do it, and if we pull it off we'll get back some prestige, and I could really move up. So now I'm wondering if that friend of yours can help—because he's one of the people they hired."

Markla's heart skipped a beat. "They hired Rune?" she said. "Are you sure?"

"Yeah," he drawled. "I heard about it from one of our spies in the government office. Rune helped you in the prison, right? And he gave us a ride. So he must be really into you. In fact, he must *love* you, so why not use that to our advantage?" Then he flashed that smug look again and said, "I mean now that you're done with me."

At the mention of love, Markla felt her face getting hot. "Forget it!" she snapped. "I can't bring him into the group if it's going to cause all kinds of tension and trouble."

Now Dru leaped to his feet, looming over her. "It's not like that!" he shouted. "This is about what's good for everyone. That's all I care about, and it should be all you care about, too."

Markla didn't step backward, though she wanted to. Instead, she looked at him and didn't reply.

The tactic worked. Dru seemed to relax, and he sat back down. He smiled, and this time he was less smug. "Markla, I'll get along fine with Rune. I always get along with people who can help us. There won't be any trouble—I promise. So when can you ask him? I'll give you a ride."

"I don't need a ride. His house backs up to the woods. I know the place."

"Great," Dru said. Then he smirked once again and motioned toward the box of pills on a nearby shelf. "You might want to take a few of those with you, just to be safe. Let me know what happens."

Markla gave him a look of disgust and walked outside. She was done with Dru—no doubt about it. In fact, she felt like she'd dodged a bullet, and she was filled with a sense of relief. The only issue now was Rune. Was this a good path for him?

Maybe not—but if he wants to join, why should I not encourage it?

Outside, the sun was rising. She'd seen a thousand sunrises, but this one was especially gorgeous. Streaks of pink and orange light were reaching across the sky like fiery fingers, and suddenly Markla felt hopeful. She smiled.

She would go see Rune. *And maybe I will take a few of those pills with me, Dru. Just in case.*

Chapter 34

Rune spent the rest of the morning in his room, lying on his bed, using his GoBug to look at mindstreams that did nothing except pass the time. Around noon he heard heavy footsteps in the living room and knew his father was home.

He felt a sudden urge to hide under the bed like he'd done when he was three years old. But he clenched his fist instead. I'm not hiding anymore, he thought. He had to face this.

There hadn't been any more questions about the prison uprising—not yet. Blog had been too busy working, but now he was here, and what did he know? Would Blog arrest him? Of course he would.

He wants me to sweat, Rune thought. *He's waiting for me to slip up and give myself away.*

Rune heard Blog's footsteps coming closer. Don't panic, Rune thought. *He's going in the bathroom.* But no, he was standing right outside the door. Don't panic, Rune thought again. *He won't come in here.*

The door was swinging open.

Rune's heart started to pound. Blog never came into his room—never. But here he was.

Blog was wearing his uniform, as usual. The bruises around his eyes weren't so black now, but he still looked like he'd been in a fight with a couple of hammers. Rune was still lying on the bed, and Blog eyed him like a hawk looking down at something small. Then he pulled out a chair from behind Rune's desk and sat down, and Rune started to panic. This was it.

Don't talk, he said. *Say nothing!*

Blog gave a little laugh. "Are you nervous about something, Rune?"

"No," Rune said, trying not to rush.

"You look nervous."

What a liar, Rune thought. He would've shrugged but he was still lying on the bed and it was difficult. He kept his mouth shut.

Blog gave a grim smile. "Believe me, it's better to be questioned here than at the police station." Then he leaned toward Rune and said, "We just captured Markla Flash, and she told us everything."

Rune's head started whirling. If he hadn't been already lying on a bed, he might have fallen down.

Poor Markla—she never had a chance! But he forced his face to remain blank. He wasn't going down without a fight. He still said nothing.

Meanwhile, Blog kept staring at him, and Rune met his stare with silence—but wait, he needed to look nonchalant, not confrontational. He glanced away and said, "That's good."

"Is it?" Blog said, and his voice got louder. "Is it good that you helped her escape? Is it good that you were with her in the woods, and you attacked police officers—and you wore a mask like someone in 20 Eyes? Do you realize what you did?"

What? Had Markla told them all that? What had they done to her?

And now he knew Blog was lying. Markla had been questioned when she'd been arrested for murder—and she'd said nothing. Not a thing. And he suddenly recalled a line from her profile, highlighted in bold, "subject shows exceptional resistance to interrogation."

"I don't know what you're talking about," Rune said. "None of that happened."

Blog stared into Rune's eyes again. "Oh, really?" he said. "She says it did."

"Why would you believe her?" Rune shot back. "She's a murderer and a liar. I ran into the woods, and I saw her running right near me. But I never talked to her, and we went our separate ways."

Blog sneered. "There's only one male prisoner we haven't captured yet, and his name is Blu Baroke. But he's tall with dark skin, and he wasn't the guy she was with, so who was that person, Rune? Someone about your size, riding a flyboard—and he was real good at it."

Rune almost smiled at the compliment—because Blog rarely gave him one. But he stopped himself. "I don't know," Rune said. "Maybe someone else in 20 Eyes. She has a boyfriend, you know. She told me that during the guided dream. So it was probably him, coming to meet her."

Blog kept studying Rune for a few seconds—and then he sat back in his chair.

"She has a boyfriend in 20 Eyes?"

"Yeah," Rune said. And he managed to keep his voice even.

"Any idea who he is? A description?"

"No. I just know he's someone in the group. That's all she said."

"All right," Blog said, and he paused. "That might be useful. She was with a guy the night I crashed my car, and I heard them talking, and that guy was not you. That was probably him."

"What did they say?"

Blog frowned and seemed to fumble a bit for words. "Nothing important," he finally said. "But someone came and picked them up. You were driving around, weren't you?"

"I used a self-car to take me home. I didn't pick up anybody."

"Right. And what would happen if I got an order to pull the car's history?"

Rune said nothing, but he felt the hair on the back of his neck stand up. The smasher script he'd used to erase the history had probably worked, but given all the other circumstances, an erased history would make him look pretty guilty in Blog's eyes. And right now Blog's eyes were boring into him like a pair of drills.

Blog rose from his chair. "Your story isn't the best, Rune—but it's good enough. I'm officially clearing you from any suspicion in this so you won't need to submit to a formal interrogation, and we won't need to do any further investigating involving your possible involvement. But if you suddenly remember something important, you better tell me. And if you see that girl around here, don't be stupid. There's only so much people will believe. There's only so much I'll do."

Blog narrowed his eyes a bit. Then he turned, left the room, and closed the door.

Rune's mind was blank. What had just happened?

If you see that girl around here? Blog's words hit Rune like a boulder. So he was admitting he'd made up the whole story! Markla was not captured. Rune took a deep breath and felt his whole body relax.

Then he was struck by another thought. *Is my father protecting me?* Yeah, maybe—incredible. Of course, Blog was also saying he'd only do so much, but how much more was necessary? If Markla was eventually captured, Rune would no longer write her nightmares, and if she was not captured, she wouldn't be around. The facts seemed to indicate he'd never see Markla again—and yet, he felt hopeful. He didn't know why.

After all, she did have a boyfriend. That part of the story was true, and it was terrible.

Chapter 35

Aldo smiled at the images of Diana flashing before his eyes. They were pictures from the Dream Center, at an office party last year where she'd looked pretty like a rose in a raspberry-colored dress—and she'd even laughed at one of his jokes. But then she hadn't wanted to stay and talk. *Would she have stayed if I'd been better looking? If I'd looked like my idiotic brother Gin?*

Gin was the president of Sparkla, and Aldo had a private GoBug meeting scheduled to happen with him in a few minutes. Aldo sighed and shook his head—and then Gin was there in front of Aldo's eyes. Gin was sitting in a sunny office with a stunning view of the ocean, grinning and drinking a fruity-looking beverage. Aldo guessed the beverage was some sort of high-protein drink that Gin would soon be blabbing about. Gin was a few years older than Aldo and in peak physical condition. Sparkla was a nation of physically fit people, and Gin reflected this. He had typical olive skin, dark eyes, and a smile that showed a pearly set of teeth. But he also dyed his hair blond. He thought the blond hair somehow highlighted his muscles.

"Aldo, what's happening?" Gin said, sounding upbeat as usual. "When are you going to get those skinny arms in shape? Sometimes biceps are better than brains."

Aldo gave a snort. "Yes, if I'm trying to move a pile of rocks. But I can always get someone like you to do that."

Gin laughed. "I see that most of the prisoners are captured—and I see we got the vote passed for the tech enhancements. Great! What about the prisoners still out there?"

"There are only two left," Aldo said with a shrug. "One of them isn't significant—that teenage girl who killed someone at the dream station. She's just a kid with emotional problems… But the other one is Blu Baroke, our main informant who was quite helpful while he was in prison. Unfortunately, now that he's out, he's decided to go rogue and we haven't heard from him. So we might want to use his fugitive status to get publicity and help with the next vote. Or we might just want to capture him again. It's up to you."

Gin took a sip of his drink. "This is the best stuff ever," he said, holding up his perma-chilled steel mug. "It's packed with protein and it tastes great. My strength index is through the roof. Do I sound like an ad?"

"Yes—always," Aldo quipped. "And it's nothing I'd buy."

"The best things in life are free, Aldo—as long as you don't marry any of them."

"Maybe they're free for you, Gin. And I'm in no danger of getting married."

Gin laughed again. "We still have all the people from the local 20 Eyes pod out there; I'm talking about the idiots who did the dream station raid. I was thinking we'd leave them out there for a while, definitely until after the next vote. But then we'll scoop them up and claim that lessening the restrictions on surveillance tech was the whole reason we were able to make the arrests. No one has to know we've had their names and numbers all along, thanks to you."

"Yeah, that's true," Aldo said, and now he beamed a bit. "That was a great idea, wasn't it?"

"The best."

Aldo chuckled. "It's amazing what people will do to avoid nightmares—or to get them swapped for some fun-time LiveDreams. They'll betray anyone."

"Right. Plus, we just got the ability to do most of it legally. So we won't have Blog looking over our shoulders with all his law-and-order propaganda."

Aldo raised a finger and pointed it at Gin. "Blog's a barbarian but he's not stupid. I suspect he knows how we get the information, but the arrests make him look good—when we finally decide it's time to arrest people. I'm sure he'd like to see us get more of the restrictions on nightmares removed."

"Yeah, and I have a plan for that," Gin said with a grin. "Let's exaggerate the situation with Blu and the girl. Let's say if we'd been able to use better interrogation techniques, we would've gotten the girl to give us the names of the dream station raiders—but we couldn't do that, and now they're still out there, and so is she—probably conspiring to do something even worse. Then we'll get a few of our people to post a petition. We need to pave the way for MindCore."

Aldo nodded. Gin's not a complete idiot, he thought. In fact, Gin usually came up with decent ideas when he wasn't too busy doing push-ups and chasing women with shallow taste.

"We can do that," Aldo said. "We'll pull back on our search for both of them. I can make up some false information for the police. I'll say we have a tip from a prisoner that they went south, or maybe escaped to Narna, and hopefully Blog will buy it. But MindCore might be a tough sell, assuming we tell people what it actually does."

Gin started chomping a high protein candy bar. "Yeah, but if we had MindCore, we could get all the information we needed from any prisoner and put all their friends behind bars. And people would like that... So, what about the new project? The one with the kids?"

"It's about to start. Getting kids to influence kids is a great idea. The future always wins, Gin. It'll be a big success."

Aldo disconnected the call and sighed. Would helping Gin make him feel less alone? No. But then he had another thought, and it made him tingle. This new plan with the kids involved Diana, and he'd be talking to her soon.

Chapter 36

It was a cool autumn evening. There was a light breeze blowing, and leaves were scattered all around, and Rune was in his shed banging on his drums. As much as he loved GoBugs, LiveDreams, and flyboards, there was something satisfying about banging on a drum. A drum was one of the most primitive things in the world. It was one step ahead of hammering a stone with another stone. But that simplicity was what made it beautiful.

He was thinking about Markla, of course. Maybe she'll hear my drums, he thought. Yeah, the drumming was like a call out to the wilderness. Then he imagined her with that smug-looking stormtrooper, and he banged a little harder. He played until his hands were throbbing. He played until there was no sun outside, and the only light in the room came from an orange orb that cast heavy shadows and made the shed seem like a cave. Finally, he stopped drumming and sat back against the wall. And that's when he saw the door to the shed opening—and his eyes went wide.

Standing in the shadows was Markla Flash.

For an instant, Rune stopped breathing. She was wearing a fleece-lined flannel shirt over another shirt, and denim pants, and her moccasin-style shoes. She was quiet, as usual. If he hadn't been looking right at the door, he wouldn't have known she was there.

He wanted to speak, but no words came.

"Hi, Rune," she said, and he heard her voice quiver a bit, like she was nervous—and this made him feel better because he felt the same way. He was shocked to see her, and he was thrilled to see her, and he wanted to tell her. But all he could manage to say was, "Markla, what are you doing here?"

She hesitated. "You told me to come see you. So here I am."

"Oh. Are you alone?"

"Yeah. I broke up with that guy."

Just like that, Rune felt the world move beneath his feet. "Really? Why?"

"I didn't want to be with him, not like that. It was never that serious." Then she seemed to squirm a bit, and she said, "I don't know if it matters to you."

Rune stood up and took a step toward her. He was standing right in front of her now.

"It matters," he said, and he looked into her eyes. "I don't want you to go to Narna. I want you to stay here."

She smiled and stared back at him. "I want to stay. I don't know how it's going to work out—or for how long. But I'm here right now."

Rune was done thinking, and he wrapped her in his arms. Their lips touched, and she tasted sweet, yet spicy like cinnamon, and she kissed him with gusto. She hugged him hard and held him tight. Rune felt the blood pounding in his ears. He felt like he was floating. How long did they continue to kiss? He lost track of time. And then she was removing her shirt, and pulling her undershirt over her head, and they were fumbling with their clothes, and they were down on the floor.

There was a rug but it was still a hard floor. Rune didn't care and neither did she.

He'd never done this before but he pushed that thought out of his mind. He knew she'd been involved with someone else, but it didn't matter. She was here with him now, and he'd loved her all year—and for a lot longer than that. Maybe he'd always loved her. Yes, that was true. He'd loved her since long before he'd known what love was. He'd loved her since he'd been a child, and she'd punched Janna Krolla in the nose, and she'd made that silly monkey out of clay.

Suddenly, she stopped kissing him. He pulled his head up and looked at her.

"What's wrong?" he said.

When she spoke, she was breathless. "I've never done this before," she said. "I doubt I'm going to be very good at it."

Rune laughed. "I've never done this before, either. So don't worry—we'll be bad at it together. But it'll be fine."

Chapter 37

Markla wasn't sure what to think. *So, that was it.* Well, it hadn't been too bad. There'd been a certain amount of fumbling around, and a bit of pain and awkwardness—but all in all it had been fine. She laughed at her assessment. Really, she felt a sense of relief mixed with excitement. *There's a lot of potential here,* she thought. *And I do feel closer to Rune, and that's the best part.*

She'd been filled with anxiety concerning a possible encounter with him, but she'd also been charged with happy anticipation, as much as she'd allow herself to be—a spark of hope hidden in the back of her head, like a seed of something thrilling. When she'd taken one of those pills before entering the shed, her hand had been shaking. Then when they'd kissed, the passion had surprised her, like she'd been waiting her whole life to feel— what? That someone cared. But was Rune that someone? She was going to hope, and once she'd allowed that hope to flood her mind the rest had been easy. She used to roll her eyes at the idea that anyone would "glow" after a passionate encounter, but she couldn't deny she felt warm and radiant. She pictured herself as a gigantic firefly, and she laughed again. She and Rune seemed good together, very good. But what was he thinking? *And what happens now?*

They were still lying on the floor in a wooden shed filled with drums and shadows. Rune was beside her, also staring at the ceiling. She rolled over and put her arm across his chest. If he'd been a cat—a tiger, she thought—he would have been purring. *And that's what I want to believe!* She felt his heart beating, and she put soft kisses on his neck.

He made a humming sound and then wrapped his arm around her.

"Is this why you came here?" he said.

"Yeah."

"Really? I thought you were going to try to get me to join 20 Eyes."

"I guess this is part of my pitch."

"Oh. Your pitch is good."

"Ha, thanks. I was worried it wouldn't be."

"Why?"

"I don't know. I suppose I'm not always that confident."

"But you seem so confident."

"Rune, you don't know me. I'm not confident like you."

"Me? I'm not that confident."

"You don't think you are—but when it really matters, you are."

He crinkled his forehead, thinking it over. But he didn't respond. Instead, he said, "You were in all the news streams today—you and that guy, Blu."

"Oh, yeah? How did I look? Messy, right?" She laughed. "I'm a disaster, Rune—always."

Rune laughed back. "You looked great—you're the cutest disaster in the world. But hey, Aldo had a nightmare labeled "Blu Baroke," and I copied it, and it wasn't a nightmare. It looked more like something fun. I wonder why he had it labelled that way."

"I don't know," Markla said, and she paused. "Maybe there was more to it than you noticed."

"I noticed quite a bit. Trust me, this was not a nightmare."

"Huh, I'd like to see it."

"I'll show it to you later—but first, let's talk about you. Where are you staying?"

"Nowhere."

"You can stay here. Remember, you said you never would? But now you can. You can stay in here with my drums."

She sighed, because she couldn't. But she didn't want to mention it yet, so she changed the subject.

"Where did you get all these drums?"

"From my parents," Rune said, and then he laughed again. "I think my dad wanted to get me out of the house. He's not into music but he thinks drums are a 'manly instrument' so he got them for me. My mom's pretty easygoing. She thinks whatever I want is a great idea, as long as it doesn't interrupt her LiveDreams. And hey, why didn't you tell me you played the flute? We could've been playing together all these years. We could've formed a band."

"Sure. We could've been 'Rune and Flash.' "

"I love it!"

She smiled and then shrugged. "I'm not much of a musician, Rune. I got my first flute from Krista Cono. Remember her?"

"Yeah, of course. She drowned when we were little. It was so sad."

"Yeah, she drowned, and I had a hard time dealing with it because she was my friend. I used to go to her house, and she played the flute, and she would let me play it sometimes. Then after the accident, her mother gave me her flute—and my mom threw it away because I kept playing it at night, and it was bothering her and her stupid boyfriend. So I stole some money from her to buy a new one, and I played it every night, and then early in the morning, and whenever I thought it would annoy them, and I kept doing it—no matter what." Her voice trailed off.

Rune was quiet for a bit and stroked her hair. "Your mom sounds mean," he said. Then he paused, like maybe he was waiting for her to say more, but she didn't. Finally, he said, "Are you going to stay?"

"I can't. If I do they'll catch me sooner or later. There's no way around it."

Rune gripped her tighter. "I don't want you to go."

"I'm not going yet, okay? Let's not think about it right now."

"But we need to think about it, Markla. I really like you... I care about you a lot."

"I like you, too," she said quickly. "I care, too."

"And I like the way you stand up for things you believe in. So, what do I need to do? What do you need to tell me?"

She took a deep breath and said nothing because she just wasn't sure. She kissed him again but pulled away. She stood up and gathered her clothes while Rune watched—and her eyes fell on the collection of drums, the drums Rune's father had given him.

She found herself really studying them now. There were so many, and they were finished in shades of sunburst, aqua, and pearl, or painted in bright colors. They were dazzling, and she kept staring but still said nothing, and for some reason she thought about the wooden flute sitting in her knapsack outside. Finally, her eyes went back to Rune, and she knew what she had to tell him. She was certain.

"Rune, I don't want you to join 20 Eyes."

She studied his face, looking for a sign of surprise. But he showed no emotion.

"That's some pitch," he said. "Why not?"

"Your life is different than mine. You don't need to do what I did."

"What does that mean? I thought you wanted me to join."

"I want what's best for you. And that's something else."

Rune slowly stood up and pulled on his own clothes. He stood close to her and wrapped his hands around her hips. "I want to join," he said. "I want to talk to the people in your group about helping you. I have the original camera feed from your crime. Maybe you're not completely innocent—but you're only sixteen, and a good lawyer could build a case to change things. Couldn't they help you get a good lawyer? We could show how you were only defending yourself. You could get a new trial, and it would be on all the mindstreams. We could show how the government lied."

She shook her head. "That's not really the 20 Eyes way. Besides, no one's going to believe that feed is real. They're going to say it's a phony LiveDream."

"But we can prove it's real."

"Can we? People believe what they want to believe."

"Yeah, and that's why I want to join! I'm not interested in violence; I won't do anything violent—but I could help in other ways. If we can show how dishonest the government is we can change things. We can post petitions and people will vote."

She looked away from his gaze. "That's not what we do, Rune—and I don't think about changing things. I think about how much I hate injustice, and people stomping on other people who are powerless. I think about fighting back but I don't think about winning." Then she paused and said, "I have lots of bad thoughts in my head, things I don't talk about. There might be something wrong with me."

"There's nothing wrong with you. You're fine the way you are."

"I'm not fine. And I don't want you to join the group."

He put his hands on her shoulders and stared into her eyes.

"Markla, I want to be with you! And Diana called, and they want me to work in the Dream Center doing some new job—no torture, just propaganda. I could find out what the toads are up to! So count me in—please. This is going to be great."

She felt her resolve weakening. This is going to be a huge mistake, she thought. But of course, she already knew about his new job, and that was why Dru had told her to come here, and it was true—Rune could be a big help. Maybe.

"All right," she heard herself say. "If you're really that sure, I'll tell Dru. He's the guy you already met, and that's your first 20 Eyes secret. I don't feel like talking to him right now, but I'll signal him tonight and let him know, and we'll see how it goes."

Rune kissed her, and she kissed him back and hugged him hard. Then Rune smiled and said, "I'll get along fine with Dru. We'll be friends."

She sighed. "He's not always that friendly—or that smart."

"Don't worry about him," Rune said with a laugh. "I'm not worried at all. And I know he's not smart."

"How do you know that?"

"Because he let you get away."

The compliment made her tingle a bit but it also made her anxious. Rune needs to be careful, she thought. *But I'll be looking out for him—always!* Then she kissed him again.

Chapter 38

Aldo was humming to himself as he strolled through the Dream Center. It was an old love song that wasn't popular on the mindstreams, but so what? Most popular songs were garbage. He turned into a classroom where he knew Diana would be waiting for the arrival of Janna, Dimitri, and Rune. My sweet Diana, he thought. He was smiling—but then he stopped short. Why did she look so angry?

"Diana, what's wrong?"

She was glaring at him like a wounded animal. "What kind of person enjoys torturing someone?"

"What?" he said, and his voice felt weak.

"I tortured Carla—and I liked it. And now I feel so guilty. I feel like a monster."

Aldo tried to catch his breath. "But Carla hurt your son," he said. "You were just getting revenge."

"My son loved that girl, and he would hate me for what I did to her! Besides, none of it can bring him back—and it's all your fault!"

"My fault?" Aldo sputtered. "How is it my fault?"

"You're the one who suggested it. You're the one who had her chained up in that room. You're a bigger monster than I am!"

Now Aldo felt his heart pounding. How could this be happening?

"But you said you hated 20 Eyes. You said you wanted her dead—and Markla Flash, too."

"I was just talking. I didn't mean it! You have no heart, Aldo."

"But I do! I was trying to do something good for you."

"You made me hate myself! That's what you did."

"Diana, I'm sorry. I'm so sorry."

She gave him a look of disgust and shook her head. "I'm

sorry, too—and I don't want to talk about it anymore. The kids will be here in a few minutes."

"We can talk about it later!" he blurted. "We can have dinner tonight."

"I don't think so. It's just not the right situation—you and me. Please don't call me."

She stormed out of the room, leaving Aldo alone.

He could barely breathe. He felt like his heart had been yanked from his chest and squashed. He stood still for a few agonizing minutes. As Janna and Dimitri arrived, he staggered out into the hall.

Chapter 39

Rune's mind and body were bubbling with memories from the night before. Despite his interest in LiveDreams, he was having a hard time concentrating on his new job at the Dream Center. Meanwhile, his friends were determined to talk to him.

"Rune, you're too quiet," Dimitri said with a grin. "It's almost like that prison riot changed you."

They were in a classroom, sitting together at the same table and waiting for Diana. No one had seen her yet.

Janna elbowed Dimitri. "Do you ever know when to stop talking?"

"What do you mean? I just started."

"Yeah, and it's already time."

Dimitri just laughed and said, "So, seriously, Rune—what happened that day?"

Rune just shrugged and said nothing. He wasn't annoyed; his mind was just far away. Then Diana walked into the room, and he saw the dark circles under her bloodshot eyes, and he guessed she was more tired or upset than usual—but she seemed to make an effort to smile.

"Rune, I'm glad you're here," she said. Then she added, "I'm glad you're all here. You're going to be part of something new."

Dimitri grinned once again. "Are we going to change the world?"

"You'll be part of a change," she said. Then she paused and added, "I guess we'll see how it goes. Follow me."

She led them to another room with multiple dream stations and then explained their task. They'd be given lists of popular mindstreams where they would post LiveDreams about different topics. The LiveDreams they'd create would be short, and they'd be built around information Diana gave them—and Rune struggled to hide his rising anger. Would these LiveDreams be called LiveDreams, or would the government try to pass them off as real? A good dream writer could make a LiveDream look exactly like a film clip recorded with a camera, and this is how Aldo had created the misleading images of Markla's crime. He'd created a LiveDream and then declared it to be actual camera footage—and he'd gotten Markla sentenced to 20 years of torture.

But they were not creating those kind of dreams, and Rune's anger was short lived. The LiveDreams Diana wanted seemed harmless if not downright beneficial; they were messages about education and why it was important for every young Sparklan to value it. So now Rune's expression brightened, and he dove into the task—because more than anything, he loved to write LiveDreams. With great enthusiasm, he created a clownish loser named Blotto who dropped out of school, and a message that said, "Don't Blotto away your life." As Rune worked, he kept muttering that the dream could be better—but in his heart, he was proud of his work, especially when Diana was impressed. Everyone worked on their LiveDreams all morning and into the afternoon, and then they were finished for the day and Rune headed outside. Rune was happy about his first day on the job, but now he couldn't wait to get home—would he see Markla tonight? It was the only thought in his mind.

"Wait a second!" Janna said. Rune was about to hop on his flyboard and head toward the prison gate but now Janna had other ideas. "You're just going to fly out of here and leave me alone with Dimitri?"

Dimitri was right behind Janna. He grinned at her joke, but it was a weak grin.

Rune laughed. "I'll walk to the gate. But then I'm gone."

"Okay—my mom is picking me up, anyway, and we're going shopping. So what did you think of the job?"

"It was fine. I always wanted to create my own personal loser."

She laughed. "I had fun writing mine. And I learned some good stuff, too."

Janna had written a straightforward LiveDream that relied on numbers to show her cheerful characters the greater income potential for an educated person. Despite the focus on math, Rune thought she'd made it interesting.

Dimitri said, "I liked your LiveDream, Janna. It makes me want to go home and start counting."

She rolled her eyes. Then she said, "Rune, what are you doing tonight? I won't be out too long, and I got a new keyboard. Why don't you come over after dinner? I could use some percussion." She turned her head fast and looked at Dimitri, like she was anticipating a tasteless joke. "Be quiet."

"What?" he said. "I didn't say anything."

Rune laughed to himself. *And you won't get anything, either.*

"Tonight's not that good," Rune said. "I've got a few things to do."

Janna opened her mouth in mock indignation. "You have something better to do than play with me?" Then she whirled again toward Dimitri. "Don't talk."

"What?" he said, throwing up his hands. "I didn't say anything."

Rune knew Dimitri was getting annoyed. Janna wasn't exactly taunting him, but she probably knew he wouldn't like being left out.

"I could come, too," Dimitri blurted. "I could be the audience. If no one hears it, did it even happen?"

Janna looked at him but didn't respond, and now they reached the gate. As it slid opened, Rune saw Janna's mother waiting in a silvery anti-grav car. It was a luxury model, for sure.

"Sorry, Janna," Rune said. "Maybe another time."

She made an exaggerated pouty face. "Okay. But call me if anything changes."

"Sure."

Rune watched as she ran to the vehicle. Then he glanced at Dimitri who was staring after the car as it drove away. Dimitri made no attempt to hide his forlorn expression. He looked sad like a lost puppy.

Poor guy, Rune thought.

"Hey, Dimitri, if I play with Janna I'll give you a call, okay? You're right, we could use an audience."

"Really?"

"Yeah, but I'm not going to play with her. Not tonight, anyway. But when I do, I'll call you."

Dimitri shook his head. "Rune, are you crazy? What are you doing? Who's better than Janna?" Then he laughed. "Have you got Markla stashed in your shed?"

Rune gave him a cold stare. "Dimitri, why do you always have to mention her?"

Dimitri hesitated. "I don't know," he said, and he looked away. There was a long pause, and then he shrugged and spoke in a soft voice. "Maybe I'm just jealous of the way all the girls like you. Maybe I know they'll never like me that way—because I'm not that likable." He turned his head back toward Rune, and for once he did not have a silly grin on his face. "I'm sorry about all the Markla jokes," he said. "I know you really liked her. I'm sorry she got arrested."

Suddenly, Rune felt less anger toward his old friend. "Lots of people like you," he said. "We've been friends a long time, right? Anyway, Janna's not the girl for me."

Dimitri's ears perked up. "Oh, yeah? Why not?"

"She's just not. Maybe it could work out for you."

"Do you really think so?" Dimitri's face lit up.

"Sure, why not? Hey, the bus is here."

"Yeah... Okay, Rune. I'll see you later."

Dimitri smiled and boarded the bus while Rune hopped on his flyboard.

***

By the time Rune got home his whole body was crackling with anticipation. Would Markla return? That was the plan. But how long would she stay? She'd talked about going south, or going to Narna, or going somewhere. The thought of her leaving made Rune's stomach feel like it was doing somersaults.

Blog wasn't around, but Rune went into the house and found his mother in the living room, submerged in a LiveDream. All he saw was the back of her head and her messy hair sticking up above a sofa cushion. He didn't bother interrupting her. He ate some rice and beans and went outside to the shed where he activated two orange lighting orbs. They didn't provide bright light, but Rune liked it on the dark side. He thought Markla would, too.

He waited. He played the drums. Rune mostly played *bolla drums*, a type of drum that had been around for thousands of years. He would sit on a small stool and lean one of the drums back a bit between his knees and then bang on a few more that were within reach. He banged along with music that played through his GoBug, and then he GoBugged for a while in a non-musical way, holding his breath while checking every stream for news about Markla's capture—but he saw none. Every instant seemed like an hour. As it got darker outside, he heard the thump of a car door slam, and he knew his father was home. He felt a flash of fear but then told himself to stay calm. His father wouldn't find it odd that he was in the shed, and he wouldn't know he was out here, anyway. He'd just know Rune wasn't in the house, and Rune often wasn't in the house. It wouldn't mean he was rendezvousing with a fugitive, especially one who'd supposedly left the area.

More time went by. The clock was crawling. Finally, there was a knock on the door—and his heart leaped. Markla was here.

Her black hair was windblown and tangled as usual. She wore the same flannel shirt, open like a jacket, and a simple brownish shirt of cotton, as well as faded denim pants and moccasins—typical Markla. She stepped into the shed quietly, as always, and Rune considered how she'd make a wonderful assassin. He hadn't heard any sound outside, even though dry leaves were scattered all around.

"Hi, Rune," she said. But she wasn't smiling, and she was standing stiffly. "I'm back."

Rune felt a jolt of uncertainty, and he wondered if something had changed. Where had she been—and who had she been talking to?

"Hi, Markla. Are you okay?"

"Yeah. I'm fine."

"Is something wrong?"

"No."

"Why do you look unhappy?"

She shrugged. "I'm not. I was just wondering."

"Wondering what?"

She hesitated. "If anything changed since yesterday."

He laughed. Then he stepped toward her and wrapped her in his arms. "I hope not. I'm really happy to see you."

Now she smiled. "I'm happy to see you, too. I was worried… I thought you might come to your senses."

"No chance."

They kissed, and it was a long kiss. He hugged her as he did it, and it was a long hug, and he wanted it to go on and on—but then the moment was broken. He felt her stiffen and pull away.

"What?"

"Sh!"

Now Rune froze and listened. Someone was coming, crunching through the leaves outside. Markla glanced around, and Rune could see the alarm in her eyes—there was only one way out of the shed. Then they heard more crunching, and someone was at the door, and the door had no lock. Rune had never thought it was necessary.

Markla moved fast, pressing herself against the wall beside the door. Rune stayed closer to the center of the room, near his drums. The door opened outward—and it was moving.

"Hello?" a deep voice said.

It was not a voice Rune recognized—but he saw Markla's eyebrows go up. But she didn't speak. Her eyes looked wild, and Rune felt his heart start to pound. Then a stocky guy appeared in the doorway. Rune had never seen him before. In the dim orange light, he appeared to be short with cropped dark hair, and he was at least a few years older than Rune. He stepped into the shed.

"Who are you?" Rune said. Rune was standing behind a few drums. They offered little protection but they provided a token barrier.

As Rune spoke, the guy took another step forward and clearly did not see Markla in the shadows behind him. Okay, that's good, Rune thought. Now she could easily slip past the guy and run from the shed—but she did not run.

"I guess you're Rune," the guy said. He was studying Rune as he spoke.

Rune's mind worked fast. *Was this guy in 20 Eyes?* He was still just looking at Rune, but then he was reaching for something, and Rune's heart skipped a beat—it was a gun. And then Rune could see Markla behind him, and she had a dagger in her hand.

"No!" Rune said.

The guy hesitated and then started to turn—and Rune lunged, grabbing the wrist of the hand that held the weapon. The gun went off as two drums tumbled to the floor.

"No!" Rune shouted again. He had both hands on the gun now, and the guy was trying to yank himself free, and the gun fired another shot. Another drum tumbled over, booming as it hit the floor—and Markla was there, slipping her left arm around the guy's chest. In her other hand was the dagger—and now it was at the intruder's throat.

"Drop it!" she said.

The guy froze. He didn't turn his head.

"Markla?" he said, and now his voice was a bit high-pitched as she tightened her grip. "What are you doing here?"

"I'll kill you, Stono," she said, and her voice was low and menacing. "You've got one second."

Rune held his breath. Would she do it? Yeah, he was sure she would—and apparently, so was Stono. He released the gun and it clattered to the floor.

"Rune, pick it up," she said.

He reached down and grabbed the weapon. It felt heavy in his hands yet strangely comfortable. Well, he'd fired a gun before. Blog had insisted he learn—it was something "a man needed to know." Rune took a few steps back and pointed it at Stono.

"Get down on the ground," Markla said. "Now!"

She loosened her grip on Stono and stepped back—but Rune could see she was ready to strike. Her eyes were like fire.

Stono got down on his knees. Markla said, "On your stomach with your hands out where I can see them."

He did as he was told. "Markla," he stammered, "I didn't know you were going to be here."

"And why does that matter? Do you think I want you to kill Rune?"

"No. I guess not."

"*You guess not?* Maybe you should stop guessing, Stono, and start thinking. But that's the problem with you guys. You're all stupid."

"But he can identity Dru!"

"Dru? The guy you just named?"

"Well, yeah," Stono said and his voice trailed off.

"Stupid again," she said. "A never-ending pile of stupid—that's you, Stono." She knelt down and poked the point of the dagger into the back of his neck. "When did Dru tell you to come here?"

"This morning."

She swore softly. "What else did he say? Tell me something."

"There's nothing else! He told me to…take care of Rune. He said Rune was the Centurion's kid, and his house backed up to the woods. I didn't know he'd be here. I was just scouting around but then I saw someone in here so I checked it out. That's all."

Rune wasn't sure what he should be doing, so he continued to scowl and point the gun at Stono. But he was sweating. What would he do if Stono suddenly made a move? He wouldn't kill the guy—no way. But he wouldn't let him hurt Markla, either. Maybe aim for an arm or a leg—yeah, that was the plan. Get up close, so he couldn't miss, and shoot the guy in an arm or leg. Of course, that was assuming Markla didn't kill the guy first.

She stood up, and Rune breathed a sigh of relief. But then they both froze and stared at the open door—there were more footsteps outside. Rune swung the gun at the doorway—and now he heard a voice he recognized.

"Rune, what's going on? Put down the weapon."

Blog was standing in the doorway, and he had a gun of his own.

Rune hesitated, and now Blog roared. "Put down the weapons! Both of you!" He stared at Markla. "Put it down and go stand against the wall with Rune. Don't be dumb and make me shoot you."

Rune looked at Markla, and for one horrible second he thought she was going to attack his father—and Blog would kill her. But she looked back at Rune, and she dropped the dagger. She went to stand beside him as Rune dropped the gun.

Blog stared at the guy on the floor. "Slide back a bit," he said. "And keep your hands where I can see them."

As Stono followed directions, Blog pulled out a stun stick. He reached down fast and jabbed Stono on the back. There was a sizzling sound, and Stono let out a yelp, and then he was unconscious.

Blog put the stick back on his belt and stood beside a drum that was still upright. He eyed his remaining two prisoners.

He shook his head. "Rune, what did I tell you about this girl? I warned you. So, who's the guy on the floor?"

"I don't know," Rune said.

"I was talking to her."

Markla stared straight ahead and said nothing.

Blog laughed. "That's fine. I'll get the story later." Then he aimed the gun at Markla. "You were tough when they interrogated you but you won't be so tough against a bullet. So tell me, who is the captain of the local 20 Eyes pod?"

Markla remained silent.

Blog gave a low laugh and shook his head. "Markla, if you don't tell me, I'm going to shoot you." He raised the gun a bit.

"No!" Rune said, and he leaped in front of her. "You're not going to hurt her! You'll have to kill me first."

Now Blog cocked his head, apparently amused. "Is that so?" he said.

"Yeah," Rune said. Then he let out a scream and charged at his father.

Markla shouted, "Rune!"

Rune was blind with rage; he wanted to rip Blog apart. But Blog swore, and his left hand shot out and smashed hard into Rune's neck. Then he snarled, gripping Rune by the throat. Rune punched Blog's arm, but Blog used his other hand and slammed the gun down on Rune's head. For an instant, everything went black, and then Blog kicked Rune's feet out from under him. Rune heard Markla shout again as he hit the floor. He opened his eyes and saw Blog with the stun stick in his left head. In his right, he still held the gun, and it was pointed at Markla. She was closer to Blog now.

"Get back," Blog said. She hesitated and then slowly moved backwards toward the wall. Blog looked down at Rune.

"That was pathetic," Blog said. "But I guess they don't teach you anything useful in dream school. Do that again and I'll put you to sleep and shoot the girl. Do you understand?"

Rune stared up from the floor with his chest heaving. He felt like he was burning up. This wasn't just about Markla and 20 Eyes. It was about everything.

Blog gave a grunt. "As dumb as that was, Rune, I didn't think you had it in you. You must really like her. But is she worth it?" He aimed the gun at her head. "Give me a name, Markla. I mean it."

Markla glanced at Rune and then gave Blog a vicious glare. "I'm not afraid to die," she said. "Go ahead."

Rune thought his brain would explode. *"No!"* he shouted.*"Don't do it!"*

Blog gave a short laugh—and then lowered his weapon.

"Maybe she is worth it," he said. "This one's a warrior, Rune. Maybe you will be, too, one day." He paused and said, "I was awake, Markla, lying on the ground when that friend of yours wanted to kill me. I heard him say your name, and I know what you did. You saved my life, and I owe you. You can go."

Rune's mouth dropped open.

Markla raised her eyebrows a bit. She hesitated for an instant but then quickly bent down and retrieved her dagger. She eyed Blog yet made no move toward the door.

Blog pointed at Stono. "This guy is trash," he said. "Some of what you're fighting for is good, but as a whole the group is trash. They talk a lot and blow things up but they have no honor—no code. Do you think this guy would die to protect you? You could do better."

Markla said nothing but she once again glanced at Rune.

Blog laughed again. "I suppose he has potential," Blog said. "But your future isn't here, Markla—it's somewhere else. Narna is a primitive place but you'd probably do well there. The best way is to head north, through the woods, until you come to the hover-train yard in Sliver. When the trains pull out, they aren't going at full speed. If you're quick and you're careful, you can hop on. The security is weak at the border. When the train stops for inspection, you can probably get off and slip through. That's one plan, anyway. You should go now. In a couple of weeks it'll start getting cold."

Markla shrugged. "I'm not sure what I'm doing yet," she said.

"Don't overthink it. The truth is usually the most obvious thing. Do you understand?"

Markla stared at the weapon in her hand and then slid it back into the sheath on her belt. "Yeah, I do," she said. Then she added, "Thank you."

Blog took a GoBug from his pocket and placed it behind his

ear. "You're welcome, and here's some more advice: Don't come around here again. I'm giving you a break, but if I see you again I won't be so nice." He pointed at Stono. "In a few minutes, I'm going to be making a call about this person, so it would be a good idea for you to leave. I'll give you a chance to say good-bye, but that's it." Then he looked at Rune and said, "Be in the house when the police get here. And don't say anything."

Blog walked out of the shed. Rune rushed to the doorway and watched him walk into the darkness to a place near the house. He guessed Blog was making his call to the police, and they'd be arriving soon. What would the story be? Right now, he was more or less alone with Markla. Stono was sleeping like a rock and certainly wasn't going to hear anything. Rune spoke fast.

"Markla, he's right. You should go to Narna."

"I don't want to go to Narna!" she spat. "And I can't believe Dru sent someone to kill you. I signaled him last night and told him you wanted to join, and he said everything was great. What a liar! I guess he figured we were together and he got jealous."

"Forget about Dru. You need to get out of here."

"I can't forget about him. I trusted him—you want me to go?"

"No! But I want you to stay alive. I want you to be free. I can join you there."

"Rune, you have a life. You have school, and I don't want you throwing everything away for me." Then she paused, and she cursed. "But maybe you're right about Dru. I should forget about him and 20 Eyes and leave them behind. After all, they left me."

"Right!" Rune said, and now his heart felt light. "But we could stay in touch."

"We could. And if you still feel the same way in a year, you'll be done here. You could come to Narna, if you wanted to. Maybe I could get a new identity."

"Yeah, let's do it! But we'll need a way to communicate."

"We can use radio."

"Radio? I've heard of that."

"No one uses it now because of GoBugs—but 20 Eyes uses it. The government knows we use it, but it's got different frequencies, and if you keep changing the one you're on and keep the conversations short, it's almost impossible to trace. It could be good."

"How does it work? Do you have what we need?"

"It's like this: I monitor a certain channel. If I get a message from someone in the group, we use codes to tell each other what channel to switch to, and when—just in case someone's listening. We switch the monitor channel every week. This week it's channel 25."

"Okay, great. What channel would we go to?"

"I don't know, and it doesn't matter—channel 2, because there are two of us, ha. But we can worry about that later. I have to get you a radio first. Then I'll come back tomorrow."

"That's not a good plan. Don't come here."

"Okay, I'll meet you in the woods, near the prison. You could go there after work—to that spot by the stream, that tree I climbed. Can you find it?"

"Yeah."

"All right," she said. Then she laughed. "Just make sure Janna doesn't follow you."

"Why would she do that?"

"I'm joking, Rune. But you're so naive. I'll see you there."

They kissed. Then they did it again—and then once more.

"Bye, Rune."

"Bye."

She gave him one last look, and he could see in her eyes that she didn't want to leave him, and he thought that if he never saw her again, he would keep this memory etched in his mind forever. Then she slipped out of the shed and disappeared.

Chapter 40

Rune sat in his room, straining his ears to hear the conversation between his father and a couple of knobbers in the living room. One of them was Stoke, a tall guy with dark skin, a beard, and a tattoo of a rattlesnake on the side of his face. He was a fierce-looking friend from Blog's military days who usually talked to Blog about trimming trees, growing grass, and drinking ale. Rune guessed the talk was different tonight but despite his best effort he couldn't hear any of it. Meanwhile, a couple of other troopers hauled Stono away in a police car. The official story was that he'd been at the house to assassinate Blog, and there was no mention of Rune or Markla. Rune guessed Stono would say nothing. The people of 20 Eyes never cooperated with the authorities.

Where was Markla right now? He'd only seen her tonight for about half an hour, and it had been the fastest half hour of his life. He wondered if Blog had told the truth about the best way to get to Narna—and he couldn't believe his law-and-order obsessed father had allowed her to go free.

I don't know my father at all, Rune thought. Then he heard Stoke and the other trooper leaving, and Rune started to sweat. Should he wait for Blog to come into his room? No, not this time. Rune stood tall and walked into the living room.

His mother was sitting on the sofa in her usual spot but for once she was not immersed in a LiveDream. Her worried eyes were rimmed with red. Blog was in the kitchen, opening a bottle of ale.

At the sight of Rune, Maya's eyes got wide. "Rune, you need to stay in the house from now on, until the situation with these people is over. They wanted to kill your father!"

Rune shrugged. Maya only knew the official story.

"I'll be careful," he said.

"You need to be more than careful. You need to stay inside. They could target you, too! After all, you know Markla Flash, and who knows what she told them? Maybe that's why they came here tonight. Maybe they really wanted to kidnap you."

"Markla doesn't want to kidnap me."

"How do you know what she wants?"

Blog walked into the room with a bottle in his hand and a smirk on his face. "Don't worry, Maya. Rune's done some research, and kidnapping isn't what's on her mind."

Maya hesitated. "Okay," she said. "Maybe that's not what's on her mind—but Rune, you need to forget about her. You can't be involved with her! Promise me."

"Don't worry about it," Blog said, now distinctly smirking in Rune's direction. "It's an issue for law enforcement, Maya, but it'll work out. Rune's not in any danger, but Rune and I need to discuss it. These aren't things you want to know."

Maya got up. She stood in front of Blog and grasped his hand with both of hers. "Be careful," she said.

He gave her a warm stare. "I will be."

Maya disappeared into the bedroom and closed the door, and Blog sat on the sofa. "Sit down, Rune. Let's sort things out."

Rune sat in a chair across from his father, determined not to be intimidated. But the air was charged with tension, and Rune felt like Blog was going to say something shocking. He'd been full of surprises tonight.

Blog took a swig of ale. "I didn't want to involve you in any of this, but since you decided to find a girlfriend in 20 Eyes, and since you decided to take a job inside the prison and the Dream Center, you've involved yourself. Maybe it's time for you to become a man." He put down the bottle. "Did you join the group?"

"No."

"Good," Blog said, and he nodded his head with approval. "Now start talking. Tell me what happened and don't leave anything out."

Rune talked. But he mostly talked about things he thought Blog already knew or would soon realize. Yeah, he'd helped Markla escape from the prison, and he was with her in the woods—and he'd rescued her and someone named "Dru" from a car crash. He hadn't known Blog was the trooper on the ground, and Markla had changed her mind about trying to recruit him, and apparently Dru was the person who'd sent the assassin. But despite his father's warning, he did leave a few things out—like his intimate encounter with Markla in the shed, and how he was planning to stay in touch with her, and the way he was plotting to run away with her to another country. He especially didn't mention that. But how much would Blog guess? At least some of it.

When he was done with his confession, Rune sat back in the chair and waited. All in all, Rune felt good. Blog was quiet for a minute. Finally, Blog said, "Dru Nava is the captain of the local 20 Eyes pod. Stay in the house until we arrest him."

Rune blinked. "You know him?"

Blog gave a low grunt. "I appreciate Markla saving my life, but do you really think I'd let her walk out of here if I didn't already have his name?" And then a picture of Dru appeared in front of Rune's eyes, sent via GoBug.

"That's him!" Rune said.

Blog gave a satisfied grunt. "So he's the guy who was with Markla the night I crashed my car, right? And he's also Markla's boyfriend." Then Blog paused to smirk yet again and added, "Or is he an ex-boyfriend now?"

Rune hesitated. "She broke up with him," he said.

Blog laughed. "Of course she did." Then he said, "We know who Nava is. We know who a lot of them are—but sometimes there are advantages to not arresting them. Sometimes it helps change public opinion if a few people are out there causing trouble, do you understand?" Then Blog sneered and said, "But this guy crossed a line. He tried to kill my son, and I won't leave him out there to try it again. So I don't care what Aldo and Gin think about this one. He's going down."

"You mean Gin Xantha, the President of Sparkla?"

"That's another thing we need to discuss. Aldo and Gin are up to no good, and we need to stop them."

Rune hesitated. "We?" he said.

"Yeah. Me, you—and the people of Sparkla. I'm talking about the good ones who reject trash like 20 Eyes but who also know the system isn't working. It's being manipulated by people who want to destroy it. There was a time when I went along with it because I liked the results we were getting—but that was a mistake, and those days are over." He leaned forward and stared at Rune with his hawk eyes. "We need to find out what's going on inside the Dream Center. We need to know everything Aldo is planning. Since you're going to be there every day, I'm thinking you can help. So, are you in or out?"

Rune was stunned; he felt like he'd been hit with a brick. But he didn't think about it long.

"I'm in," Rune said.

Blog nodded. "Good. We don't need you to do anything drastic or stupid. Just snoop around, but be careful. Tell me everything you see and hear."

"Are you part of another group fighting the government?"

"Yeah, but it's a small group—small, but smart. We don't have a catchy name or a mindstream filled with advertisements. We stay out of the spotlight. We're just a group of people who've had enough, and you don't need to know more than that right now."

Rune figured this was as much as he'd get out of Blog tonight.

"Okay," he said. He wasn't even sure how much he wanted to know, since he planned to finish his last year of school and join Markla in Narna. But then he had another thought.

"What about the assassin? Are you sure he won't mention Markla to the interrogators?"

"It's unlikely but it's not a problem either way, since I'm going to be handling his interrogation." Blog sighed. "I might bend the rules occasionally, Rune, but I take my job seriously. I'm an officer of the law." He paused and added, "I was never going to shoot Markla. That's not what I do. I arrest people, and I leave the justice to others, and then I hope for the best. That's my duty—and my officers feel the same way, and we don't abuse suspects, and we don't abuse the truth. But Gin and Aldo have different ideas. They do it all the time."

"I know they do!" Rune said. "And by the way, I have copies of all the LiveDreams Aldo created. Maybe they could be useful. I also have a script that opens doors in the Dream Center—a 'bunker' and some others."

Blog's eyebrows went up. "Why do you have them?"

"I stole them," Rune said, trying to sound casual. "I wanted to see if Aldo used LiveDreams to change the images of Markla's crime—and he did."

Blog's eyes flashed with anger. "That's what they do! That's exactly what they do. How did you steal them?"

Rune told him the story, and how he'd almost been caught. Blog actually grinned.

"Good job, Rune—you've got guts. Send them to me. They might be useful."

Rune felt himself swelling with pride, and it shocked him. Why did he care what his father thought? For some reason, he did.

Blog picked up his ale and took a final swig. "Still, it was risky, and why did you do it? I know why, even if you won't admit it. Life is full of choices, Rune, but don't fool yourself—that girl is an extreme choice. That doesn't mean she's a bad choice—sometimes the extreme choice is the best thing ever. But other times it'll wreck your life, so think about what you're getting into with someone like her."

Rune continued to say nothing. Obviously, Blog suspected Markla was still around. It didn't matter.

But Blog seemed done with the topic. He put down his empty bottle and said, "You might need to contact me from inside the Dream Center, or from somewhere else, and you might want to make sure no one can trace the message. So I'm going to give you something, a way to communicate that's difficult to trace. It's something you've never used before. It's called 'radio.' "

"Radio?" Rune said. He tried to sound surprised. "That sounds interesting. How does it work?"

Chapter 41

Markla slipped into the woods when the police arrived but she didn't go far from the shed. She crouched behind a clump of trees and observed from the shadows, and once again she felt that longing, like a part of her was being ripped away. Soon, she thought, *we'll be together again soon.* She stayed close to her flyboard, ready to run, as a couple of knobbers dragged Stono's unconscious body away. Then she started thinking about the radios.

She hadn't exactly lied to Rune—she did want to forget about Dru. But she only had one radio at her mother's house, and she'd need another one, and Dru had it. But I need to be careful, she thought, and she pushed some horrible thoughts of revenge from her mind. She wanted to meet Rune tomorrow, near that happy stream and under that tree. It was important to keep thinking about that moment. It was a thought that could keep her from doing something reckless.

She took a deep breath and headed to Dru's place. It was a dark night, with the moon and stars smothered behind a dense wall of clouds, and this was convenient—but unfortunately, Dru's place was located across the river and on the outskirts of Turnaround, and that meant going through Cooly Strip and then crossing a bridge. Luckily, the landscape was covered with trees, and the bridge was the only part of the trip that was dangerous. She ruled out crossing the river on a flyboard at night. That was a plan for a more desperate day.

She went slowly on the flyboard, trying to look casual. She had a black hooded jacket she'd gotten from Dru's place, and with her hair tied back and stuffed under the hood she could pass for a boy—a young boy, in fact. Being tiny and not overly curvy has some advantages, she thought, and then she laughed. *Janna could never get away with this.*

She made it to Dru's greenhouse without incident. She walked past a wall of windows filled with fluffy pink flowers, and then stashed the flyboard behind a twisted old tree. She saw a light in the building out back.

She paused to think. It wasn't that she had no plan—it's just that she didn't have a good one. Certainly, she wasn't planning to physically attack Dru. Markla didn't consider herself to be much of a fighter. The way she saw things, all her incidents of violence had been unplanned. Every one had been about survival and the effects of an uncontrollable anger. As a small child, she'd spent many jittery hours imagining the moment when she'd strike out at her attackers—but she'd never done it. And then when she'd gotten older, and those incidents had stopped, she still hadn't done it. Instead, she'd acted outwardly calm while her inside bubbled with fury. She'd never slept much. On some days, she'd gone to school in a daze while kids wondered what was wrong with her. Then one night at the dream station all her rage had erupted, and she'd murdered someone, and now she doubted she'd ever sleep well again.

No one knew about these things, no one except Tommi, and even he didn't know everything. But Markla wanted Rune to know. She had no idea if she'd even tell him—but she imagined telling him one day. She wasn't looking for pity. She just wanted one person to really know her.

All these thoughts bombarded her mind as she went to the door of the building adjacent to the greenhouse. She listened and heard no sound. The dirty glass door was unlocked, and she opened it just far enough to slip inside.

Dru was sitting at his cluttered desk with a GoBug behind his ear. Among the many items on the desktop, she saw a bottle of ale and a plate of spicy noodles. Every hair on his pretty head was perfectly in place, like he was expecting a photographer.

He always has to look sharp, Markla thought. *If I cut his throat, he'll run a comb through his hair before he dies.* She watched him closely, and when he looked up, he was startled. But it was only a slight reaction, like he hadn't heard her enter. Then he smiled and seemed normal enough.

"Markla, where have you been? I was worried about you. I figured you were in here yesterday while I was at work."

"I was—thanks. But just now I was at Rune's house, watching Stono try to kill him."

Dru's grin vanished. "What are you talking about? You weren't supposed to be involved."

"I wasn't! I recruited Rune last night, remember? It was your idea, and then you send an assassin?"

He put down his fork and gave her a hard stare. "Markla, I know you're mad—but try and understand. I changed my mind about Rune. Sure, he's your friend, but he can identify me, and his father is a Centurion, and there's just no way around that stuff. So think about it like that, okay? Stono wasn't there to hurt you. I specifically told him about that a while ago."

An alarm sounded in Markla's head. "Why would you need to tell Stono that? Did he want to hurt me?"

Dru hesitated, and Markla knew the answer.

She shook her head in disbelief. "Are you serious? You had a conversation with Stono about me? Why, because I got arrested? Other people have been arrested, and no one talked. Why would I be any different?"

"Markla, it's not like that. Stono wasn't going to do anything. It was just a thought he had—and hey, what happened? Where is he?"

Markla didn't hear him. She was in a daze. And then she was in a rage.

With a shout, she swiped his ale and food onto the floor,

breaking the bottle and the plate. Then she snatched the GoBug from behind his ear and flung it across the room.

"I thought this was my family!" she said, and now her head was spinning. "I thought I had people I could count on. *How could he want to hurt me? And how could you want to kill Rune?*"

"Hey! Calm down."

"I'm not going to calm down, Dru!" But then she took a deep breath and stopped shouting. "I want a radio."

He looked at her and shook his head. Then he crossed his arms. "Where's Stono?" he said. "What happened over there?"

"He was arrested by Blog Roko. I got away, obviously—and Rune is fine."

Now Dru leaped to his feet.

"What?" he said, and he waved his hands in the air. "That's terrible!" He started pacing around the room, his boots crunching on the broken glass. "What if Stono talks? I can't believe this."

"Dru, the prison is full of people who can identify you. If Blu never talked, or Carla, or Rose, why would he? They didn't get anything from me, remember?"

"He's not like those others, Markla! And he's not like you. You're a lot tougher than he is."

Markla crinkled her forehead. Why did everyone think she was so tough?

"I should've killed him!" she snapped. "I almost did—but then I didn't, because Rune was there."

"Oh, really? And why do you care what Rune thinks? Doesn't he already know you're a killer?"

"That was different! And admit it—you wanted him dead because he likes me. After I recruited him you guessed we were together and you got jealous and you wanted him dead!"

"No! I wanted him dead because he's a threat to us all, and you would see that if you didn't like him so much yourself."

Markla struggled to keep her temper in check. "I want the radio, Dru. I'm leaving."

His face flushed. "I gave you a radio. Why do you need another one?" Then he narrowed his eyes. "Who are you talking to?"

"Tommi," she said. "I'm giving him mine, but I need another one to communicate with him while I'm here. When I go, I'll give it back to you."

Dru was quiet for a second, also calming himself down. "Have you talked to Tommi yet?"

"No—why? Is there something I should know?"

"Yeah. He already has a radio. I gave it to him."

His words stung Markla like a slap. Obviously, Dru had plans for her stepbrother.

With an effort, she kept her face blank. "I need another radio," she said. "I just do."

"Is that so?" he said with a smirk. "Go ahead—take it. There's one in the desk."

She opened the bottom drawer of the desk and removed the device. It easily fit into her hand except for the collapsible antenna. "Thanks."

Dru started to reach out and touch her the way he always did after an argument, but she took a step back.

"I'm done here," she said. "I'm quitting the group."

Dru rolled his eyes. "Why? Because of Rune?"

"Yeah, exactly. You lied to me."

He threw up his hands once again. "I would've told you, but I figured you'd get upset."

"How did you think I was going to feel when he turned up dead?"

He shrugged. "I thought you'd eventually understand."

"You thought wrong, Dru." *And it wouldn't be the first time.* Then she said, "Rune knows you're after him, and so does his father. So don't try it again."

"You don't make decisions for the group. I do."

Markla looked at him as the full force of his comment hit her.

He was going to try it again. There was no doubt in her mind—and they both knew it. But she just stared and said nothing. The silence was deafening, and she stayed very still. Her instincts told her a sudden move would trigger a fight—and she would lose.

"I have to go," she said. She turned and opened the door, walking fast toward her flyboard.

He called out to her. "Markla, wait! Don't leave."

He was coming. She slid her dagger from its sheath and held it close to her body. She kept walking.

"Markla, wait!"

She walked faster—but his footsteps were close now, almost close enough to kill her. Was that his plan?

It didn't matter. She stopped short, whirled to her right, and stabbed him in the stomach.

He gasped. She pulled the blade back and saw his eyes wide with shock. She also saw he was unarmed, and that was fine—with a grunt she plunged the dagger into his heart. Because a stomach wound might take too long.

He staggered backwards. He was staring at her as he fell to the ground, clutching at the weapon buried in his chest. An instant later his eyes were dead and staring at the sky.

Markla took a deep breath and squatted down near his body. She felt sick, and her eyes filled with tears as a pool of blood spread across the ground. A thousand thoughts whirled through her mind—but two of them stood out. He wanted to recruit Tommi, she thought, *and he wants to hurt Rune. And I can't let those things happen.*

She yanked the dagger from Dru's chest and wiped it on his shirt. Then she heard a sound, and she looked up fast—and there was Blu Baroke. He was walking out of the greenhouse.

Run! I should run!

But she did not run. Instead, she kept the dagger in her hand and stood up. Her heart was pounding, and her feet were itching to dash away, but her grip on the weapon was light. She knew it worked better that way. He stopped about six or seven paces in front of her.

He was dressed in a pair of denim pants and a flannel shirt much like her own. Even in the dark, she could see his face was scratched and there was a bruise over his left eye. In his hand was a gun. She held up her dagger and stared into his eyes. This is it, she thought. *I'm going to die.*

He looked down at Dru's body, and then back at Markla. He eyed the weapon in her hand.

"Lover's quarrel?" he said.

"It was a little more than that."

He paused and shook his head. "I got here about an hour ago. Dru was letting me hide out in the greenhouse. I'm not going to hurt you, Markla—although maybe I should be the one who's scared."

"No," she said. "I'm not like that."

He raised an eyebrow, glanced at Dru again, and then looked at Markla once more. "You're young," he said. "I am, too—but I'm getting old fast. And what I've learned is this: It's easy to do certain things—but living with them later, that's the hard part."

"I'll live with this."

He nodded. "Yeah, you might. I was talking about me."

"What have you done?"

He shook his head. "Things I'm not proud of."

She narrowed her eyes and considered the strange nightmare Rune had mentioned. She recalled how so many people were easily captured after the prison break—a sure sign of betrayal from someone. Then he motioned with his head toward the road. "You should probably get out of here before someone else comes around."

She was quiet but backed away from him, moving slowly. He didn't follow. When she was far enough away, she put away her dagger. Then she reached for her flyboard and hopped onto it and rode toward the shadows.

"Be careful," he called out.

She didn't say anything. In a few seconds she was gone.

Chapter 42

Aldo glanced at the time and sent Gin a GoBug message. He tried not to look smug when Gin answered with dirty look. Gin was holding a white towel and standing in an airy room lined with shiny exercise equipment.

"Aldo, why do you always send me an 'urgent' message when you know I'm working out?"

"Do I? I didn't notice. But this is more important than your muscles. Dru Nava is dead."

Gin swore and tossed his towel on the floor. "That's not good!" he said. "I thought we were saving him for a dramatic moment—something we could shout about."

"I guess someone had other plans."

"Who? Someone in the Eyes?"

"We don't know yet. We do know he was romantically involved with the girl who's still on the loose—Markla Flash. That's one of the things we got from Blu when he was in prison. So maybe it was a case of 'love gone wrong.' " Then Aldo frowned and added, "But that's a common situation, isn't it?"

Gin laughed and took a sip from an insulated water bottle. "Not for me; I don't fall in love. But I hear it's a real problem for my girlfriends and definitely for my wife. So, is she in good shape?"

"Who? Your wife?"

"No, you idiot—this girl you're talking about. Nava was in good shape, right? So if she killed him, she was probably in great shape, unless she used a gun. Was it a gun?"

Aldo sighed. Gin's fascination with everyone's physical fitness was exhausting. No doubt a serial killer would be less horrific if he could do 20 pull-ups.

"She's small and thin," Aldo drawled. "Other than that, I'm not aware of her physical condition. But Dru was killed with a knife, just like the person she killed at the dream station, so maybe she's small and thin and likes to stab people. Don't go getting any ideas, Gin—she's too young for you. Besides, it seems that Blog's son, Rune Roko, might also have a relationship with her."

Gin grinned. "Of course he does. Hey, Blog's kid is in the Eyes?"

"I don't think so. But based on what Diana has said to me, it sounds like he's got a serious interest in this girl."

"Right, and who could blame him? There's nothing sexier than a cute little girl with a knife."

Aldo rolled his eyes. He knew Gin was only partly joking. When it came to women, Gin was a twisted guy. *And yet, all the women like him! Why?* But there was a serious point to this conversation.

Aldo said, "Blog isn't really on our side but he has strong support among the police. Maybe arresting his son would be a good way to take him down a few notches—a son in 20 Eyes won't look good."

"Yeah, great plan. I don't trust Blog at all. But how far do we go with it?"

"It depends on how much Rune knows. We could talk to him and see. Or maybe we could do something more effective."

"MindCore?"

"Yes. We know it works but there are issues. Right now, when it retrieves memories, it tends to only find the ones the subject thinks are most important, and those aren't necessarily the ones we want. We need to be able to target the selection better. I have some ideas that might fix this problem but we'll need to test them out."

"All right. You get on that, and I'll finish blasting my triceps."

Chapter 43

Markla woke up before the first bird chirped. The moon was shining now, all yellow-gold, and she had no memory of falling asleep. For one beautiful instant, her mind was unaware of where she was or what had happened—but then things came into focus, and the world came crashing down around her, and she recalled Dru's dead body and then heading into the woods. She remembered sailing back over the bridge at night on her flyboard, and being reckless, and not really caring if someone spotted her.

But now she cared because she wanted to see Rune this afternoon—yet how could she explain what had happened? It was bound to be on a news stream, and when Rune saw the picture of Dru he would fill in the blanks, and they would be covered with her bloody fingerprints. He would think she was a vicious killer after all. This was never going to work.

He won't want me anymore, she thought. *And it makes perfect sense. There were good reasons no one ever wanted me around.*

Then again, Rune might think she was innocent. After all, Rune knew Dru was in 20 Eyes, and the group was known to be violent. So maybe in his mind, someone else could've done it. But did she want to lie to Rune? No, she didn't, just like she'd never lied to Dru. She put her head in her hands and wiped her teary eyes. She wasn't sure what was more upsetting—the fact that she'd killed him, or the fact that he'd deceived her. It was all such a mess. She threw off her thin blanket and examined her surroundings.

She was at the edge of the forest, across the street from a few squat wooden houses. The one she was interested in was the one in need of the most repair. The paint on the shingles was cracked and peeling, and there was a broken window covered with a burlap bag, and the three front steps looked more like a pile of stones. The house had always been this way, for as long as Markla remembered. In a best case scenario, her mother would go to work, and Markla would be able to sneak in and maybe see Tommi. Also, she would grab her radio and maybe eat something.

She had some rations in her knapsack, along with a toothbrush, toothpaste, and other hygiene and toiletry items. She took care of those tasks and then brushed her hair mainly to relieve nervous energy. She tossed the brush into her knapsack and considered the best approach.

Was the house under surveillance? There was a single streetlight near the first of the three houses but it was dim, and it mainly cast lots of shadows. Still, she didn't see anyone around. She knew there were all kinds of surveillance devices that could be used, but the toads would need a court order. But since she was a fugitive from the most dreaded anti-government group in the country, they might have one.

This is stupid, she thought. Trying to sneak into the house was a bad move, and why bother? She was risking a lot just to get a radio for someone who was probably going to leave her anyway—and rightfully so. Then again, he'd forgiven her for her crime at the dream station, and really, that one had been worse. Besides, hadn't they both been cases of self-defense? Sort of.

I'll get the radio, she thought. *If Rune rejects me, I'll be sad—crushed, really—but I'll just move on. Or maybe I'll go down fighting somewhere, somehow.* It seemed like a logical way for it all to end.

There was no point in waiting, and besides, the darkness had some advantages. She moved out of the woods and ran across the road. The house was the last of the three on the street. One side of the house had a neighbor—but the other side was bordered by trees. She went into those trees, carrying her flyboard. She left it at the edge of the tree line where she could quickly find it if necessary. If the house was under surveillance, fine—she wouldn't stay long.

She crept through the overgrown grass in the backyard and then stopped; her cat Pepper was sitting on top of the weathered picnic table, watching her with a curious expression. Pepper was a big tomcat, all black except for a tuft of white on his neck.

For an instant, Markla was thrilled. "Hi, Pepper," she whispered, and she scratched him between the ears. "I guess Tommi's been feeding you. Where are the others?" She had four cats—Blink, Pepper, Raz, and Coco—but there were quite a few others that came around because she would feed them all, much to her mother's annoyance. After a few quick seconds, she narrowed her eyes and stood up. She headed for the back door.

She moved quietly up two crooked steps and then grabbed the knob on the storm door that was missing a panel of glass. She had a key for the back door, but it wasn't locked, and it creaked a bit as it swung open. Once again, she considered the stupidity of what she was doing. But she kept going.

She was in a narrow area between the back door and the kitchen, a place her mother had appropriately called a "muck room," and it was dark, and she knew the room was cluttered with shoes, umbrellas, and random junk. In fact, the whole house was filled with junk. But Markla had a light step, and she was well aware of her surroundings—and it occurred to her that this is where she'd learned to be so quiet, sneaking around this house at night, hoping no one would hear her enter or leave.

The kitchen was just big enough for a round table with four chairs, a refrigerator, a few cabinets, and a sink. Above the sink was a hazy window with no blind or shade, and it filled the room with shadows and dim light. Markla resisted an urge to pull out her dagger. Really, let's not do that anymore, she thought. In fact, she didn't want to hold the weapon ever again. But of course she hadn't thrown it away.

Had it only been a couple of weeks since she'd lived here? The thought amazed her. Her mother had no boyfriend at the moment, unless she'd found a new one recently. So she was probably asleep, passed out from too much wine.

Markla left the kitchen and entered the living room. To her right was an arched doorway that led to a hall. If she turned one way down the hall, she'd come to Tommi's room. If she went the other way, she'd end up in her mother's room. In the middle of the hall was a door that led to the home's only bathroom.

Her mind flooded with memories, and they hit her like a brick wall, and she had a quick vision of killing Sharli in her sleep. This had been a common fantasy when she'd been younger, but she had no intention of doing it now because what would happen to Tommi? Also, it was probably wrong to kill her own mother, so there was that, too—and she laughed to herself. Don't kill your mom, she thought. *Don't cut her miserable throat and watch her gag and bleed to death! Don't do it, Markla!*

Once again, she laughed to herself, and considered how twisted her mind really was. But it wasn't going to happen—not unless Mom woke up. And she laughed yet again.

She walked through the living room to a staircase that led upstairs. Like everything else in the house, the stairs were creaky, but she knew how to step on them and they hardly made a sound. The upstairs was a partially finished attic with raw beams across a pointed ceiling, an unfinished wooden floor, and two narrow dormers with windows. These dormers were significant, since they faced the back of the house and allowed someone to open a window and step onto the roof. There was a crooked tree growing close to the building that would allow someone to go from the roof to the ground, and Markla had used this route a few times. This had been her room.

There was also a window at each end of the room, and a skylight that tended to leak when it rained. On the upside, the windows and skylight combined to make this the brightest room in the house. It was still dark now, but there was more pale light up here than downstairs. It was just as she'd left it, the one room in the house that was not cluttered. There was a rug that looked like a patchwork of bright colors on the rough wooden floor, and some shelves made from pine. There was a bed, big enough for one—and there was someone sleeping in it! Markla caught her breath. It was Tommi.

She glanced around, and saw that none of his belongings were here. He hadn't moved up here, he was just sleeping in her bed. For an instant, she felt like crying, but she didn't. He's probably just trying to get farther away from Mom, she thought. *It probably has nothing to do with missing me.*

There was a dresser against the wall, and she opened the top drawer and rummaged around, looking for the radio. She found it—and then she frowned. There were two radios in the drawer, and they were identical. They were the kind used by 20 Eyes.

She shoved one of the radios into her knapsack and then glanced at Tommi. Her heart skipped a beat. His eyes were open, shining like the eyes of an owl.

He was staring right at her. He sat up in the bed and whispered, "Markla, you're here."

She whispered back, "Yeah, but only for a minute. I wanted to get my radio. And I see you have one, too."

"Dru gave it to me."

Right—Dru.

"I told you not to join the group, Tommi. There are lots of things you don't know about them."

"Like what? I want to fight the toads."

She hesitated. Where had she heard this kind of talk before? She felt sick but she moved closer to the bed and said, "It's a violent group, and they have no loyalty to each other." Then she blurted, "Have you gone through your test yet?"

"No. But soon."

"Okay, so you haven't met many of them."

"Just Dru and Stono—and you."

Now a wave of hope rippled through her. His connections to 20 Eyes were severed.

"I see," she said. "Well, Stono was arrested last night, and Dru is dead. And I quit the group."

Tommy's mouth dropped open. "What happened? How? Did they go on a raid?"

Markla hesitated. "No," she said. "Stono tried to kill my friend, and the knobbers got him. Dru tried to kill me."

"What?" Tommi said, and he gasped.

"He thought I might talk and identify him—even though I never said a word and never would… Those are the kind of people they are. Not real friends. Not people you can count on." She put her hands on his shoulders. He seemed to be in a daze. "I have to go," she said. "I hate the toads but 20 Eyes isn't the answer. I can't tell you what to do anymore—but try to be smart, okay? I'll miss you."

"Where are you going? I want to go with you."

"You can't. Maybe someday you can visit me. I'll try to contact you if I can."

"I don't want you to go."

She smiled. "I know, but everyone makes choices, Tommi, and some of mine weren't so good. Try to do better than me—please."

She turned and headed for the stairs. But then he whispered in a fierce voice.

"Markla!"

"What?"

"I love you."

She paused and stared at him through the darkness. "I love you, too," she said. Then she blinked back a few tears and hurried down the steps.

She had to get out of here quick—but as she reached the bottom of the stairs, she heard the door to her mother's bedroom open. Markla stopped short and pressed herself against the wall of the stairwell. Had her mother heard them talking? Markla felt her heart pounding—she hadn't asked Tommi if Sharli was alone. It's true her mom had no real boyfriend at the moment but there were several different guys who could be with her.

But no. Apparently, Sharli was alone, and she was stumbling into the bathroom. Markla breathed a sigh of relief. Sharli stumbling around was fairly typical—and that's why Markla had never had a sip of alcohol. She'd never done any kind of mind-altering drug, either. It was one of the few things about Sharli that Markla appreciated; she'd shown Markla what she did not want to be.

For a moment, Markla had another violent fantasy involving her mom, and while she wasn't serious about carrying it out, she was a little more serious than she'd been with her last fantasy. Her conversation with Tommi had filled her with emotion, and hearing her mother bumbling around filled her with rage. She hated to leave Tommi alone with his mom—but then again, he was too young to live on his own.

What she really needs is some kind of help, Markla thought. But Markla also knew she wasn't the one to do it. Forgiveness wasn't her strongpoint, especially when it came to her mother. *There's only way to cure someone like Sharli—and I've committed enough atrocities for one day.*

Markla shook her head. I'm so deranged, she thought. *I'm the one who needs help.*

She slipped through the back door of the house. She paused and listened, and all she heard was a chorus of crickets and a breeze rustling through the trees, and she wondered if Narna was as pretty at night as Sparkla.

Pepper was now sitting near the back steps where he'd been joined by Raz, a precocious gray female Markla had found wandering in the woods a few years ago. Markla had guessed the cat had been abandoned, and she'd always been Markla's favorite.

Markla bent down and petted Raz. "Thanks for coming out to see me off," Markla whispered. "Watch over Tommi, okay? He thinks he's watching over you, ha."

Raz looked up at her and purred. Markla found her flyboard and took off.

Chapter 44

Rune didn't sleep much. He spent the night staring into the darkness and imagining scary possibilities. Would Markla see Dru again? If he could have one wish come true, it would be to see Markla tomorrow and she would be safe.

He thought about the radio Blog had given him, and it was so tempting to call her—channel 25, that's the one she was monitoring. But what if someone in 20 Eyes heard the call, or someone in the government? What if his Dad heard it? It was too risky. Be patient, he thought. *I'll see her soon!*

Finally, the birds were singing, and a sliver of daybreak was slicing through the blinds, and Blog was clomping through the front door. Rune fumbled with his GoBug and once again checked the news streams, but he saw nothing concerning last night and no news of Markla being captured. He breathed a sigh of relief and leaped out of bed.

Blog had told Rune to stay in the house until Dru was arrested, but that wasn't part of Rune's plan. Living in fear of Dru wasn't an option—and the prison was close to where he planned to meet Markla, so that's where he was going. He ate his oatmeal and strawberries the same as always, and then he jumped on his flyboard. Soon enough he was at the Dream Center.

As he walked into the building, he was tingling with the thought of being a spy. How strange that working with his father could make him so excited; he could hardly wait to start snooping around. Then he saw Diana, and he felt his muscles tighten. She was standing in the small galley-style kitchen near the classroom, sipping hot tea. Her eyes were red and weary, and her face was pale, and she seemed to be staring into space. But when she saw Rune her eyes opened wide, and some color came into her cheeks, and she smiled.

"Rune! Are you all right? I heard 20 Eyes tried to kill your father!"

Rune smiled back at her, and he thought about his mission. "Yeah, they missed," he said. "But it wasn't in the news. Who told you?"

"Aldo," she said, practically spitting his name. "But how did you get here? You need to be careful. Do you want a cookie?"

"No, thanks."

"Did you eat breakfast? You should eat something. You look tired, too."

"I ate. I didn't sleep much."

"I'm not surprised. I didn't sleep much, either. By the way, Blog wasn't the only one attacked last night. Someone in 20 Eyes was also killed."

Rune froze. "Who?"

"No, not her," Diana said, obviously annoyed. "It was someone else, someone the troopers have been tracking for a while. But he was never arrested. As far as the media knows, he was just another citizen—until they dig up more facts."

Now Rune thought of Dru—and then Blog.

"How did he die?"

"Someone stabbed him in the chest, or at least that's what Aldo said. He was in here early this morning, working on MindCore, but then he left in a huff. I'm not sure why, and I didn't ask."

Blog didn't kill Dru, Rune thought. Blog had a gun, and knife wounds create lots of blood and potential evidence. But then again, maybe he wanted to make it look like a 20 Eyes dispute. Or maybe it had been Markla.

This idea hit Rune hard. He imagined Dru attacking her, and was she all right? *She might need help!*

Diana banged her teacup down on the counter. "Why do you care so much about that awful girl? You could do a lot better. But I suppose you'll have to, since she'll be killed or captured soon."

Rune felt a surge of anger—but he stayed calm and held his tongue. I need to get information, he thought. *Don't argue!*

"I don't care about Markla," he said. "I used to like her but now I don't."

"Really?" She gave him a sharp look but then seemed to relax. "I'm glad to hear that, Rune. What made you change your mind?"

"I thought about the things she did, and the way she acted during the nightmare, and then I saw her differently."

Diana paused and then nodded with approval. "Seeing people for who they are is part of growing up. Falling for the wrong person can change someone's life in a terrible way. I know because I did it, and then years later my son did it."

"I'm sorry to hear that."

"It's just the way it happened, and so I hate to see other people go down the same road—especially someone as young as you."

Rune took a cookie from a box on the counter and spoke in a casual tone. "So, what is MindCore? You mentioned Aldo was working on it."

"MindCore is amazing," she said, and she seemed happy to change the subject. "It uses LiveDream technology but it's much more powerful. Right now, we feed a dreamshell into someone's mind, and that's where the LiveDream happens—inside that person's mind. We can feed the same dreamshell to multiple people at once, and we can put in placeholders that will cause that dream to be different for each person—and we can guide the dream, too. But everybody is experiencing the dream inside their own consciousness. There's no interactive connection between multiple people using the same LiveDream.

"With MindCore, we feed the dream into your consciousness, but then we send your thoughts about the dream into an artificial dreamspace—an artificial consciousness that can be connected to an unlimited number of people—and then we feed those collective thoughts back into each individual consciousness. So everyone connected to MindCore not only sees the same dream, but they see each other in the dream. You're all in the same dream together. You can experience a dream adventure with people you know."

Rune's eyebrows went up. "That's incredible. It sounds like fun, too."

"That part is fun," she said. "But it does other things, too. The same technology that brings part of your consciousness into the artificial dreamspace can bring more than just the part necessary for dreams. It can bring a lot of other stuff into that space, too, and people can sift through those things and view them. It can dig up thoughts you forgot about—or wanted to forget. It can regurgitate the worst memories you ever had, and it can let other people view them—and it can put those memories on a loop. People can be subjected to the most stressful moments they can remember, over and over again. It could be used as a brutal interrogation tool, or maybe misused."

Rune grimaced. Then he said, "What about good memories?"

"It can find those, too. The search feature isn't perfect yet but it can be done, and MindCore can cause a person to relive any happy experience. But keep in mind, the human brain doesn't record memories like a machine; it doesn't assign them all equal importance. If something had a bigger impact on you, it has a much greater chance of being remembered. Also, your memory isn't 'picture-perfect' like a machine; people often remember what they want to believe. So if your memory of something is better or worse than what actually happened, that's what you'll see using MindCore."

Rune thought about his mom and her LiveDream addiction, and he wondered what memories she would choose to relive over and over again, and how they would appear to her—better or worse. And what about Blog, or Markla? What sort of secrets would it show about each of them, if any?

"Can it load standard LiveDream shells?" Rune said. "I'd like to try it sometime."

"Yes, it can run those. Maybe later today we can experiment with it."

Rune's eyes lit up. "Really? That would be so great. Are you sure Aldo won't mind?"

"I'm sure he *will* mind—but I won't mind. And Dimitri and Janna won't mind, either."

They were both walking through the door. Dimitri had a goofy grin on his face, as usual. Janna looked more serious and glamorous but she was still smiling.

"What won't we mind?" Dimitri said. "Naked mud wrestling?"

"No," Janna said. "I would definitely mind that. I don't get muddy."

Dimitri laughed, and Rune smiled a little. Then Rune told them about MindCore, and naturally they wanted to try it.

"Later," Diana said. "First we need to create some LiveDreams. Here are your assignments. Before we use MindCore, you're going to write about 20 Eyes."

Rune felt a jolt, and he narrowed his eyes. Obviously, this was not another innocuous project about education.

Janna frowned. "What are we supposed to say?" she said. "I don't know much about that group—most good people don't."

"You don't need to know much," Diana said. "We want something general aimed at streams that are popular with teenagers. We want to make viewers feel rage about the damage the group has done, and we want people to not be fooled by their propaganda—because once someone joins the group, it's too late. They can never be saved." Then she glanced at Rune and said, "Here are a few possible ideas."

For an instant, Rune felt like everyone was staring at him, and his face felt hot. I need to stop being paranoid, he thought. *They don't know what's on my mind!* Then a series of storyboards with dialogue and character descriptions appeared on the dream station screen. Without another word, Rune started on his LiveDream. He didn't feel like talking; he wanted to make a LiveDream, and he wanted it to be the best one in the room.

His dream wasn't like Dimitri or Janna's. It wasn't just a few apathetic characters followed by generic images of death and destruction. Rune's LiveDream told a story using a series of fast images interspersed with dialogue. It showed two young people unhappy with their world and looking to change it—and they joined 20 Eyes. Then there was death, and there was destruction, and they were responsible. There was guilt and a sense of betrayal. There was the horror of being naïve, and when he watched the final version he shivered because it had almost happened to him. *I was almost in this dream.*

Diana loved it, and Dimitri sucked in his breath when he saw it. Janna closed her eyes and said, "Very real—too real." Dimitri and Janna were still working on their LiveDreams when Diana said, "So, does everyone want to try MindCore?"

Of course they did, and now Rune relaxed and had a giddy feeling. His LiveDream had been a success, and on his very first day as a secret agent, he was going to get some major information. His dad was going to be impressed.

Using their GoBugs, Diana connected everyone to a console, and then to the artificial dreamspace she called a "dream tank." Then she loaded a LiveDream—and in an instant, they were together on top of a mountain overlooking a breezy ocean. Rune's hair was blowing in the wind, and the waves were crashing against the rocky shore below, and in every other direction there was only lush forest as far as the eye could see. They were all together, and it felt very real, and they stared at each other in disbelief.

"We're all here," Dimitri said.

"This is incredible," Janna said. She reached out her hand and touched Rune's arm. "You feel totally real. We can definitely interact."

"I'm real, too!" Dimitri said, and he held his hand out toward Janna. She shrugged and touched it, and he grinned. "What other dreamshells do we have?" he said with a laugh. "I doubt too many people will want to live in the real world anymore."

There's some truth in his words, Rune thought. He envisioned a day when people would park their bodies for long stretches of time and LiveDream together in fantastic settings while the world went on around them.

They experimented a bit but Rune kept watching the clock—and he kept wondering about Markla. He kept searching the news streams on his GoBug, and then Dru's face was in front of his eyes—and yes, he'd been murdered. But as Diana had said, he was not named as a person in 20 Eyes. It was being investigated as a murder with "no clear motive." Well, he wasn't a very nice guy, Rune thought. *Maybe that was motive enough.*

Now Rune felt even more anxious, like he was on the edge of a cliff. Meanwhile, Diana left the room to do something else, and Janna looked through some dreamshells. She wanted to guide a dream for two people at once, and she'd found one involving race cars.

"Come on," she said. "Rune, you and Dimitri can race. I'll guide."

Rune looked at the clock and once again thought about Markla. But his day here wasn't over yet, and she wouldn't be at the rendezvous point yet, and maybe this would help pass the time. So he and Dimitri connected their GoBugs to the MindCore stream, and Rune instantly found himself in a blaring red hover-car shaped like a rocket, right beside another car manned by Dimitri. Dimitri's car was emerald green, and he was laughing and making boasts, and then a light flashed and Rune hit the accelerator. It was a guided dream, so Janna could make anything happen—and Dimitri got off to a fast start and blazed ahead of Rune. Rune gritted his teeth and kept his foot on the floor as he swung the car into a tight turn. Sure, he had other stuff on his mind, but he still didn't want Dimitri to beat him. He pulled to within a hair of Dimitri, and they were side by side again, and then they roared out of the turn and headed down the straightaway. Rune snarled at the sight of the glowing finish line—and then he grimaced because it looked like Dimitri's car was a bit faster, and Dimitri was going to win. But then a boulder fell from the sky and landed on the hood of Dimitri's car.

It was completely absurd, but Dimitri's car swerved and smashed into a guardrail. Then the car spun around, shot across the track, crashed into an opposite rail and exploded. Rune raced past the wreck and breezed across the finish line. Game over.

Dimitri swore while Janna laughed hysterically. Then Dimitri staggered out of the car, and his body was black and smoky like a piece of burnt toast, and he swore again. Apparently, there was no pain because Janna had not made the burns painful—at least not physically. Dimitri left the dream and ran over to her.

"Not funny," he said. "That wasn't funny."

"I thought it was hilarious. You win, Rune!"

Rune left the dream, though he was still hooked into MindCore and ready for the next one. He gave a short laugh. It had been funny, but a little cruel, too—and Rune's heart went out to Dimitri a bit. Dimitri really liked Janna, and he almost looked like he was going to cry.

While Rune was watching Dimitri, he felt something strange

inside his head. It wasn't painful; it was merely odd. It felt like an itch inside his brain.

"Hey, what's going on?" Rune said.

He heard no sound.

"Hey, what's happening?"

Rune got an inkling he should disconnect himself, but he didn't because he was curious and it seemed harmless enough. Dimitri and Janna were using their GoBugs, staring at something synced to MindCore. At first, they were giggling—but then they stopped, and they were watching something in silence. And then their eyes were wide, and their mouths were hanging open.

Suddenly, Rune knew something was wrong. He ended the connection. Janna and Dimitri were staring at him, but they still said nothing. And the silence seemed ominous.

"What's going on?" Rune said.

Dimitri glanced at Janna. "That's amazing. There's no way I'm going back in there."

"What happened?" Rune said. "What is it?"

Janna's eyes were tearing up. "Rune, how could you?" she said. Then she turned and ran from the room.

Rune looked at Dimitri. "What did you see?" he said. When Dimitri didn't respond, Rune asked again in a louder voice. *"What did you see?"*

Dimitri hesitated. "Rune, she didn't do it on purpose. She was fooling around, and somehow MindCore showed memories of you and Markla. They were…things you'd probably want to keep private. And then you two were talking about meeting today, near a tree by a stream—and then you disconnected it."

Rune raced over to the console but there was nothing there—until he noticed one of the settings and realized it had brought more than his thoughts from the LiveDream into the dream tank. He felt a cold chill go through his body. Diana had mentioned

MindCore could do this but she hadn't demonstrated it, and was it really that easy?

He cursed to himself, and then he was filled with anger, like he'd been violated in a perverse way. But he didn't have time to worry about it.

"I've got to go," Rune said.

"Rune, wait!"

"What?"

Dimitri hesitated again. Then he shrugged and said, "Be careful. And good luck."

"Thanks."

Chapter 45

Rune's heart was pounding as he rode his flyboard through the main gate of the prison and down the gravel path leading through the woods and then to the street. Don't panic, he thought. *Stay calm!*

He didn't want to head right for the forest and make it obvious he was going somewhere other than home. So when he reached the main street, he followed it for a few seconds. Then he glanced around, and seeing no one, he veered off into the woods.

But wait! His GoBug was still active, so he decided to stop and pull the power crystal. As he did, he saw a call coming in from Dimitri—and his instincts told him to listen. Dimitri's voice filled his head.

"Rune, you're in trouble. Janna called the police."

Rune's jaw dropped. "What? Are you serious?"

"I tried to stop her! I told her the machine might not be accurate. I told her you were her friend—but she still did it."

Rune swore and shook his head. "All right... Thanks, Dimitri. I have to go."

He didn't wait to hear what else Dimitri had to say—he'd heard enough. He pulled out the power crystal and he was off, moving as fast as the flyboard could go. He cursed at himself for taking the longer decoy route. All that time wasted! He had to get to the rendezvous point as soon as possible.

But now he was unsure of the way. He'd thought it would be easy to retrace his steps from that day—but it wasn't. *All these trees look the same!* And he couldn't call out to her because someone might be looking for her, closing in.

He steered his board around a few trees and then a few more and then avoided some thorny plants—and he started feeling frantic. Where was he? Stay calm, he thought. *Find the tree line!*

And he did, bursting into the clearing near the prison. All right, he was back to a place he knew, and he remembered running through the grassy field that day and entering the woods right about...there. So he flew along the line to that place and then headed back into the forest, and he recalled how they'd covered a fair amount of ground before reaching the stream—yeah, the stream! If he found the stream and followed it, he'd come to the right place. Things were getting easier—but there wasn't much time. If only he could contact her! And suddenly he thought about the tiny radio his father had given him.

At this point it was worth the risk. He yanked it from his back pocket and set it to channel 25.

"Markla! Markla, are you there?"

He heard a sound, and he looked up. Two black hover ships were flying low over the trees. Why were they black? The police used white hover ships. Rune came to a quick stop and pressed himself behind a wide tree.

"Markla, are you listening?"

They're after her, he thought. Janna really had turned her in, and it was disgusting—but now he was off again, steering the board while shouting into the radio. He knew she'd hear those ships, and she would run. So they'd still have to catch her in the woods—and she had a flyboard, and she was quick and crafty.

"Markla, can you hear me?"

Suddenly, he heard her voice and his heart jumped.

"Rune, is that you?"

"Markla, run! They know about us! They used a device to read my mind!"

"Rune, what are you saying? Go to our channel."

"No, run!" But then he was frantically switching the channel to—what? Channel two—that's right! And then he was shouting the same message.

"All right," she said. "I'll go."

"Good! I'm on my way."

"What? No—don't come here. You'll get caught, too!"

"Just run! I'll find you."

"Rune—no!"

He snapped off the radio and tore through the forest.

He heard more noise from above and saw the black ships dropping down like spiders. They were close to where he was and his heart sank. They were all around—but at least now she'd be moving, not sitting by a tree. He could help her. But then he heard the roaring hover-bikes, and shots being fired, and he realized they might actually kill her. Markla could be dead right now, and the thought made him sick—but then he saw her, moving fast on her board with her black hair flying. She was swerving through the forest. He angled his flyboard through some dense undergrowth and suddenly he wasn't far behind.

Then he saw the troopers and their hover-bikes, coming from up ahead and converging on all sides.

Markla spun the board around—a nice move—trying to double back. Rune did the same—no good. The troopers were everywhere, and two shots whizzed past Rune's ear. Then he looked at Markla, and she looked at him, and for one instant the world seemed frozen. For one instant, they were alone. And then something struck Markla in the chest and she tumbled from the board.

"Markla!"

Rune leaped from his board and ran to her. The hover-bikes were pulling up all around. Troopers were aiming their guns at him and jumping from their bikes. Markla was lying in some weeds.

Rune slid down next to her—and her eyes fluttered open, and a wave of relief washed over him. She was alive! She'd once again been shot with a rubber bullet. She seemed groggy, but she was okay.

He cradled her head in his arms, and she looked up at him.

"Rune, I told you to stay away. Why did you come?"

"Because I love you."

She laughed. "I love you, too," she said. "I love you a lot."

Then someone shouted, "Put your hands in the air!"

Rune glared at the ring of troopers. He didn't put his hands up—he didn't move at all. Then one of the troopers pulled out a stun gun. Rune felt a jolt, and everything went black.

Chapter 46

Markla's eyes were closed while chaos drifted through her mind. She recalled being in the woods, and Rune was on the radio, and police were all around. Then she was down, and Rune was there, and he was shot with a stun gun, and they were grabbing her, and she was lashing out with her fists, and they were beating her and forcing her face into the hard ground. Her hands were cuffed behind her back—and there was a jolt of electricity, and then nothing. But now she smiled because there was one more thing, one more memory coming through the brutal haze, and it was brighter than the rest.

Rune said he loved me. Is it true?

She opened her eyes. She was lying on a metal bed inside a prison cell, but this cell had no bars. This cell was narrow and smothering with dark gray walls, a thick wooden door, and no windows—except for a window built into the door, but it had a sliding metal cover that was closed. There was a slot near the bottom of the door but it was closed, too.

She was wearing the same clothes she'd worn in the woods. So no yellow jumpsuit yet. Well, that was good because she hated that putrid shade of yellow. She moved a bit and groaned because every part of her ached. But she stood up, anyway, and saw a metal toilet and a tiny sink. There was also a mirror, and this surprised her. They want me to see how terrible I look, she thought. She glanced in the mirror and saw her face was red and puffy in a few places. There was a crimson bruise on one swollen cheek, and her lower lip was bloody—but her teeth and eyes were fine. She lifted her shirt and saw a deep purple splotch on her upper ribs where she'd been hit by a projectile. It was sore and painful to the touch but she knew nothing was broken. All in all, the toads hadn't done much damage. She'd endured worse beatings, for sure.

She sat back down on the bed and frowned. Of course her dagger was gone, and that was tragic because how was she going to kill herself? She sighed. Did she really want to do that? Maybe, but maybe not. She clamped her teeth together and scowled. If she did die, she wasn't going to die alone. She was going to take as many of the toads with her as she could.

She laughed to herself and shook her head. *When did I become so murderous? Markla, get a grip!* But really, she'd had violent thoughts her whole life. She'd just hidden the worst of them. She'd never wanted anyone to know about the raging battlefield inside her head—except for Rune. For some reason, she'd wanted him to know. Maybe that's what love is, she thought. *Letting someone know your scariest thoughts and hoping they'll still want you around.*

There was a clanking noise, and the window in the door slid open. She saw a man with a face like a weasel.

"Don't get up," he said. "Stay away from the door."

The door opened, and now there was a woman with two men behind her. One of them was the weasel-faced guy, while the other one looked like a generic thug. They both had stun sticks and clubs on their belts while the woman was unarmed. Her hair was perfect and her expression was blank.

"Hello, Markla," she said. "I know your history, so don't do anything stupid. If you try anything, we won't kill you. But we'll hurt you more than you can believe, do you understand?"

Markla shrugged but said nothing. She had no intention of doing anything "stupid"—but they were the stupid ones to believe her greatest fear was physical pain. It wasn't. Then Aldo appeared behind the other three, and it was comical watching him maneuver his way to the front.

Markla almost laughed. Despite all her bruises and injuries, and despite her situation as a captive about to be tortured, she thought the scene was hilarious. *All these people for me?* Not only were they heavily armed, but they were standing back behind the doorframe like she was the most dangerous creature in the world. She wondered if this was how an animal in a cage viewed its captors—with a combination of amusement and disgust.

Meanwhile, Aldo was studying her through his InfoLenses. "So, Markla, how do you like your new surroundings?"

She said nothing. But the toad kept talking.

"You're not in the prison, Markla. There are too many rules in there. You're in the Dream Center. We're going to do some experiments on you."

Instantly, she felt a shiver of fear, followed by a seething rage. But she still showed no expression.

Aldo gave a smug chuckle. "You don't seem to have much to say, but I can gauge your mood by certain biological reactions that are readable with my InfoLenses. You're scared and furious—and it doesn't matter because you can't change anything." Then he sneered and said, "What's your fascination with Rune, anyway? Is he so beautiful that nothing else matters? Take a good look at yourself, Markla. You're nothing special. You're like a dirty little animal, and he'll leave you when he finds someone prettier—maybe a nice girl who hasn't stabbed anyone to death." He paused and seemed to force a smile onto his face. "We're going to learn a lot from you, and then we're going to tear your mind apart. So get ready to tell me about Rune's involvement with 20 Eyes. Get ready to tell me secrets you never wanted anyone to know."

Markla stared at the wall and tried to push the smoldering thoughts to the back of her mind. When she finally spoke, her voice was low, almost a whisper. "I don't care what happens to me," she said. "But if you hurt Rune, I'll kill you."

Aldo laughed again. "Rune, Rune, Rune—love is so pathetic.

You'd do anything for Rune, wouldn't you? But you have no control over what's going to happen—none. You'll be helpless against MindCore, Markla, and no one will care." He turned to the others. "Bring her to Room B. I want her awake, so if she resists, don't stun her. Do what you need to do but get her there in one piece."

Markla was still sitting on the bunk as the two men squeezed into the room. She stood up, and they shackled her wrists and led her away. She didn't resist at all. Not yet.

Chapter 47

Aldo stopped in his office to get some cookies. As he reached into a desk drawer, he found himself thinking about Diana—but this was normal, since he was often thinking about Diana. Then suddenly she was storming into the room.

His heart started racing. She looked tired and pretty and vulnerable, like a broken flower, and he couldn't deny it appealed to him. But her eyes were hot with anger.

"Aldo, why is Rune here?"

Stay calm, Aldo thought. *Stay in control!*

He bit into an oatmeal cookie. "Why wouldn't he be here?" he said, keeping his tone casual. "He was aiding a member of 20 Eyes, and we know about it because of you. You should be thrilled he was arrested."

"Not because of me!" she snapped. "Because of a student playing with MindCore. You're deliberately trying to hurt me. It wasn't my fault!"

"I don't know what you're talking about. Why do you make it sound like a bad thing? No one ever hated 20 Eyes more than you."

"I don't care about Markla! But Rune's only guilty of falling in love with her."

"Love?" Aldo stopped chewing. "What is love, Diana? It's a mirage. It's a thing that breeds disappointment."

"This isn't about what you feel—or what I don't feel. Let him go."

"He's a criminal, and it's not my decision. Besides, Rune won't be harmed—unless, of course, true love turns out to be elusive and agonizing."

"So this is who you are, Aldo—a bitter little man who's going to get revenge against me by torturing a kid."

"What?" Aldo's face turned red. "Do you really believe

that's true? I think you overestimate your importance; I'm not bitter at all!"

"I hardly find this endearing."

"Well, you weren't too endeared anyway, were you?" he spat, and instantly regretted his bitter tone. But he still couldn't hide his smugness when he said, "Don't worry about it, Diana. This is all about testing a new technology. If this happens to prove how fragile love can be that will just be a bonus. Where are you going?"

She was turning away. "I don't want to watch."

"Wait!" he said, and now he was sputtering. "This is a great moment for MindCore. Don't you want to be part of it?"

She stared at him and swore. "Are you really asking me that question? Are you that out of touch with reality? You spend too much time playing with your LiveDreams, Aldo. If Rune gets hurt, I'll never forgive you. You disgust me!"

She left the room, and Aldo gulped some air—he was having trouble breathing. *Disgust?* How could she walk out on him like this? *Why doesn't she love me?* He blinked back a few tears. I can record it, he thought. *I can record it, and she can watch it later—whether she wants to or not!* Then he heard a beep on his GoBug. He listened for an instant and watched an image in front of his watery eyes. On a wall screen, a two-dimensional version of the same image appeared.

Blog Roko was walking into the Dream Center.

For an instant, Aldo felt a jolt of fear. But then he gave an angry snort and muttered, "He's a caveman, and there are no more caves." Then he frowned, because the caveman might still do something crazy. Aldo switched his thoughts to a secure mindstream and barked a few orders.

He swore and tossed the bag of cookies into a trash can.

Chapter 48

Rune sat up and looked around. What was going on? He was in a dingy cell, and he was groggy, and he was alone. Also, his radio was gone. He banged his fist down on the hard bunk.

Did his father know he was here? Maybe—but then again, the people who'd attacked him had not looked like regular police. It was possible no one knew he was here, and he felt his stomach quake. Then he heard a clanging noise, and the heavy door swung open, and there was Aldo.

Aldo seemed smug as he walked into the cell. There was a big man behind him, but he stayed outside. Aldo was wearing his white lab coat along with his usual InfoLenses, and he looked exceptionally bug-like.

"Hello, Rune," he said. "I hear you've been consorting with an enemy of the state—or did you just like her a lot? Falling in love with the wrong girl can be tragic. But maybe they're all wrong in the end."

Rune said nothing.

Aldo shrugged. "I'm guessing your involvement with 20 Eyes was minimal but it doesn't matter. I need to test MindCore, and I need to accomplish a few other things, and you and Markla are going to help."

At the mention of Markla, Rune's heart leaped. "Where is she?" he said.

"Don't worry, you'll see her soon. But she's not in a good mood."

"What did you do to her?"

"Nothing yet," Aldo said with a tight smile. "But you should be careful with that girl, Rune. She's emotionally disturbed, and she murdered Dru Nava last night. Also, she's a bit grubby and dirty-looking, don't you think? I'm sure a popular kid like you could do better."

Rune gave Aldo a blank look. What was he talking about? And had Markla killed Dru?

"Anyway," Aldo said, "I thought you might be getting lonely. So we've got someone to share your cell." Then Aldo stepped back out into the hall. He motioned with his head—and two huge men brought Blog Roko into the cell.

Rune's mouth dropped open.

Obviously, Blog had been in a fight. He was barely conscious, and the two men tossed him down onto the hard bunk and left. Then Aldo nodded his head and the door slammed shut. But Rune heard Aldo say, "Don't get too comfortable. We'll be back."

There was silence.

Rune rushed to his father's side. He saw the crater-like wound on Blog's head, like his skull had been smashed with an iron pipe. His face was also battered and bloody, and one of his eyes was purple like a plum and swollen shut, and for an instant Rune felt like he couldn't breathe. For the second time in a week, Rune was shocked by his father's mortality—but he knew he had to be strong. *Stay calm!*

"Dad, are you all right? Say something!"

He grabbed Blog's shoulder and shook him a bit.

"Dad!"

Blog's one good eye opened. He spoke in a whisper.

"Rune, is that you? Hang on. Help is coming."

"What?"

"There isn't much time—not for me."

"That's not true! You need a doctor."

Blog managed to shake his head a bit. "This isn't the way I wanted to go out, Rune. But you'll be fine."

"You're not going anywhere! And I won't be fine."

Blog reached out and grabbed Rune's hand, and his grip was firm. "Stop talking and listen," Blog said. "I've always said you weren't tough enough or strong enough—but it's not true, and it never was. You've always been your own man. Stay that way."

"Dad, you're going to be all right."

"No, I'm not. But you'll know what to do. You'll know it when you see it."

"I'm going to get you out of here!"

Blog shook his head again. "Tell your mother I love her—and I love you, too. I'm proud of you." Then he grunted, and his head rolled back a bit, and he stared at the ceiling. Rune was looking right into his one good eye when the light went out.

"Dad... Dad?" Rune shook him. "No!" he said. "No!" Then he shook him some more—and then he slumped down to the hard stone floor. Rune put his head in his hands and sobbed.

At first, his mind was empty. But then suddenly it was a storm of emotion—sorrow, regret, and rage. He threw back his head and screamed, and he wanted his scream to shake the building. He never should've taken the job at the Dream Prison, and he should've left Markla alone, and he never should've gotten so involved... This is all my fault, he thought. *This is all my fault!*

He clenched a fist and slammed it down on the floor. He felt cold, like a block of ice, and everything seemed hazy and far away. It seemed like a long time passed.

Finally, the door opened, and a doctor appeared. Rune stayed on the floor and watched in silence as the doctor reached a quick conclusion. Then two men came and carried Blog out, and Aldo returned. The cell door opened and he was standing there with his InfoLenses, looking once again like a scrawny insect. He frowned.

"I'm sorry that had to happen, Rune. We didn't want Blog to die, but he was causing lots of trouble, more than you know—or maybe you do know. Well, we're going to find out. You're going to help me test MindCore—you and Markla."

Aldo's words bounced around inside Rune's head for an instant—and then Rune leaped to his feet, and Aldo yelped, and Rune grabbed Aldo's throat.

"You'll pay for this!" Rune shouted. "You'll pay!"

Aldo gave a shout, and then he gagged, and two big men rushed into the cell. A flurry of fists slammed into Rune's head, and he was snarling and ignoring the blows, and there was a moment of blackness and Rune was tumbling back down to the floor.

Rune opened his eyes. The two men were standing over him, and Aldo was gasping and trying to compose himself.

"Where's Markla?" Rune said. "You better not hurt her. You can do what you want to me—but leave her alone."

Aldo took a deep breath and scowled. "Is that girl all you have to worry about?"

"Yeah—that's all."

Aldo sneered. "You'll see her soon, very soon. Comb your hair, Rune. She's just a dream away." Then he looked at the two men and said, "Bring him to Room C."

Rune rose to his feet and they led him out.

Chapter 49

Rune was strapped to a chair in a dimly lit room. He saw the silhouettes of two more chairs that were both empty, and a desk equipped with a console. The chair was comfortable but his arms, legs, neck, and torso were definitely immobilized by heavy restraints. There was a GoBug behind his left ear, and there was no sign of Markla. But he had a feeling he'd see her soon—in a MindCore nightmare.

Rune took a deep breath and braced himself. He'd experienced many LiveDream nightmares but this would be different. When people purchased nightmares, they rarely wanted to feel actual pain. It was the threat of pain that made the dream exciting—but when the pain arrived, it came in a weakened form. If someone drowned in a nightmare, it would only be a taste of the true experience. If someone was boiled in oil or burned alive, the nightmare would fade quickly. The game was over and it was time for another round.

This nightmare was no game, and it could be horrific. The pain and terror would be intense, and while he could refuse to play along, it was unlikely he'd be able to completely resist. It wasn't human nature to stand still and be consumed by an impending horror. It was human nature to fight and to hope. But still, it was only a dream. *Remember, it's just a dream!*

Aldo isn't going to break me, Rune thought. *No way!* Then he heard a chiming sound and everything went black.

Rune squeezed the arms of the chair and tried not to think about the worst possibilities—but his brain still flashed with the images of a dozen horrible deaths. Then the blackness vanished and he looked around, expecting to see something terrifying. But he did not.

Everything was still and quiet.

He was outdoors, and it was night. There was a moon in the sky, like a slice of reddish onion, and he was standing on a dark street lined with trees. There were only a few houses on the street, right near a stretch of dense and untended woods. A breeze was blowing, and he heard the rustle of leaves, and in front of him was a dilapidated little house that looked vaguely familiar. Hey, this was a street in Sparkla, and wasn't this Markla's house? He'd never been inside her house but he knew where her family lived. Even in the dark, he could see that the house was in desperate need of repair—and Rune knew what he was seeing was not a fabrication on Aldo's part. He knew Aldo had taken this image directly from Markla's mind. Aldo had invaded her memories, Rune thought. *I wonder if he'll do the same to me.*

Rune considered not moving because why should he? He might end up running and fighting and screaming but there was no reason to do it yet. Then he heard a scream from inside the house—and his heart skipped a beat. He knew it was Markla.

He dashed across the street to the house. He leaped up the broken front steps, yanked the front door open, and raced inside—and there she was, standing in a cluttered living room with her disheveled hair, flannel shirt, and a necklace made of pebbles. She was staring at him, yet her eyes seemed far away. He stopped short and stared back.

"Markla, are you all right?"

He resisted an urge to hug her; his instincts told him this was not the time. So instead he took a few steps and stood closer to her, less than an arm-length away.

"Rune, I'm fine," she said.

"But you screamed."

She shook her head. "No, I didn't. That was part of the dream." Then she paused and said, "I'm in a dream…with you?"

"Yes, we're in here together. This is MindCore; it can do

this. It can see your memories, too. That's how Janna saw that I was going to meet you, and then she reported it to the police. We were experimenting but I didn't know she was going to do that... I'm glad to see you."

Now he hugged her, and she hugged him back and said, "Ha, I told you to watch out for that toad."

"Yeah," Rune said with a little laugh. It was good to hear her sound like herself. "I should've listened. I was afraid you were going to think I turned you in."

"I didn't think that—but it doesn't matter. I would've forgiven you."

"You would? Why?"

"I've caused you so much trouble."

"I like being in trouble with you," he said. It was only a dream, yet her body felt so real pressed against him. But then she stopped returning his embrace. She pulled away and her gaze looked distant.

"Markla, what is it?"

She looked around with jumpy eyes. "This house," she said. "Aldo went through my memories. He pulled things out."

And now Rune saw that she was scared—more scared than he'd ever seen her. In fact, she seemed far more scared than she'd been in the nightmare he'd written.

"It'll be okay," Rune hissed. "It's only a dream. We can handle the pain. We'll do it together."

When she responded, she sounded distant and spoke in a whisper. "There are things worse than physical pain."

Rune had never seen Markla look so frightened or intimidated. What could be so bad about her memories? So far it was just a house, and hadn't she been living in it not too long ago? But this probably wasn't the house from last month or last year. This might be a version of the house from longer back, from a far away place in her mind—and Rune sensed this was true. What had happened here? Was it going to happen again?

He narrowed his eyes; he was ready for a fight.

He heard the sound of a door creaking in the nearby hallway, and then footsteps. He clenched his fist—and a man appeared. He was tall and bony with a slippery-looking ponytail hanging down his back. He wore old work clothes smeared with dark stains, like he'd been fixing something greasy. His eyes were rimmed with red.

In a flash, Markla's fear vanished and morphed into rage. Rune swore he could see it exploding inside of her as she pointed a finger.

"You!" she spat. "What are you doing in my dream? I'd kill you if I could."

He laughed. "Well, you didn't hurt me when you had the chance."

"I was six years old! How much of a chance did I have?"

"Maybe you'll get your chance now."

He smiled and unbuckled a heavy leather belt from around his waist. He folded it once, so it was even thicker. "If you don't shut your mouth, little girl, I'm going to teach you a lesson."

What was Markla thinking? It was hard to know as she scowled and deliberately stepped toward him. But she didn't get far. The belt lashed out and hit her in the face.

Rune felt a flash of anger, and he tried to rush toward the guy—but he couldn't move. His feet were stuck to the floor, and the guy hit Markla again and knocked her down. Rune guessed she was also frozen now, and the guy was beating her with gusto.

"Stop it!" Rune screamed.

The guy's face was red with rage as he swung the belt. "You little monster!" he said. "You never know when to shut up, do you? And where's my drink? Did you hide it? I'll teach you for real! We're going to do this whenever you need it. That's how it was, right?"

The guy uncurled the belt to its full length now, and the blows rained down. Markla was curled up a bit, trying to avoid the blows, but it was impossible. Markla was gasping, and Rune wondered if the pain was amplified in the dream, and he guessed it was. Markla was wearing a thin shirt, and the sound of the belt striking her was sickening.

Rune screamed again but there was no end in sight. The beating went on and on, and Rune had never been filled with more fury. Then finally it stopped—and a woman entered the room.

She was bigger than Markla, and Rune had never seen her before, but Markla obviously knew her.

"Mom," Markla said. "Make him stop!"

The woman was younger than Rune's mother, and he assumed this was the way she'd looked about ten years ago when Markla had been six. She was wearing a bathrobe, and she looked like she'd just rolled out of bed, and her bed had been outside in a pile of trash. She turned to the guy and said, "Rod, stop hitting her. I'll put her in the closet and she'll be fine."

A door on a nearby wall swung open, and Rune could see there was a closet there. But it was a small space, barely large enough to hold a child.

"No!" Markla said. "I don't want to go in there again." Then she said, "How could you? How could you put a little kid in there?"

"You're not that little."

"But I was! I was just a little kid! And I was so scared. And you didn't care! Why didn't you care about me?"

The woman sighed. "Always complaining, Markla. Always causing trouble… You need to learn how to behave. Now get in there before I give you a good beating myself." Then she looked at Rune. "Or maybe someone else will do it."

Rune felt his blood run cold. No, he thought. *That can't happen.*

But it did happen. Rune lurched forward, and with a sinking feeling he realized he had no control over his body in this dream—and now he was reaching down and picking up the belt.

"No!" he said. "No!"

He couldn't stop himself. As Markla looked up at him he swung the belt. It hit her cheek with a loud *splat!* He instantly felt sick to his stomach.

He let out a scream of anguish but swung the belt again—and then again and again. Pink and purple splotches appeared on Markla's face. She gasped as the blows landed, and Rune felt like his body would burst from rage. He tried to speak but only a strangled whisper came from his mouth, and now he began to strike her continuously, faster and faster and with more intensity. She grimaced and clenched her fists and turned her dark eyes toward him as tears streamed down her cheeks, and Rune knew they were tears of frustration. He felt the same way—and then he had a horrible thought. How would this change things between them? It was only a dream, but would the memories linger and destroy what was real? Rune now felt his own eyes swelling with tears. And then the beating stopped.

Rune's arm went limp, and the belt fell from his hand. He saw Markla relax, yet he felt only a small sense of relief. The damage has been done, he thought. But then he set his jaw and glared. *Don't give up! Maybe not!* He tensed his muscles, knowing that the next thing to happen could be even worse—and then the house was gone.

Suddenly, he was in a forest.

He vaguely considered how seamlessly a new dreamshell had been loaded. He blinked a few times and tried to adjust to the new setting while his eyes jumped around. Where was the new danger?

He knew this place. It was a sunny spot near a bubbling stream. It was the spot near the Dream Prison where they'd been arrested—and now he discovered he could not move. He struggled to raise his hands and realized he was secured to one of the trees by heavy straps. He grimaced and then realized he could still move his head, so he kept scanning the area—was Markla here?

Yes, she was. She was on the ground not far away, lying like a pile of crumpled clothing. It's a dream, he thought. *If she's dead, it's just a dream.* But it felt so real, and she was not dead. She was rising to her feet, and he winced as he saw her. Her face was swollen and bloody. Then he saw the dagger in her hand. She was coming toward him.

"Markla," he said. "This is a dream. I would never hurt you."

Her eyes smoldered with fury. "You're like everyone else," she said. "You hurt me like everyone else."

Were these her words? Rune's mind turned furiously, and he realized his thoughts were his own—and MindCore did not seem capable of changing them. But could the dream trigger things deep in Markla's mind, some fears and insecurities she'd always had? Yes, of course it could. Maybe that was Aldo's game.

She was right in front of him now, holding the blade close to his throat.

"Look at my face, Rune," she hissed. "You let this happen. You made this happen!"

"No," Rune whispered. "It wasn't me."

"You never really loved me," she said. Then she started sobbing, and Rune felt his heart breaking.

"Markla, I do love you! This is just a dream. I'll always love you!"

"No!" she screamed, and she took a step backward. "You'll never love me! And why should you? This is all my fault, Rune! I caused all this to happen to you—I did it, and I hate myself! I can't be with you! I can't be with anyone!"

"That's not true!" Rune said. "I want to be with you, Markla—and I'd do it all again. Aldo's trying to manipulate us. He wants us to believe these lies!"

She stared at him in silence. Then she stopped crying, and she tossed away the dagger, and she wiped her eyes with her sleeve. "I know that, Rune," she said. "But what if some of it's true?"

"None of it is true! We can think our way out of this."

She was quiet once again. What was going through her mind? What would she believe?

Rune waited. And then he was yanked from the dream.

It was like being hit over the head. There was a jolt, and then a feeling like falling, and then blackness. For an instant, Rune was confused. *Is this a transition into another dreamshell?* But he knew it was not, and now the blackness was fading, and he felt dizzy, and everything was blurry—and then things came into focus, and he was back in the room where he'd started.

He was no longer strapped to the chair, and he was no longer in the dream. He was free.

He leaped to his feet and looked around. The room was still dark but he could see Diana's shadowy outline behind the desk, near the glowing console. She was watching him. Then he heard the noisy sound of gunfire, followed by some shouting. It was somewhere outside.

"Diana, what happened?" Rune said. "What's going on?"

"I stopped the dream," she said, and her voice was calm. "You need to go, Rune. Someone is attacking the Dream Prison, and the Dream Center. I set you free but you need to get out of here now. Please, listen to me."

"Where's Markla?"

"She's in the next room down the hall. I stopped the dream for her, too."

An explosion sounded, and the room shook. Rune started

to walk but felt dizzy—he put his hand out to grab the chair to steady himself. He also felt sick to his stomach.

"It's MindCore," Diana said. "It can have that effect on you. You'll be okay in a minute or so. It will affect Markla more, since she had more of her memories accessed."

"I need to find her."

"I know you do," she said. Then she paused and blurted, "Follow me! Hurry."

The lights came on and she ran to the door. Rune could see her face was streaked a bit. As she opened the door, he was shocked to see she was holding Markla's dagger.

She saw the alarm in his eyes. "Just a precaution," she said. "It's this way."

More sounds of gunfire crackled—were they coming from inside the building now? Was this the help Blog had promised? Or was it 20 Eyes—or maybe even another prison uprising?

They didn't go far. Diana stopped in front of a door and said, "She's in here."

Rune dashed into the room. He turned on the lights, and it was much like the room they'd just left. Markla was strapped to a chair. But her eyes were closed, and she wasn't moving. Rune raced to her.

"Markla!" he said, "Markla, talk to me! Wake up!"

He shook her, and her eyes fluttered open. Rune held his breath.

She looked dazed. "Rune," she said, but her face had no expression. Then she tried to move and discovered she was still strapped in. He saw a flash of panic in her eyes—but he put his hands on her shoulders and said, "It's okay! I'll get you out."

Then he was helping her to her feet—but she fell back down onto the chair.

She put her head in her hands. "Something's wrong."

"You'll be okay," Diana said. "You might need a few minutes."

"Where's Aldo?" Rune said.

Diana shook her head. "Revenge is a bad plan, Rune. Just go."

"I have to find him."

"Aldo didn't kill your father, Rune. Blog got himself killed, and if you're not smart, you'll get yourself killed, too. I don't want to see that."

"I'll be fine! I need to find him."

"You're not your father. You're a different person."

"I know I am! But the people attacking the prison—I think they're friends of his. Where's Aldo? Is he in the bunker?"

He could tell by her eyes that the answer was yes.

Meanwhile, Markla was still holding her head. Then there was a loud burst of gunfire, and an explosion, and two people ran past the doorway and down the hall.

"The bunker is sealed!" Diana said. "You can't get in."

"Maybe—maybe not. Where's my GoBug?"

She glanced at a nearby cabinet. Rune ransacked it, and there it was! He put it behind his ear. He also found some other things—things that had belonged to Blog, including his badge and a pair of handcuffs. He grabbed them both. Then he ran back to where Markla sat, and he reached down and took her hand.

"Markla, are you okay? How do you feel?"

"I'm dizzy. But nothing hurts."

"Do you remember what happened in the dream?"

She seemed to think about it—and then she looked up at him. What was she thinking? Rune held his breath.

"Don't worry, Rune," she said. Then she reached over with her other hand, and placed it on top of his, and she squeezed it. "I know what's real."

Rune felt a rush of warmth, and he breathed a sigh of relief. "Good!" he said. "But don't move! I'll be right back, do you hear me? I'll be back." He pulled himself away.

"Rune, wait!" Markla said. "Maybe Diana's right." Then she tried to get up and once again fell down onto the chair.

Rune shook his head. "Just wait here. Everything's going to be fine." Then he whirled and headed for the door—but Diana stepped in front of him.

"Rune, please!" she said. "Your father wouldn't want you to die."

"He wouldn't want me to run, either."

Rune raced around her and bolted down the hall.

Chapter 50

Markla blinked a few times but everything was blurry. Then suddenly her vision cleared, and how much time had passed? *I need to find Rune!*

She tried again to rise from the chair—and this time she did it. The dizziness and nausea were gone, and she felt a wave of relief. She scanned the room, looking for her backpack. She noticed Diana eyeing her with what seemed to be a combination of sympathy and suspicion.

"Thanks for helping us," Markla said. "I know you don't like me, Diana. But thanks."

Diana's stare seemed to soften a bit. "I don't like some of the things you've done, Markla, and I hope you don't cause Rune any more trouble—but that's unlikely, isn't it? Because he's crazy about you."

Markla felt a flush of warmth, and she distracted herself by tossing back her messy hair and grabbing her backpack from the floor. "I care about Rune," she said. "Is that so terrible? Maybe he cares about me, too."

Maybe he loves me. He said he did!

Diana sighed. "It's not terrible," she said. "I watched the dream, and I understand you better now. You've been through a lot, and you're still here. You're a tough girl, Markla. I suppose that's something I admire about you. I think that's something Rune admires, too."

Markla said nothing. She didn't have time to explain that she wasn't that tough, and that she questioned herself often, and that she suffered from panic and nightmares—and she'd cried about more than a few of her choices over the years. *I'm softer than you think, Diana.*

"I'm not like that," Markla said. Then she paused and added, "Not all the time. Hey, is that my dagger?"

"Yes," Diana said, and she held it out toward Markla.

Markla snatched it from her hand and attached it to her belt. "Thanks," she said. "Where's the bunker?"

"It's the heavy gray door down the hall." Then she paused and spoke in a shaky voice. "Rune shouldn't have gone. Aldo's dangerous, and he might do something terrible."

"He used my memories against me!" Markla said. "He tried to ruin everything."

"Be careful, Markla."

Markla didn't answer. She was moving fast

Chapter 51

Rune raced down the narrow hallway. He heard more shouts and gunfire from another part of the building. He also heard the whooshing roar of police hover-ships outside, but whose side were they on? Then he saw the door to the bunker. It was a common gray door set into the wall but Rune knew it was made of heavy steel and sealed shut. Using the GoBug, he loaded the security script he'd stolen from Aldo's office—and the door opened.

He saw a long stairway leading deep underground. He dashed down the steps and reached another door and used the GoBug to open that one, too. Now he was in a dimly lit hallway where he saw yet another door, and it was partially open. He listened for an instant and then burst inside.

He found himself in a sparsely furnished office, and on the wall were a series of lighted screens. Near the door was a metal desk equipped with a LiveDream console, and sitting behind the desk was Aldo. He was holding a gun.

Aldo's eyebrows shot upward as he fumbled with the weapon. He fired two wild shots.

Rune heard the shots strike the doorframe to his right. He moved to his left and hurled the handcuffs. They struck Aldo in the face.

Aldo swore, and in an instant Rune was there, grabbing at the weapon. They were on opposite sides of the desk, and the gun fired again, but Rune was holding Aldo's wrist. Aldo leaped to his feet, and they struggled. Rune had both hands on the gun now. Aldo was trying to punch Rune with his free hand but his blows were feeble. Then he lost his grip on the weapon and it flew across the room.

Aldo's jaw dropped. He grabbed a lamp from the desktop and swung it at Rune's head but Rune easily blocked the blow. Then Aldo scrambled toward the gun but Rune tackled him and they both tumbled to the floor with the gun out of reach. Aldo's InfoLenses fell from his face.

Aldo was smaller than Rune, and Rune could tell he was weak. They wrestled for an instant, and then Rune was on top of Aldo, pummeling his face with punches.

"You killed my father!" Rune said. "You tortured Markla!"

"No!" Aldo said. "We didn't mean to kill Blog—and that was just a dream with Markla. It was just a dream!"

Rune kept pounding him. "You wanted to hurt her!" he shouted. Then he wrapped his hands around Aldo's throat.

Aldo was gagging. He was turning crimson and purple. His eyes lit up with wild desperation—and then Rune caught sight of someone and he turned his head fast.

Markla was standing in the doorway. Her eyes were wide.

"Rune, are you all right?" she said.

Rune froze, and he stared down at Aldo's bulging eyeballs— and then he loosened his grip.

I'm not going to kill him! I'm not like that.

Rune took a deep breath and stood up. "I'm fine," he said. Then he looked down at the battered man and said, "Aldo, get up. You're under arrest."

Markla ran toward him. Rune picked up the gun and pointed it at Aldo, who was coughing and gagging. His nose looked broken and his face was bloody. Rune also retrieved the handcuffs.

Aldo struggled to his feet. He was breathing hard as Rune cuffed his wrists behind his back.

Aldo's face was red with fury. "You're a fool, Rune—you and your horrible girlfriend." He glanced at Markla with a look of disdain. "She'll turn on you eventually. No animal can be trusted—and no woman, either." Then he motioned with his head at the screens on the wall. "Besides, you're wasting your time. Your father's friends have lost."

Rune looked at the images on the wide screens and then at Markla—and his heart sank. It was true; the wrong people were winning. Through the fire and smoldering destruction, he could see the prison and Dream Center were being secured by regular government forces. Then there was another explosion outside and the screens went black. But he'd seen enough.

"Rune, we need to go," Markla said, and she tightened the straps on her backpack. "We need to get out of here now."

"Yes, go," Aldo said in a mocking tone. "But I'll see you two again—because your 'great love' won't save you. We can identify your faces, your DNA, your eye prints, your fingerprints, your brain wave patterns, and what can you do about it? Nothing! You'll end up in MindCore again, and you've got no power to stop it. The future always wins."

Rune took a few deep breaths. His fist itched to start punching Aldo again but he didn't. Instead, Rune stood up a little taller and eased his grip on the man.

"You're not the future," Rune said. "The future is going to be something better. And we're going to leave you here to see it."

Aldo smirked. Then he gasped and crashed against the desktop. Rune blinked and stared at Markla, who was standing there with a bloody dagger in her hand.

Rune's head started spinning. This is a dream, he thought. *She did not just do that! She did not!* But then he watched as she stabbed him again—a savage thrust into his back. This time she left the blade there.

Aldo gasped once more and dropped to his knees. His body quivered, and his handcuffs rattled, and then with a groan he toppled onto his stomach. His mouth moved but no words came out. His gaze rolled upward to stare at Markla—and she stared back at him, and her eyes were cold. But she didn't say a word. She just watched him die.

Rune's whole body felt numb. He looked at Markla but couldn't speak.

"Rune, I'm leaving," she said.

"I'm going with you!" he blurted.

There was a moment of silence. "Are you sure?" she said.

"Yes."

Markla didn't quite smile, but the icy rage vanished from her stare.

"I'd like that," she said. And now she did smile, just a little.

He stepped toward her, and they kissed. It was a short kiss—and then it was longer, and she tasted spicy like she always did—like a strong dose of cinnamon. Then she pulled herself away. She knelt down and yanked the dagger from Aldo's back and wiped it on his hair. His blood was creeping across the floor. She didn't let any get on her shoes.

"Let's go," she said.

Rune nodded and headed toward the door—but then he stopped. He ran to where Aldo's InfoLenses were lying, and he stomped on them and heard them break. Markla watched with a look of approval.

They ran up the stairs and hurried into the Dream Center. Rune had Aldo's gun in his hand, and his mind was racing because they were sure to be stopped. But they heard no shooting as they headed down the hall, and they saw no one. Rune glanced around, looking for Diana, but there was no sign of her. When they reached the main door, Rune opened it a crack and peered outside.

A thick haze of smoke filled his vision and burned his nostrils. He could see the ground around the building was a chaotic mess filled with bodies, broken vehicles, and destruction. But the violence seemed to be over, and he saw people emerging through the smoke, talking on radios—and Rune's jaw dropped.

This was not the scene from the screens downstairs. This was something different.

"What's going on?" Markla said.

Rune opened the door. He stepped outside and shook his head. "It wasn't true!" Rune said, and he smiled. "The news stream on Aldo's wall—it was a phony LiveDream. The government didn't win. We won!" Then he saw his father's friend Stoke walking through the battle zone. Stoke spotted Rune and came over to him.

"Rune!" he said. "I'm so sorry about your father. We were a little too late. But he would be happy to know what we did today."

"What did you do? Did you overthrow the government?"

"No, but that wasn't our goal. We're taking the LiveDreams off the streams. All across Sparkla, we attacked key targets. The new reality is going to be the truth—at least for now. We'll see what happens tomorrow." He glanced at Markla and said, "What are you two doing? You should get out of here."

"But we can help," Rune said.

"I don't think so," Stoke said. "Our attack was meant to send a message, and we did that. But now it's up to the people—and you need to get out of here quick. You can come with me in a hover-ship."

Markla was shaking her head. "I'm not going with them, Rune."

Rune hesitated. "I think we'll go our own way," he said.

Stoke paused. "Okay," he said. "But be careful."

Rune and Markla headed through the main gate and across the grassy field. A strong breeze was blowing but the sun shined down. As Rune looked back at the bombed out wreckage of the Dream Center, his head was swimming with a mix of emotions. He kept glancing at Markla, who was silent.

Finally, he said, "Are you okay, Markla?"

For a moment she stayed quiet. Then she said, "I'll never be okay, Rune. But I'll never be powerless, either. That won't ever happen again." She stopped walking and looked at him. "I want us to be together. That's the only thing that's real to me right now."

Rune suddenly felt warm, like he was filled with sunshine. "I want us to be together, too. We're together right now, aren't we? And it's going to be great. I know it."

He put his arm around her, and they walked into the woods.

The End

About The Author

Joe Canzano is a writer and musician from New Jersey, U.S.A. For the latest news about Joe's books, subscribe to his newsletter. You can find it at www.happyjoe.net, where you'll also find more information about Joe than you'll ever need.

He invites you to email him at happyjoe800@gmail.com

Thanks for reading!

Novels by Joe Canzano

MAGNO GIRL
SEX HELL
SUZY SPITFIRE KILLS EVERYBODY
SUZY SPITFIRE AND THE SNAKE EYES OF VENUS
RUNE AND FLASH

For more information check happyjoe.net.

Printed in Great Britain
by Amazon

84662913R00181